# Who Killed D.L. Phillips?

**A Leyla James Mystery, Volume 1**

A. Eveline

Published by A. Eveline, 2020.

WHO KILLED D.L. PHILLIPS?

First edition. September 15, 2020.

# Contents

# CHAPTER 1: The Discovery.

On the following Monday morning, Graciela made her way past security and into the old North Building of the Radio Frequency Administration in Southwest Washington, D.C. As always, she loaded her cart and pushed it into the elevator. While vacuuming the halls on the second floor, she felt unusually distracted, distraught, worrying about her six-year-old son, Matias, and his school problems. Last night, he had cried at dinner, saying in Spanish, "Nobody likes me. Sammy told me to go back to my country." He looked down at the table and rubbed his eyes.

"Did you tell him that you were legal and that this is your country, too?" He shook his head no, his eyes still downcast.

"Well, tell anyone who says those bad things to you that this is your country now. This is your home."

Graciela felt sick. She had tried so hard to come to the US, to bring her boy here to be safe. And now he wasn't safe from unkind words. His little face pinched up, tears rolled down his cheeks. She felt his pain of being ostracized.

"Are there any other kids like you in school?" She meant brown-skinned and Hispanic.

He shook his head. She wondered if that was true. She got him ready the next morning and dropped him at his school. All the way there, he sobbed that he did not want to go, that he hated going to school. He wouldn't hold her hand or look at her. She sat in the car, he got out and she watched him trudge into school with his little backpack, his head down.

Now, in the hall in front of the largest conference room, Graciela wondered who she could turn to for help with him. She would ask her amiga at lunch. Maybe she should go to the school, complain. But the problem was her English. Maybe she would take a friend to help her. She sighed. She had tried so hard to make his little life better.

She pulled at the door handle to get into the conference room but found the door locked. Strange. She tried her keys but none would work. The door seemed to be stuck. She was a small woman but forceful. You had to be strong to be a custodian and do what she did. Cleaning was hard work. She threw her whole body against the door while slamming down on the handle. The door clicked open.

She stepped inside the room, bringing her cart with her. When she looked up, she saw a woman in a chair, slumped over the conference table, her red hair spread over the table top where her head rested. Graciela gasped. "Excuse me, I—"

The woman didn't move. In front of the body on the table was a small rectangular device. A piece of paper lay beside it.

Graciela moved around the table to see if the woman was just sleeping. She could see from this new angle some dried blood on the front of the bright green suit. Blood had also seeped into the carpet beneath the chair.

Graciela screamed.

She ran into the hall and called her supervisor on her two-way radio. The supervisor called his supervisor who called the agency police. The RFA had its own police force, used chiefly for security in the building. A murder was beyond its authority. The agency police had never had a homicide in its building, let alone a very bloody one. Shortly, Graciela's supervisors came to the conference room and stood in the hallway with the shocked, silent Graciela. She had seen bloody bodies before, in the streets at home, in El Salvador. That was the reason she and Matias came to D.C. to live with her sister, to save her boy from the gangs. She never expected to see murdered bodies in the place where she worked, with such tight security.

The RFA officers dutifully ambled into the room, eyed the woman's cold, stiff body. She heard one of them refer to her as D.L. It appeared that she had been dead for at least a day maybe more. Killed over the weekend. They began quizzing Graciela.

She was nervous and flustered, making her English worse than usual. "No one in the hall. Door stuck. I crash it. See her." Graciela collapsed on a chair near the door facing away from the body, hands over her eyes.

She realized now that the dead woman was a frequent visitor to the agency. Graciela and her friends, both male and female, on the cleaning staff had made comments about this mujer caliente, who hung around the offices of the agency staff. Graciela had glimpsed her once or twice as she cleaned the RFA restrooms, but she didn't know her name. There was nothing else that Graciela could tell the police about this murder. Because, of course, it had to be a murder. It was all there in front of them. A dead bloody body, a strange device, and a note.

The supervisor and officers mumbled to each other. It was clear that outside help was crucial. They called the Federal Protection Service who watch over federal buildings, the employees, and the visitors. Here was a dead visitor.

Fifteen minutes went by. The five live people in the room were suddenly silent. All, except Graciela, were focused at the corpse. Then, two officers of the Federal Protection Service sauntered in, a man and a woman, both heavyset and armed with walkie-talkies that screeched and mumbled.

"Hey, guys," the female officer said. "What do you have for us?"

One of the supervisors stepped up. "The cleaner found the body about a half hour ago. She said she didn't see any activity in the hall and the door to the room was locked. She forced her way in."

The two FPS officers walked silently around the bloody scene, kneeling on the floor around the chair and eyeing the dead woman in the bright green suit. They each heaved themselves up, then looked at each other and shrugged. "We need some guidance from higher up on this one," the female officer said and called their supervisor. Graciela didn't want to hear the conversation, but until they let her go she had no choice but to stay in the room. The smell of blood made her stomach heave.

"Sir, we're at the RFA, North Building, large conference room. There's a body of a woman in her 30s. Looks like a knife wound to the chest. Massive bleeding. Could be dead for a couple of days." The officer paused, listening. "No, no sign of a continuing disturbance." She looked at the agency staff. "Were there any reports of a stranger in the building this morning?"

The two RFA police shook their heads.

"They're putting me on hold." She told her partner. All the officers looked at each other again and shook their heads. "Sounds like no one knows what to do."

"What's new?" said one, shrugging.

The supervisor came back on the line. The officer listened intently and nodded her head and hung up.

"There won't be a lock down since we all agree that the event occurred at least one or two days ago. The killer probably left the building immediately after the murder. I'm supposed to call the FBI; he gave me a name and number."

"Why didn't he call the FBI?" The male officer shook his head. "Doesn't want to be part of this?"

Graciela knew why. No one wanted the responsibility. An investigation into a murder on government property was not in their job descriptions. Murder investigations were left to the experts.

An hour later, they still hadn't told Graciela she could leave. The FBI team showed up and took command of the room. This time, the officers were pleased with the Bureau's officiousness. They wanted out of there as much as she did. But the lead FBI agent, a woman, pointed to a corner and said to them, "Stay over there and we'll talk with you soon." Graciela was commanded to remain where she was, in her chair.

Two FBI agents began talking to the agency police, the custodian's supervisor and the protective service officers.

"Who discovered the body and when?" one asked.

The supervisor pointed to Graciela. "She did. About 9:30. She was doing her regular check of this building. It's not being used now. She found this door jammed and she broke into it by force."

A slender dark-haired female agent came over to Graciela. The agent was gentle and bent over her. She softly introduced herself and told Graciela that she would like some information. She motioned and said, "Come with me."

They went over into a far corner of the conference room. The agent asked where she was from. "El Salvador. I, permiso de residencia," said Graciela. By then, she was in tears, speaking half Spanish, half English, trying to explain that she had nothing to do with this crime. The agent speaking Spanish said she understood Garciela's concerns. The female FPS officer was watching, maybe wondering how the FBI knew to include a Spanish speaking agent.

Another agent was taking names and brief notes from the group. The FBI crime scene investigators entered, dressed in white hazmat suits and booties. They surrounded the body. Graciela watched as the team set up their kits and took fingerprints from the table, the device and the victim's handbag and cellphone. One of the team picked up the device with gloved hand and said, "Looks like a simple listening device that can be bought off the net." The note was tucked away in an evidence bag.

"Well, from the blood, it's likely that she was murdered right here in the chair. The angle is strange though, the perp needed to be behind her. He must have grabbed her around the neck. Are there marks there?"

Another team member, pushed aside the chair next to the body, got on the floor and looked up. "Yep, there are marks." The room was thoroughly examined, and photographs taken. Eventually, the body was removed for autopsy. The room was cordoned off. Agents continued their investigation.

Graciela's interview was finally winding down. She felt exhausted. But at least she got a sense that the FBI agent believed she knew nothing about the murder. She just was doing her job by checking and trying to clean the conference room. The interview ended.

"You may go," said the agent with a kind look at Graciela. "Please, do not discuss this with anyone. We may want to talk to you again later."

Graciela's supervisor came over. "You should take the rest of the day off but stop off at Human Resources. They will give you the name of someone to talk to today."

Graciela left to find comfort from her amiga and to ask for her help with her boy.

# CHAPTER 2: Unbelievable.

I learned of some of the murder details—where Delilah Lydia Phillips was found and by whom—later that morning. The victim went by D.L. A mass email arrived from one of a group I belonged to, women who practiced telecom law and met occasionally for networking and support. The sender worked at the Administration and gleaned some details from discussions, most likely gossip, in the hall.

A young Hispanic woman cleaner had found the body. Most of us knew D.L., some more than others. I was sure that there would be little grief when the news was formally released, not in this town or anywhere else. D.L. was a pain to anyone who crossed her path, including me, Leyla James. But murder? In the Radio Frequency Administration conference room? It was bizarre for so many reasons. The question was—who hated her badly enough to risk a murder? Most of us simply tolerated or avoided her, if we could. We were shocked. But also intrigued.

In the afternoon, I ran into a couple friends at a neighborhood deli. As we stood waiting for our orders, we swapped information. Jean, a former firm colleague, and now an Administration staffer who I knew well from our young lawyer days, said, "My clerk overheard some of the cleaning staff gossiping about the conference room. The name of cleaner who found D.L. was Graciela Lopez."

"I know Graciela!" I said. "She has a part-time job at my gym on the weekends. I recognized her one Saturday and said hi and asked her if she worked at the RFA. You'd have thought I'd given her a compliment just because I acknowledged her." I couldn't imagine that her life as a cleaner brought her much joy, but she always looked happy.

My friend went on, her eyes bright with excitement. "They say there was a lot of blood. Soaked into the chair, the rug."

"Gross," I murmured.

"Yeah, well, the cops kept Graciela waiting in that room for an hour or more. Can you imagine? Then the FBI questioned her forever. Poor thing." Jean sighed. "You know, it could have been any one of us that went in there."

"I heard it was almost three hours later before they took the body."

"Oh," Jean interrupted. "There was something else. One of them said an electronic device of some sort was on the table in the room and a piece of paper. Wonder what that was?"

"Who knows," I said with a shrug. "The thing is, it takes some kind of chutzpa to commit a murder in a federal building. I wonder if it was planned, like a professional hit, or she just finally sent someone over the cliff. And what's that device all about? Do you think someone's office was bugged and she had something to do with it?"

My friend Beth wondered how the murderer got D.L. into the North Building. "It had to be someone who knew the layout. I wonder if someone on the Administration's staff was involved."

"She had so many enemies," Emily said. "It could be anyone! She was always making life miserable for someone. One more filing at the Administration by her, castigating the staff, and someone decided to drive a stake through her alleged heart."

We all laughed. This was not exactly how I would want to be remembered. It was more like the Scrooge death scene, with vulgar comments about the deceased.

My order was called, and I picked up my lunch. "But Jean," I asked, "what is the staff saying?"

"Aside from being appalled, not much. Apparently, she was supposed to have a meeting with Sam Watson on Friday afternoon. He had another meeting before hers. It ran late. D.L. must have gotten impatient. She wasn't waiting when the meeting broke up."

Our small niche in the regulatory law "industry" in Washington, D.C. is the Radio Frequency Administration, the RFA. That agency regulates interstate communications by radio, television, wire, satellite, and cable. This means that anyone who wants to use the commercial airwaves to provide cell-phone service or broadcasting service, for instance, has to go to the RFA to get permission. I am one of those people who helps clients get what they need from the federal government labyrinth, but we also attempt to make our clients follow the rules. Sometimes they do, sometimes they don't. And if they don't, we are there to defend them, vigorously. Bad behavior helps pay the bills.

I had been involved in this practice of law for fifteen years, three as a paralegal, then a summer associate and finally as a full-fledged associate in the law office of Jesse Harris. The partnership came almost eight years later, after we merged with a bigger firm. Jesse was a longtime D.C. resident. He had come up from Alabama to D.C. to go to college. He then worked as a Senate intern for an Alabama Senator and after that line on his resume, he went to law school in D.C. Jesse had lost his southern accent over the years, but he retained his love for southern cooking. His take-out lunches filled the halls with mouthwatering smells from the Deep South, fried things in contrast to my usual stark salad, often without dressing. My reward was that I was slim. But sometimes I thought that my workday life consisted only of getting up, working out, sitting down all day for work, eating lettuce for lunch and dinner and going to bed. Some life.

But I was lucky to have found Jesse shortly after he left a large firm in disgust. He needed a helper in his new solo practice. I came on as a paralegal during law school. Working with Jesse, I met a lot of characters: lawyers, clients and vendors of all types, but D.L. was a piece of work that defied description. She was one of Jesse's clients when I was wet behind the ears. She had formed a partnership that aimed to get licenses through a RFA lottery to provide cellphone service. Her partner, Matt, was supposed to run the business end of the cellphone operation, once a license was granted by the government. D.L. would be...whatever she wanted.

At our first meeting, I thought D.L. was attractive but attempting to be too clever for her own good. There was coffee, tea and water, which Jesse offered her. She instructed me that she wanted coffee with milk, no sugar. I was startled since everything was on a side table within her reach. Jesse just smiled when he saw my dismayed reaction. I had just gotten the first taste of the D.L. treatment.

The money person, Matt, relied on D.L.'s government "expertise" as a license speculator (really a get-rich-quick artist who puts investors together into partnerships and then applies to get airwave licenses). At the meeting, whenever Matt tried to contribute his considerable expertise as a senior accountant, she shut him down. Throughout this meeting, D.L. disagreed with him on everything.

"Look, you don't have the experience with the government to know how to handle this," she told him.

"But this is just common accounting practices," he protested. She cut him off. "Not with me!"

I thought he made sense. He was the money man, after all. Jesse thought so, too. I sat quietly at the end of the table, watching the show. Jesse was the pacifier and tried to ease the tension between D.L. and her partner. At some point in the discussion, Jesse said, "I can see Matt's point. It would make more sense, from a financial point of view."

D.L. slowly turned in her chair and stared at Jesse, scornfully. "Stick to your expertise of law. It's clear that you know nothing about my financial plan. Matt's ideas do not fit any of its requirements." Jesse sat back resigned and folded his arms on his chest. D.L. did not like to share the stage with anyone.

I learned by network gossip that she was at odds with practically everyone she came into contact with, except her current boyfriend. I imagined it would only be a matter of time before she kicked him to the curb.

Anyway, the matter that Jesse had handled in those early days was finally resolved several months later, with Jesse smoothing out a little wrinkle in a partnership that would have gotten D.L.'s winning lucrative wireless licenses bounced. And lucrative it was, for D.L. A few years later, she made a multimillion-dollar settlement with her accountant/partner. She had made his life so complicated that Matt finally bought her out.

By the time I ran into her again, I was no longer a baby just out of law school. I'd survived the bumps and bruises every maturing lawyer suffers while becoming proficient in her skills. D.L., however, never acknowledged that change. She seemed to think she was an even match to any attorney, even without portfolio.

That afternoon following her murder, many lawyers, including me, called our clients throughout the country with the news. Many were indirectly or directly battling D.L. I just got off one such call when Adam Ross called. Adam was another long-suffering lawyer who, like me, had protracted and acrimonious dealings with D.L. Phillips.

"So, Leyla, what do you think about D.L.?" Adam asked. "Did she have it coming?"

"Well, some would say that." I laughed.

We talked about the sketchy description of the murder and D.L.'s obituary in the newspaper stream that afternoon. "It's interesting that the obit mentioned she was the daughter of a prominent Washington attorney, who had himself mysteriously died in a single-car crash one night in Rock Creek Park last year."

Adam made a hmmm sound in the phone. "You think that implies some sort of connection with her death?"

"I don't know," I said. "I remember when it happened. I thought he had been drinking before it happened. But the coroner's office reported almost no alcohol in his blood." Both father and daughter involved in unexplained deaths? Odd.

Adam's misfortune was to represent a company that attempted to broker a spectrum-sharing deal with D.L. Fights between D.L. and Adam's client, over the money and the quality of the license that each side held, made life miserable for everyone involved. D.L. thought her license was superior; she demanded more money. Even after both contracts had been signed, she made stabs at extracting more money and perks from the deal. When things didn't go her way, she filed complaints at the Administration claiming fraud against Adam's client.

You can't make this stuff up. She was bound to make enemies. But would the enemy actually commit murder?

"So, what do you think?" Adam asked. "Did someone off her?"

"I really don't see how. Not in that building."

When I was first practicing, I could walk over to the building, nod at the receptionist in the lobby and go directly to the staffer I wanted to see. An undetected murder might have been possible then. Now, everyone has to sign in at the front desk with one of the two guards, present identification and tell the guard who we are visiting. A verification call is made. Only then is a visitor's badge given out by the guard and the visitor passes through a screening device, manned by another guard. At the end of the meeting, visitors are escorted to the elevator and instructed to give back the badge at the lobby exit door. It would be almost impossible to commit a murder, without leaving an electronic trail and eyewitnesses to a presence in the building.

"I heard she had a meeting with Sam Watson the afternoon of her murder," I said. Adam was a friend of Sam's and he would know.

"Yes, it was a meeting with Sam," Adam said. Sam was often the target of D.L.'s threatened lawsuits against the staff. She complained of sexual discrimination and favoritism, harming her constitutional rights. Watson bore her abuse with grace and tried to maintain a balanced approach in his orders while dodging complaints and veiled allusions to staff stupidity.

"Well, Sam isn't a killer," I said with certainty.

"Sam? Of course not," Adam agreed. Watson was the epitome of diplomacy and level headedness. He was a young looking, attractive, mid-level staffer who was well groomed and well-mannered. He was equally helpful to everyone, although my law partner Jesse groused that Sam sometimes played lawyer for D.L. She boasted about her phone conversations and emails with him and other RFA staffers, often inserting their email excerpts into her filings to create the impression that the Administration supported her arguments.

"I ran into Sam on Saturday morning at the gym." That gym was a popular venue for other D.C. lawyers including me. "Sam was ticked off because there was supposed to be a meeting between him and his deputy and D.L. on Friday afternoon."

The Administration staff never met alone with outsiders, particularly with a loose cannon like D.L. But that threesome also meant that the meeting was only about D.L. and her businesses, not with parties in her litigations. So, I thought, the question here is—why would D.L. meet with staff alone? Why no clients? What was she up to? Did her murder have anything to do with her scheduled meeting?

According to what Sam told Adam on Saturday, the guard at the elevator claimed D.L. arrived at a reception area a few minutes before 3PM on March 28 on the fifth floor with her badge and she waited in a chair near the conference room. Watson told Adam that apparently no one had notified D.L. that Watson and his deputy were in another meeting and that it was running late.

"That's unusual that the staff didn't tell her to wait," I said.

"Right. Sam said that it might have been because it was so late on Friday afternoon. Or because the staff was unaware there was a delay. Anyway, when Sam and his deputy finally came out of the meeting with Leon Gallagher, Phillips was gone, and there was no message from her. Funny thing was, the visitor log showed that she hadn't signed out or left her badge."

"Definitely puzzling. So how did she end up on the second floor in the North Building?"

"According to Watson, the Administration police conducted a search of the entire Administration building, floor by floor, interviewing staff as they went. No one had seen D.L. later that afternoon. When they reached the eighth floor and had not found any evidence of her presence, they called off the search. They assumed that she had slipped out without notice, perhaps in a huff, without leaving her badge."

But that didn't make sense either, I thought. How could she have gotten past the guards without them noticing her?

Adam gave a little laugh and shook his head. "When Sam talked to me on Saturday, he sounded as if he knew he would catch hell from D.L. on Monday morning, about being stood up." Adam said.

"Surprise!" I said. "No kidding."

# CHAPTER 3: A Little Context.

"Well, you came back from vacation at a dramatic time," I said to Jesse as he slid into the chair in front of my desk the following day. "Have you heard all the gory details?"

"Quite the scene, I guess," he said. "Quite the gossip going around."

"Yeah, I heard."

It is amazing to me that Jesse always knows everything. I could witness a car crash in front of our office, and five minutes later Jesse would tell me who the victims were and the degree of injury. I was incredulous.

"How could you possibly hear that news in the Yucatan?

Jesse laughed. "I ran into Carlton Edwards on an airport shuttle from Tulum yesterday."

That made me even more nonplused.

"Carlton Edwards? Yesterday? The news only got out here yesterday morning."

"Carlton was talking to his D.C. lawyer yesterday, before his afternoon trip to Mexico City."

"What's up with Carlton, these days anyway?"

Jesse told me that Edwards had retreated to Mexico to regroup after a series of legal disasters resulted in jail terms for him in various prisons, simultaneous with an acrimonious divorce.

"He seemed proud of himself for getting through it all in a good frame of mind and in decent financial shape. He said that was thanks to his friend, Andrei Ceban, who he was going to meet in Mexico City. He reminded me that he had introduced me to Ceban at a telecom conference in Spain long before Edward's problems. I don't really remember him. But Edwards said that Andrei was his great collaborator and introduced him to a lot of productive contacts in Europe and Mexico."

"So, he is still into con games?"

Jesse gave a non-committal shrugged. "He said that he was going to see Ceban about some business deals. He was also mulling a new approach to making money at the Administration. He seems to believe that he didn't do it right in the past."

"Hmm. Well, how is he going to do that since he's been disbarred and banned from appearing before the Administration?"

Jesse laughed. "Don't put anything past that guy. This time he said that he would be careful choosing his clients. He says they were the ones who had caused him all his legal problems."

I laughed, too, because I have in my file an Administration release from a few years ago that detailed Edwards' problems. The document also served as a reminder to me about the trouble that a lawyer could get into before a government agency. Carlton Edwards had ultimately been convicted of committing fraud at the Administration and with the Securities and Exchange Commission. According to the release, he sold interests in wireless applications to investors with promises of unparalleled returns. Clients were told that for only $20,000.00, they would be part of a federal lottery that would give them a hundred thousand annual payout forever, if their application won.

According to Administration estimates, the scams brought in a half billion a year to the organizers. The Edwards Proceeding had a multitude of twists and turns with trips up to the Court of Appeals and back down to the Administration over a period of several years. At the same time, other Edwards' transactions were being litigated (and appealed). That ended in Edwards pleading guilty to conspiracy to evade securities and banking reporting requirements in Tennessee. He was sentenced to 21 months in federal prison, followed by three years of probation, and $20,000 in fines. Two years later, the SEC won a judgment of nearly $13 million. Later that year, Edwards violated his federal parole and his state probation by traveling to St. Croix to engage in the same activities relating to securities and federal licenses. Edwards was sentenced to six additional months in federal prison and four years in state prison. You might say that he was incorrigible.

"Well, I know one person who won't be able to help him in his endeavors at the Administration." I said.

"Yeah, Darius Phillips." Jesse said. He shook his head.

Darius Phillips, D.L.'s father and an old friend of Edwards, had died last year. According to the newspaper account at that time, another motorist had found him, crashed in his car in Rock Creek and he called the police. There was no evidence of what had caused his car to hit a tree, bounce over an embankment and end up in the creek. No skid marks on the road. No signs of a physical illness that had caused him to lose control. The car was inspected and found to be without defects. It had had a recent tune-up, but no significant repairs had been made. The death was still unsolved.

"I have so many stories about that guy." Jesse shook his head.

I had heard his reminiscences before. They both practiced telecommunications law when that practice consisted of 25 or 30 white males. No one outside of their circle knew what they did. It was still basically a male practice even when I started, but then so was most of law. It was always hard to go to a meeting with twelve men and, maybe, two women. It was difficult to be acknowledged or even heard in male discussions.

"You know," Jesse said. "I was always skeptical about Darius. But I never had any proof. With Edwards, there was proof of his squishy ethics."

Jesse had told me that Darius Phillips and Edwards had met at a telecommunications conference in Las Vegas over 25 years earlier. Both were interested in the frequencies that the Administration had set for lottery. Both were soliciting interest from parties that might want to form groups which would contribute money for a chance at winning valuable spectrum. Their idea was to retain some type of indirect interest, prohibited by the government, hoping that their groups would win the lottery for licenses worth millions of dollars.

The hustle was not too costly. At that time, the government charged no fee for the filing of these applications and the lottery was free. So, the government gave away its resources worth millions of dollars to individuals who would then resell them to eager buyers for astonishing amounts of money.

The process had begun simply with only a few insiders knowing of the profit to be made. But not for long. Soon the word got around and frequency speculation became a small industry.

"Yeah, back in the good old days," I said. "I remember them well."

I knew about that era because our firm had handled lottery applications. I was a paralegal then and Jesse taught me about the process. I dutifully put together the government applications containing specific information on the applicant and hundreds of pages, including the required strict ownership information, and then put it into huge binders. The applications were stacked in our firm's hallways as I completed binder after binder, and duplicates for different US markets.

"Hope you are making money on that!" Passing lawyers needled me, because it was just so much busy work. Our courier soon cleared out our halls by toting the binders to the Administration, which soon became clogged with thousands of these "lottery tickets" from our firm and the other telecommunications firms, application mills, engineering companies and law offices in D.C. and around the country. Each application filed with great hopes of hitting the government jackpot. And some of our clients did. And then, we did make money.

"You know, from the beginning," said Jesse. "Phillips and Edwards were really interested in each other's ideas. Although Phillips was wary, they did have a rapport. It might have been because each had angles to keep some kind of financial interest in these applications, which got around an Administration ban, that the other could appreciate and possibly use. I think that in the beginning, Edwards leaned closer to the prohibited line, but they both saw ways in which these applications could be profitable to them, as well as to their clients."

According to Jesse, Phillips and Edwards kept in touch on a regular basis. "I guess they became sounding boards for techniques to acquire licenses and get resale commissions from them. Phillips always said that he was more involved helping his clients to acquire these licenses than wanting to make millions like Edwards did." Jesse raised an eyebrow at me.

"Sure, but Phillips also made a lot from it, too. Don't kid me."

"Yeah, more than we did." Jesse sighed.

"Well, we followed the law."

At some point, Phillips' daughter D.L. dropped out of her freshman year at American University in D.C. and joined her father in his law practice as an assistant on a temporary basis. According to Jesse, Darius was adept at finding investors who were familiar with Administration offerings, but he needed help in packaging the lottery applications. D.L. coordinated the information with the clients. Her name appeared as the contact on the applications, his did not.

The Edwards-Phillips bro-fest continued for a while but as Edwards' troubles deepened, Phillips apparently started losing interest. He remained uninvestigated for any of his ventures and he intended to keep it that way. By schmoozing investors, Darius helped his daughter keep their clients happy and out of trouble. At this point, Darius distanced himself from discussions with Edwards, but he remained alert to the investigations, as a learning experience in ways that he, Darius, might with a tweak put his dealings on the right side of the line.

Later, the Administration realized that there was another, more profitable, way for the government to distribute spectrum: the auction. This time the government was finally going to get paid for its airwaves. But it did allow small applicants to get a credit and pay less for small business that was prohibited to larger companies. There basically were no rules, other than a short holding period, that prohibited the after sale of these licenses. Lottery winners would resell their licenses to non-speculators, often large companies split off from AT&T, Ma Bell. These companies actually wanted to build and operate a radio system. And sometimes they were even accused by other auction participants of setting up the small business applicant. Some investigations were done, and quiet settlements were made. There are always ways to get around any system.

Although father and daughter shared an office and the just-this-side-ofthe-law mentality, they seemed to despise each other. Jesse had a daughter, too, and sometimes, over drinks, Darius would download his complaints about D.L., looking for sympathy. Jesse told me, "Darius was divorced from D.L.'s mother years ago and he had women friends in the past that D.L. called floozies. But it was a two-way street. Darius disapproved of D.L., too. He couldn't stand her lack of interest in returning to college; her obsession with designer clothes that she couldn't afford; and her current boyfriend who Darius called a thug. Darius always thought the guy had ties to organized crime. They fought about that a lot."

According to Jesse, D.L.'s relationship with her father might have soured her attitude toward men, although she professed to like them. Certainly, her romantic life seemed to confirm that, as I heard from my peers. Gossip had it that she had had relationships with various men who obviously had money and liked to share it with good-looking women. In one instance, according to Jesse, Darius had heard from a friend about an "undignified" scene at Eden's, a highly visible D.C. lobbyist gathering place. D.L. and her current flame had been confronted by the flame's ex-girlfriend. Wine was thrown, followed up by name calling.

"I just can't control her," Darius told Jesse. "Sometimes, it is just embarrassing."

As a result of this scrapping, assistants rotated through their office on the way to more stable firms. There was a lot of gossip about the dueling twosome. Jesse always counseled patience to his friend Darius but knew that any truce would not last long.

My friend Adam represented one of D.L.'s partners, who finally filed suit against her, claiming mismanagement. D.L. immediately called Adam demanding, "What were you thinking? Didn't you read the partnership agreement? It clearly states that the parties have to arbitrate."

She had been litigating before the Administration for at least 15 years. The years spent in her father's law office had convinced her that Administration filings had to have less legalese and blunt language was needed.

D.L. sneered at both lawyers and Administration staff and she was disliked by one and all. At least everyone that I know except for one: her father's employee of 15 years, Louise Richards. Richards is a courteous woman in her thirties, slightly crunchy with Birkenstocks and flowing clothes, who does not resort to name calling and is forever patient. She is a gentle woman, a single mother with a child to support. My client met her following his deposition in a D.L. litigation and said Louise was a very pleasant person.

Louise was often left to sort out the office disruptions, which according to past employees, was done with aplomb. Louise would first soothe Darius and then softly counsel D.L. Soon, father and daughter were speaking again, and Louise faded into the background. We wondered why this pleasant person stayed on and what secrets she held about D.L. and Darius. Maybe some of those secrets would be revealed in the murder investigation.

# CHAPTER 4: The Investigation.

"Leyla, you will never guess who the FBI agent is on D.L.'s murder investigation!" Adam said as we exited together from a very unsettling settlement meeting in the Administration's office. Our clients were allied, and we had been brought into the Administration in an attempt to strike a bargain with our clients' adversary. After an hour of posturing on both sides, the meeting adjourned in a stalemate. We were walking down the hall from the conference room.

"I have no idea." I sighed. "My guess is that the agent would have to have some knowledge of the agency. And because of its high profile—murder in a government agency—this case is on a fast track."

"Remember Ida Cramer? She was brought in almost immediately and she is in the process of making a list of individuals that she wants to interview."

"I'm not sure that I know her," I said, trying to remember the name. "What's her connection to telecom?"

"Oh, she tried it for a while and then joined the FBI," Adam said.

"Hmm, that was a career jump. So, what about the list? I would think that Sam Watson is on it, as well as a Judge Morrissey."

Administration Law Judge Dean Morrissey was a lifer on the verge of retirement. ALJ Morrissey, white-haired and stooped, was stern and did not take to impertinence well. He had had many altercations, both verbal and written, with D.L. who "starred" in her perverse way, causing the lawyers at the conferences or hearings in the most current proceeding to grimace or silently suppress snickers like school kids.

Also on the list, according to Adam, was both the CEO and the owner of Radio Biz, Jack Taylor, who D.L. had taken to court multiple times along with my client. D.L. ultimately had driven Radio Biz into bankruptcy.

Adam pushed the elevator down button. Out of the corner of my eye, I saw Graciela stop her cart by the woman's room and enter with rolls of toilet paper. "You go ahead," I told Adam.

I stepped into the woman's room and walked to a sink to wash my hands.

Graciela came out of one of stalls still carrying some toilet paper. "Hello, Graciela," I said. "I hope that you are doing okay."

She looked at me and then with a small smile said, "From the gym."

"Yes," I said. "I heard about you and the murder. I am so sorry that happened to you."

She nodded, eyes tearing. "Afraid."

"I just wanted to say that I am sorry. If there is anything I can do, let me know."

"Yes. My boy." She was emphatic. I was astonished, this woman saw her chance and she took it. Good for her.

"What's the matter with your boy?"

"Bullies, la escuela."

I was at a loss. I practiced telecom law. I knew nothing about anything involving kids and school. On the other hand, I do research all the time. I could find out something. I did remember reading an email from the D.C. Bar a day or two ago about the D.C. Volunteers Lawyer Project. I saved it out of guilt, thinking that I really should contribute something someday. On my todo list.

"Give me your phone number. I'll see what I can do. What's your son's name?" I said.

She dictated her number, gave me the boy's name and the name of his school. I added the information in my contacts list.

"I'll be back in touch with you soon. I hope that you feel better." I handed her my card.

She took it, nodded and said, "Gratias."

Coming out of the restroom, I decided on a whim to drop by my friend Jean McInerny's office on this floor. I walked past the elevators and turned right, into a hall full of small offices. I walked by a few doors, reading familiar names on the nameplates but not stopping. I didn't want to be pushy and unexpectedly invade a business acquaintance's space. Jean and I were longtime friends. In our early years at the law firm, Jean introduced me to the concept of "punitive billing" for bad-acting clients. Neither of us practiced it, but it was worth a laugh when a client was giving us a hard time. We laughed a lot in those years, to keep our sanity.

Jean was in her office, typing on her computer, several books and papers in front of her. I tapped lightly on her open door. She looked up, surprised.

"Sorry," I said. "I was in a meeting down the hall and thought I would drop in for a minute. It looks like you are busy, so I won't bother you. Good to see you!"

"Come in," she said. "I was just a little startled. Just lost in my writing. Have a seat."

"I do that too," I agreed. "Someone drags me out of the zone and I have to figure out where I am."

"Yep. What brings you here?"

"Just a swipe at a settlement agreement. It's hard to try to settle with a cantankerous adversary."

"Not one of D.L.'s, obviously."

"No, but people get irritable arguing about settlement money. We need to find a way to let the staff do its thing on this one. Daddy steps in." I laughed.

"Good luck with that." She paused and said, "Why don't you shut the door?" She put her index finger up to her lips.

I shut the door and sat down, wondering what she was being so cautious about.

"Off the record," she said softly. "I found out there were several lawyers on the FBI's list. I can't tell you who they are, but the list will be released tomorrow, so everyone will know soon enough." She pointed at me and mouthed 'you.'

I was stunned. The FBI was going to ask me to explain my relationship to a murder victim?

"How many other lawyers?" I whispered incredulously.

She lifted her hands, holding up seven fingers. That may me feel a little better, but not much.

Understanding that she could not talk about it further, I got up and moved toward the door.

"It was good seeing you, sweetie. Let's get together soon."

I went back to my office in gloom. There was a message from Adam, asking me to call him as soon as possible.

He picked up the phone on the second ring.

"Hey, Leyla, I just got more word about the FBI list. There are eight lawyers on it. You are one of them."

"Wow," I said. I was glad that I had heard it from Jean. It was shocking, but at least I could control my reaction. "Who else has the honors?"

He gave me a few other names.

"Well, it makes me feel a little better that I will have company in the pen."

Adam rushed to assure me that it was not a big deal. "It will be a one-shot cameo and you will be checked off the list."

"How did you know who was on the list?" I asked.

"Word gets around," he said simply. We hung up and I pondered this development. How did Adam know these names?

More importantly, what about my interaction with D.L. had caught the FBI's interest? It is true that D.L.'s and my filings at the Administration had descended frequently into name calling. But I was not the only lawyer who jousted with her.

Actually, I had only met her in person at any length over ten years ago and at that time, I also had had several phone conversations with her. But, ultimately, Jesse handled this matter alone, and in his magical way, the problem disappeared at the Administration. If the problem went away, that was fine with me. Bottom line, D.L. left our firm with a resolved matter and an unpaid bill.

Jesse and I had a discussion about the bill. "Leyla, it's not much money. I don't think it's worth pursuing." Jesse was easygoing about fees.

"But I spent a lot of time on the phone with her. It's the principle of the thing."

In the end, Jesse's decision ruled. He had heard that at least three other law firms had tried to collect fees, in various courts. D.L. was more in debt to them than she was to us, and she always countersued for malpractice. Jesse thought such suits were too messy and lengthy — she would only settle after much pain, financially and psychologically, to her adversary. I researched those cases and realized that our exposure was minimal, and finally agreed we should leave it alone. Our policy since then was to minimize client debt by never letting the client get very far ahead of the retainer. We had joined the expanding ranks of former Phillips attorneys.

I had seen D.L. in person rarely since that time. My last contacts with her were through written filings at the Administration and one phone call the previous year that I had tried to avoid, but through some fluke, it happened. There she was.

The call came through the firm front desk and I answered. It was Louise, D.L.'s assistant. "Is this Leyla James?"

As soon as I said, "Yes." D.L. was on the phone. I was horrified. I did not want to speak to her. And suddenly she was asking me for advice about her litigation in a case that included my client.

"I can't advise you. You should have your own attorney in this litigation. I have a conflict," I emphasized.

"Well, let's just talk on a general level. What options are in any litigation?" She was pleading with me. "I just need another point of view."

I offered three obvious alternative endings: drop the suit; resolve the suit by settlement; continue litigation.

The phone call ended with me referring her, again, to another attorney. But to my horror, a follow-up email immediately came from her including multiple parties, reporting me for attempting, in her view, to undermine my client's settlement agreement with her. I assumed that it was a set-up and I turned over any further attempted discussions to Jesse, because he was an alfa male.

I never spoke with D.L. again.

# CHAPTER 5: Pity Party.

With the investigation list completed, Jean and I met at our favorite bar on M Street where we often unloaded to each other after a bad partner day in our young lawyer days. The Bar is a nondescript place, no frills with wooden tables and stainless-steel chairs. As soon as we sat down, ordered and got our drinks, Jean told me in strict confidence that there were now 35 names of interviewees, including Louise Richards, my client, two of Phillips' previous investor/partners, a paralegal and the two telecom peers. I was number 20 on the list and my client was number 21. I took a gulp of wine.

"I'm surprised they would pick me out of all the lawyers she tangled with." I sighed.

"You aren't alone." Jean was trying to soothe me.

To be honest, I once shared with a colleague a wish that something mysterious—and possibly deadly—might happen to D.L. to stop the abuse. I later revised it, in an attempt to rid myself of negativity, to the wish that she would find a nice person in her life to re-focus her attention from making people miserable. I also shared that thought with my peers. I had reached a point where all that hostility had begun to affect my attitude and I needed a more wholesome approach for my mental health. As I said to another lawyer/target, "I would hate to walk around with that woman's mind, seeing persecution and hatred everywhere." The problem was, when I received a filing from her or I was working on a response, I would become exactly like her, full of hatred and venom. It sometimes threatened to overwhelm my life. My longsuffering assistant listened to my rants every time I received a filing.

"I can't believe that she's saying that again!" I'd yell at Dot.

Then, I realized that I was making her as strung out as I was. When she flinched one time, I knew I should ease off or she'd become as miserable as I was. Thereafter I would read two pages of a filing and leave my desk to walk briskly around our office suite and get myself back together. I always tried to tone down my responses, but it was still infuriating to be called vile names before the agency where I practiced—and made my livelihood.

My concern was for my reputation as a lawyer and with the Administration staff. D.L. posted her filed documents on the internet, providing a link for easy access to the world, including prospective clients. Just search on my name and there they were! All they would see was that I was accused of fraud and lying to a federal agency. The effect on my life was insidious.

One night after leaving the office, I was grappling with yet another venomous filing and tangled in a D.C. traffic back-up on K Street. Some sort of police activity for yet another official entourage was holding everyone up for blocks. I became so enraged that I began pounding the steering wheel, then felt a sharp pain in my head. I feared I was having a stroke. I knew then that I had to somehow hold on to my sanity, even though I had chosen to live in a forever insane world.

So now, after ten years of nonstop litigation, I was going to be interviewed about possible involvement in a murder. It was almost a joke. Almost.

Jesse said it best. "Even in death, she's causing angst."

Unfortunately, I had no one emotionally close to rely on for support and to talk about this with, other than Jean. And God knows, between family and work, she had more than enough to deal with. My law partners discussed the business aspects of this development but were not a comfort. Of course, I would never expect that from my partners. We are a law business not a therapy group. I would never share this predicament with my friends or my family; they had problems of their own. But the biggest reason I couldn't talk about it was—I was embarrassed by it. I worried that once I started sharing, that would set people to gossiping. My reputation was gold to me, and I did not want to have it damaged, at all.

I kept thinking about my ex-boyfriend, Cam. We had shared a lot in the three years we were together, and he'd been a big comfort to me. I missed him. We had met at the M Street gym. We nodded to each other for a couple of weeks without speaking, soon after I joined. I had a knee injury from running every day, and my doctor recommended rotating exercise workouts to give it a rest. One day I programmed a stationary bike to take me on a random, somewhat difficult ride. I was building stamina for a bike ride that friends had encouraged me to do with them in a few weeks, the Sea Gull Century. Cam was running on the treadmill beside my bike. My neighbor on the bike on my other side said, "That's quite a program you're biking." I told him, between my panting, about the ride I was practicing for.

Then from the treadmill, Cam said, "I did that ride last year. It was a great trail, a beautiful day."

Something about his appreciation of that fall day pleased me. It had been a gorgeous autumn day, just the right temperature where you started out in a jacket and could peel it off at ten. At the first rest stop I'd replenished water and grabbed a banana. A band was playing. It was beautiful.

"I was there, too," I said. "I took the Princess Anne ride." That was 65 miles.

"My buddy talked me into the Century," Cam said. That was 100 miles. Then, he added, "I wish I could go again this year. But my buddy will be coming home from a conference that day and can't go."

"Well, if you need someone to ride the trail with, I'm going down with about 15 other people. A couple of the guys always ride the 100-mile. My name is Leyla, by the way."

"Thanks, I'm Cam. Is it too late to register?"

"No. One of my friends told me she decided two days ago to go, and she had no problem."

"Well, I'll think about it. Anybody need a ride? I can drive. I live in Clarendon." Clarendon was a somewhat upscale place dominated by singles, in Arlington, Virginia, across the river from D.C.

"I'll ask around," I said. "But you might want to start looking for a hotel. They're usually full, close in by this time. Last year, a friend and I signed up late and got a beat-up motel five miles away from the start. Even it had a no vacancy. If you want, I can ask my friends if they have an extra bed."

"Thanks," Cam said. "I'll trade a ride for a bed." We laughed.

The next time I saw him at the gym two days later, he had registered for the ride and I told him that I had emailed my group about an extra bed. A guy that I did not know very well, Tom McNeil, told me that his friend might not be able to go with him and that he would let me know about the extra bed in a day or two. The hotel he had was closer than I was to the race start. At least, Cam would be able to ride his bike directly to the start. I told Cam that and he gave me his email address. That was the beginning of our three-year romance.

Cam did share the room with Tom and joined the group for dinner the night before the ride. He sat next to me since I was the only other person he knew. We talked about our work and about living in D.C. He was in the senior executive service at State. He grimaced in jest when I told him that I was a lawyer. "So are about 90,000 other people in D.C.," he laughed. "You guys need to get a little original in your vocation choice."

"If it helps," I said, "I am a telecom lawyer. At least, that is a little different."

Cam is handsome. Actually he is beautiful in an Adonis way. Really. Olive skin, dark hair, 5'11" to my 5'5"W, slim like me and athletic. He was unattached, I found. I did not ask him, he told me. Then he said, "What about you?" It was so casual that I barely flinched, which I am inclined to do when some guy strays into the personal. "No, not even a it's-complicated." He laughed and did not ask why not. I could have told him, it was my consuming job that ate my life. No life balance for me, I thought sarcastically. Unfortunately, it was true.

It turned out that we shared a lot of interests, books, music—lots of music, both pre-adolescence and post. Some jazz, some hip hop. Almost anything. And what was really important to me was that my early warning system did not register. He made no effort to one-up me or put me down. He was just a very nice guy.

Of the many ways that I have met men, this was the easiest that I had experienced. Maybe it was that there was no first date to speak of. He wanted to go on the bike ride, and he went, with my help. We got acquainted at a group dinner. No pressure. More importantly, there were no lulls in the conversation. He was easy to be with. We found each other at the lawn party after the race. He bought me a beer and talked about the ride. I told him that my backside was happy to get off the bike, but that it was a great trip. Two of my friends came up, and I introduced Cam to them. My friends talked about directions to the group dinner restaurant later. "Yeah, it is hard to find. Laurie and I drove around for a half hour looking for it last year."

Then I asked Cam to join us, if he liked. He did, but he said that he needed help with those directions. "Would you ride with me?" he asked. My friends looked at each other.

"Sure," I said. "I'm at the La Quinta Inn. I'll be ready at seven."

He was there at 6:55 PM, looking great. I had tried to get myself together, dealing with my helmet hair. I liked everything about him so far. Let's see how long this lasts, my cynical self said. And it actually did last longer than most of my other romances.

We had a glorious fall, seeing each other a couple times a week, for dinner during the week and road trips on our bikes during nice weekends, when he wasn't traveling for his job. It turned out that he was a senior aide to the Secretary of State. Our whatever-it-was still seemed so easy, and he overlooked my last-minute delays at the office. He was such an even-tempered, stable guy. I, on the other hand, could be "uneven" when my stress level was up.

The way we became lovers was easy, too. I had had a rough Friday. I received a filing from D.L. ranking 8 on my Richter scale. I was a little upset and a lot angry. Cam and I had dinner at his favorite Thai restaurant down the street from my apartment. I was fuming but also a little despondent over dinner. After two months of knowing me, Cam knew all about D.L. and her effect on me. I wondered out loud how long this situation would go on. It seemed so endless and so futile, I said.

We walked back to my apartment. He shut the door, put his arms around me in a tight hug and said in my hair, "It is not worth getting this upset about that woman. That is what she wants from you. It feeds her. Can you try to forget about it for a while?" He put his hands on my shoulders and looked at me quizzically. He pulled me close to him and kissed my lips. Oh, that way to forget it! We had been dating a while without getting too physical, but now... I really wanted his beautiful body. I wanted to be close to him. My "sophisticated" mind began making a soundtrack of all the adolescent love songs I had swooned over in my life, starting with, "Let's get it on, baby. This minute, oh yeah." I even whispered those words, like an aphrodisiac. And it was to him, too. We did get it on, in a way that, somehow, I had missed with my past lovers. He got my attention, which sometimes wandered during trysts. No time to analyze this. I was a kid in a candy store and could not get enough of him. He seemed to feel the same.

Finally, late into the night came the soundtrack, "It's so hard to explain..." I singsonged, "that the sound of your voice can get me high."

Cam groaned in my ear, "Not Englebert," he said. "Anything but Englebert."

"Where in my brain did that song pop up from? The 70s jukebox," I laughed. "Yeah, it's so lame."

But yes, I did forget about D.L., all that weekend. We were together until Sunday afternoon, when we both headed into our separate offices. Things had changed now. Our relationship was headed into a direction where I had less control. I was not sure whether it was in my comfort zone. "If you're willing to play the game," the song goes. Looking back, maybe it was not there for either of us. But I am alone now and pondering my FBI interview. I wish I could talk with him.

No such luck. Cam was dating someone else. I saw her on Facebook in a photo with Cam that one of our mutual friends had taken at a party. I felt sick. They were dancing and looking as if they belonged together. I took a picture of the picture on my iPad and studied it until I couldn't look at it anymore. I couldn't even stand to look at my iPad. I also hated myself for internet stalking.

I tried to find out more information about her but none of the Facebook pages of our mutual friends were helpful. I couldn't ask them in person; it might show that I still cared. I didn't know who she was; what she did (and in Washington, that mattered); or how they met. She was tall, blonde, and athletic looking. There was a big ache in my heart. I wished that I could erase that picture in my head. Nevertheless, I occasionally went back to our mutual friends' pages to try to catch another look or to see if he was still with her. I saw no more pictures.

I will get over this, I told myself. But that and this FBI interest in me were weighing me down.

# CHAPTER 6: The Interview.

It took place in a sterile conference room at the FBI Building. I came out of the sticky heat of Washington early summer, sweating in my suit, directly into a freezing room. The cold made me start shaking, or maybe it was nerves. I hadn't slept much the night before. What else is new? I would take whatever homeopathic sleeping aid entered my radar screen at the time and still be awake at 2:00 AM. How many melatonin pills does it take to put a type A to sleep?

I did not want to be in this grim room with these grim people. I had butterflies in my stomach or, perhaps, dread. Leyla James never fears things, I told myself. I was wearing my power navy suit. But it didn't make me feel powerful. I felt small and weak. I was afraid. It had been hopeless to explain this to Jesse. He would not have understood. I just had to buck up.

I was escorted to the room by a stern guard, a stocky white guy who was only missing his polarized aviator sunglasses and a 1956 Dodge Police Sedan. He had met me at the entrance of the building, after I signed in and got the requisite visitor's badge. The two agents were already in the conference room. The lead was Ida Cramer, and her assistant was a young man, Evan Randle. She dressed like an Administration staffer—black wrinkled pants, a white cotton blouse and loafers, which some might say was dowdy. She wore no make-up. She was somewhat overweight. Why am I thinking this? I am being judgmental and sexist. She has a right to be herself.

But the truth is, there is no imperative to make oneself attractive in her world: there were no clients who needed to be impressed and no peers to evaluate you and your age on the basis of your appearance, unlike in my world. In fact, being attractive might work to her disadvantage if she did care: who knows, it might indicate that she was not serious enough, that there wasn't enough substance there to be considered a good agent. As an agent, she had her status. No need to impress me or anyone else. But would she judge me? Maybe rate me as overly concerned about my appearance and certainly overly made-up?

Too bad! I had business standards to follow.

Evan Randle was trim, neatly dressed but with non-descript brownish hair not cut well and sallow skin. He seemed like a newbie and was likely there to learn how to interview, or intimidate, people. He barely said hello. He did not shake my hand. She did, and her hands were clammy. Mine might have been, too. They both had open file folders in front of them.

Cramer began by asking, "Ms. James, in what context did you interact with Ms. Phillips?"

I told her that my client and Ms. Phillips held licenses in the same frequency bands, and Ms. Phillips claimed my client held them illegally. She alleged that there were a multitude of construction irregularities, descriptions of which she expanded exponentially over the years. Thus, she claimed, my client's licenses were invalid and therefore, they were hers according to Administration rules. Consequently, there was litigation between my client and her.

"How long has this litigation gone on?" Cramer asked.

"About ten years," I said. She and Randle looked at each other. To my perception, the look was meaningful. I began to fear the next question.

"Was there any rancor between your client and Ms. Phillips during this long litigation?" she asked.

"My client was resigned to the litigation at the Administration and in the courts. When we spoke about the litigation, he emphasized that we should be civil," I answered

"And were you civil?" she asked.

"It depends. If she wasn't calling my client or me felons, then I was civil. If she was " I spread out my hands.

"Did you ever talk about Ms. Phillips to anyone besides your client," she asked.

"Well," I paused, "if someone mentioned her to me and asked what to expect from her in a litigation proceeding, I generally gave them some background."

"What did you say, specifically?" she asked.

"Again, it depends on who it was and how much they had been involved with Ms. Phillips, or were about to be involved with her." I responded. "If they wanted insight into her, I tried to help. Not that I had especially acute insight."

Cramer thumbed through the papers in her folder. I could see some pleadings that were likely mine. I rarely lost control in my pleadings. I had my law license to protect. Ms. Phillips had no such worries. She could let her opponent have it without limits.

Cramer said, "It looks as if you had intense written correspondence with Ms. Phillips. In fact, you told her regularly that she knew nothing about the law and that her arguments were without merit."

"From my standpoint," I said, "it was the truth. To assert the truth is not a crime. Ms. Phillips dreamed up her arguments, generally without reference to any rules or cases. The arguments usually were irrational, sometimes not even understandable—at least to me and to my law partner."

"Did you ever discuss what you wanted to do about Ms. Phillips with any peers?"

"I...am not sure what you mean by that," I said.

"Did you ever tell anyone that someone should hire a hitman?"

I laughed out loud. "If I ever did, it was only a joke. But I don't remember saying that kind of thing to anyone."

"Well, one of your peers told us that you did say it."

I felt dread. In a conversation long ago, perhaps I had been indiscreet while talking with a peer. But then, everyone I spoke with about D.L. was just as likely to say such things. Was someone trying to involve me in her death? Who might have told them that?

Suddenly, I remembered the exact incident. I had been leaving the Administration building after a particular difficult group "negotiation" session at the Administration staff with D.L. on the speaker phone. In a burst of frustration, I vented: "I used to think that someone should hire a hitman, but now I think D.L just needs a more exciting love life." It was trite of me and just a bit sarcastic, given the gossip around D.L.'s amorous adventures, everything short of harnesses and whips. It appeared to me that the two FBI agents were not amused and looked dubious about my quick recall of the conversation. It seemed to me that they probably hadn't gotten the full version.

It's likely that I should have stopped the discussion before then, when I sensed that we were going down a treacherous road.

Now, I said, "This conversation is developing beyond a simple interview. In fact, I feel that this is becoming an interrogation. I think that I need to be represented by a lawyer."

Ida shrugged. "As you wish. Then we will pick up on this interview."

Did I detect a threat in her voice? I wasn't sure.

The interview ended, and I left unhinged, barely aware of my ten block walk back to my office in the sweltering heat. When I sat down, sweating, at my desk, I called Jesse, who was out of the office that day.

"Jesse," I sighed, "I think that they believe I actually was involved in D.L.'s death. They talked about things, casual remarks, that I said long ago to a group of lawyers after a meeting with D.L. They're acting as if I was serious when I said them."

Jesse was less than reassuring. "This could be dangerous for you."

We talked about how to tell the firm management about the FBI's interest in me and who might represent me. This was a nightmare scenario that hadn't entered into my calculations on how the interview might proceed. I thought the investigators would focus on D.L. and a possible perpetrator or motive that I could provide. Instead, they focused on our public disputes and name calling. They were acting as if our animosity was a motive, and I was the perpetrator.

I was terrified that the FBI was looking for a way to resolve an embarrassing political situation quickly and I had been made a target by a subterfuge. Congress had already started discussing possible hearings on how a murder could have happened at the Administration. We had heard that the Chairman of the Administration had been interrogated by the White House on the security of the buildings, the investigation of the background of the hires within the Administration and possible ineptitude of those in charge. A quick resolution was clearly required to right an untenable political situation. Those scrambling for resolution might believe that I was the nearest, easiest target.

I called the managing partner, left a voicemail and asked for a telephone conference in the morning. He emailed me back later and set up the call for 10:00 AM.

I dreaded going home that night. It would be my private hell filled with terrifying speculative outcomes and another sleepless night. Why had that agent asked about my long ago "joke?" Surely, there couldn't really be a hitman involved in the murder. It was preposterous. And would an FBI agent make allusions to such a fact to the interviewee, even if it were true, in an interview? I didn't think so, but criminal investigation wasn't my expertise.

Did the police know something about me? I couldn't imagine what. I knew nothing about the murder, except from gossip. I tried to get a grip on myself, but I wasn't able to sleep at all. I read, dozed, jerked awake in a panic five minutes later. The night crept on as I conjured nightmare scenarios. Cam and I had split six months ago, but he was the only person I wanted to talk to about this stuff. I certainly didn't want to tell Jean what had happened with the FBI. I felt completely alone. Helpless. My career was at risk because it was possible that someone might be slanting the investigation my way. Why? Or was I just being paranoid? After all, it was in the middle of the night. I always assume the worst at 2:30 AM.

At 10:00 the next morning, Jesse and I placed the call to the managing partner, Ray Locke, at the home office in Texas. Ray was a calm, gregarious man who had grown into embracing the world of females and minorities in the ranks. He was raised to hunt and fish and be a manly-man, so his effort was heroic. When I first met him, he was fairly hefty, but in recent years, the firm was focused on health and he vigorously joined in and slimmed down. The firm had an activity device contest for almost a year, and most of us were enlisted to become healthier. The reward was an iPad to the individuals who walked their 10,000 steps each day. Ray was open minded to new ideas. He was also fair.

Jesse sat in my office in a chair across from my desk. His focus was on the speaker, not on me. I told Ray about my FBI interview and that statements made by the agent seemed to imply that I was somehow involved in the murder of D.L. I mentioned that there might be a need for legal representation.

Ray was incredulous, "You are kidding, right? An agent implied that you actually hired a hitman because you were involved in litigation, based solely on a statement from another lawyer? Leyla, what kind of investigation is this? Of course, there will be acrimony in litigation. It happens all the time!" That put the situation into a clearer perspective for me. It would have been helpful if I had gotten that kind of incredulous reaction from Jesse. Maybe, then, I would have been able to sleep for an hour or more the previous night. But Jesse was the pessimist in our team, always seeing the downside of an event. I tended to take the positive view of situations. We balanced out each other in our legal analysis and case approaches. But I needed him to be positive now.

He wasn't. Sure enough, Jesse said, "Leyla and D.L. never got along. It was well known through-out our legal community."

"The question is," I said, "should I get a lawyer or not?"

"Leyla," Ray said. "Aren't you rushing into something? The FBI interviews aren't completed. From what you tell me, they haven't even started the actual investigation outside the Administration. Why don't we wait?"

Jesse cleared his throat, and I feared the worst. "Ray, I think Leyla should at least start getting some ideas on representation. Her interview sounds to me as if someone's thinking Leyla was involved in in D.L.'s death...somehow," he added lamely when he saw the look I was giving him.

We decided that I would ask around about representation, but I would keep a low profile and wait until the agents called me again. They had ten more people to interview. Hopefully, someone would give them better leads and refocus their attention.

In the meantime, I needed to write a memo and download my FBI interview to the firm's ethics partner. Eliot was not a supportive person and interrogated me on the phone as if I were a defendant in one of his litigations. He apparently had not gotten the memo about welcoming diversity and I felt decidedly like an outsider and a mess-up, even though I was a partner in the firm. The main problem was that he was at the home office in Texas, and I couldn't have an eyeball-to-eyeball discussion with him in his office. Our conversation resulted in further apprehension. What impact might this interview have on my career at the firm? I sensed open hostility from Ida Cramer, for no particular reason that I knew. Her emphasis on a single statement of mine was of deep concern to me. I promised that I would forward the transcript to Eliot as soon as I received it.

I spent the rest of the day prepping my client for his interview with the FBI, scheduled for the next morning. Ida had graciously allowed him to be interviewed on the telephone rather than flying him in from California. The next day, I listened silently on the call from my office. I was thankful for that: sitting in the same cold office with two FBI agents and staring at a speaker would have been another version of hell. The call lasted a half hour.

Ida was not at all aggressive with him and, in fact, was rather pleasant. It was obvious that he wasn't a target. But this made it difficult for me to complain to him about my negative treatment. He knew a little of my exchange in my FBI interview. I think that he just couldn't understand that I was suffering harsh treatment in the representation of his company, unless it was something that I might have provoked. My job was to keep my angst out of my client conversations. Somehow, I would have to be upbeat when we discussed his business in our regular phone calls.

# CHAPTER 7: Give Me a Break.

Before all the ruckus began, I had promised my mother I would drive home that weekend to the Delaware coast where she lived and where I grew up. Her three daughters were all busy, but I was within easy driving range, so it fell to me to periodically check in at home.

This time, I dreaded it. I didn't want to tell her about the FBI investigation and the upheaval in my life. She knew about D.L. I had ranted to her about D.L.'s tirades against me. Now, I just didn't want to talk about anything related to the investigation.

Before my father's death, my parents bragged about me, the lawyer, to the point of embarrassment. I could imagine the shame to my mother if my career went south and my name appeared in the Washington newspapers—as a suspect in a murder, no less. I could see it now on the front page, "Attorney Arrested for RFA Murder!" With my mugshot and name. Maybe it was denial; maybe it was simply protecting her from this ground-shaking event in my life.

She had worried about my break-up with Cam. I couldn't add this to her concerns over me. She liked Cam and he liked her. When I told her that he had moved out, her voice caught in a sob, "Oh, Leyla, I am so sad for you. Are you sure it's over?"

I felt guilty about the effect on her. Cam was so kind to her after my father died. He'd hug her when we came to visit, asking in the most touching way, "How are you, Lillian?" He did little repairs for her in the house and her shop. And he was concerned about her being alone after 42 years with my father. Cam was a kind man. I felt remorse.

I drove through the quiet, leafy, small towns in Maryland and Delaware on the way to the coast. I thought about the people living peaceful, simple lives there, free from my particular kind of angst. But then they probably had their own small-town complications, over what their neighbors were saying and who was misbehaving. They might even have legal problems. No place is perfect.

I was now on the part of the road notorious for bad accidents, with blind spots and stop signs that often went ignored from country side roads. Little roadside shrines to lost loved ones appeared, here and there, where fatal accidents happened. In fact, one of my best high school friends had died on this road. She was driving at night in the dark in the rain, coming back from a visit to her dad who had moved to a nearby town. She was just 17 and not comfortable with driving. She was also distraught over her parents' separation and had told me that day, "Sometimes, I just want to give up "

"Don't say that, April!" I pleaded. "Things will get better. Come to see me on the way home tonight." I waited for her. April and I were longtime friends. We'd known each other since we were five. We ran around together with our buddies in a herd, as my mother said, going from one house to another, eating any treats that we could find.

The phone rang later that night. It was one of my mother's friends calling. I could hear my mother's voice turn from happy to shock, "Oh, my God, no! Not April. Dee must be devastated. What happened?"

I sat in my room cringing, listening to my mother's responses.

"I just don't know what to say!" my mother said. "But I have to call Dee. I know she needs her friends now."

It turned out that April's car had hydroplaned on a curve. She lost control of the car in the pouring rain and hit a tree. She died instantly. I was stunned, cold with fear, wondering if April had really given up. I never told anyone what she said to me. There was no reason to believe it was anything but an accident. But still.

It was the first time I'd experienced the death of a peer. I'd look at the clock and think: Six hours ago, April was still alive. It was beyond my comprehension that she was dead.

Her mother had an open casket funeral. It tore my heart to see her there, never again to toss her hair back or turn a cartwheel in our cheerleading routines. My friends and I were inconsolable. It just seemed so cruel. It still bothers me every time I drive that stretch of road. Her death taught me an early lesson on how fragile life is.

A thought flashed through my mind that one sharp turn at the trees along that dark country road, going 60 miles an hour, could put me out of my agony. Stop! I admonished myself. I was stronger than that. I wasn't a seventeen-year-old kid anymore. I wouldn't give anyone the satisfaction, including an FBI agent, of assuming I'd killed myself because I was guilty of something. Further, if someone had deliberately made me look guilty, I wasn't going to add to their pleasure. No, suicide wasn't my style. I was taught to suck it up, and I would. I drove on.

I arrived at my mother's house, determined to keep my personal vow not to discuss anything that would upset her. She greeted me at the door. We hugged, and I could feel her loving stability around me. Some needed human kindness, at last!

"How are you?" she said. Her handsome face was cocked to the right, her green eyes focused on my face. Worry lines appeared between her eyes as she studied me. She knew that she could get something out of me face to face, if not over the phone. But she was wrong this time. She added, "Lynn is worried about you."

Lynn is my older, saner sister. She lives in Chicago. She has a life. We catch up on the phone every week, mainly as we commute. She is married, delighted not to be part of the dating scene. Her life has a different kind of stress. She is a dentist, has a three-year-old boy and is about to have a baby daughter. I try to keep our conversations focused on her, but she keeps asking about my life.

In weaker moments, I download a little to her: an old habit of confession to an older sibling. But I try to keep it general. I tell her that I'm not dating now, that I haven't seen Cam in six months and that's fine with me because I'm very busy. Now, I'm saying the same things to my mother.

"Things are good," I tell my mother. "I'm really busy; I'm not pining for Cam; and life is fine at the firm. I'm still working out, riding my bike and trying to run. I'm moving forward, no problem. Maybe that's the way it will always be." I didn't tell her that I had quit the gym because I didn't want to run into Cam. But Lynn probably told her that.

"Are you sure, dear?" she asked. "You look tired."

Obviously, she had her doubts, but I thought that maybe she didn't want to know the truth. She gets a watered-down version from Lynn and she is living a calm life now, in the off season anyway. She has a small clothing shop, called Lillian's after her. She has an amazing knack for finding distinctive clothes that have made her popular with both the locals and summer guests. She also is a striking model for her clothes. Tall, slim-waisted, with fabulous posture. She wears her blonde/white hair tied at the nape of her neck. Her elegance has not been passed on to me. I rely on the standard lawyer wear, suits or separates and heels, not stilettos. She tries to help me achieve some style since I don't have that flair.

Not like D.L. who was a red-headed knockout with vibrant designer clothes. D.L. made no secret about her obsession. She bragged about her outfit and its cost one day before a meeting: Calvin Klein (bright blue sweater dress, $2798); Balenciaga (coordinated jacket, $5350); Saint Laurent (boots, $1095 and bag, $2690); and Burberry (shearling coat, $7000). Seriously! Another lawyer and I exchanged bemused side glances. I didn't have the money, and designer fashion didn't interest me, at all. I hate to shop. I shared this D.L. story with my mother. She just shook her head and said, "That woman is a narcissist." She paused. "But she would make a very good customer." We laughed.

Right now, I just wanted my mother to have peace and quiet. She'd suffered through my father's illness for two and a half years, commuting between their house and the D.C. clinic every other week for his treatments. At the beginning there was an operation to remove a colon growth. He somehow survived. They were optimistic. Six months later, there were shadows on the liver and pancreas. It became a nightmare of finding and trying to stamp out spots that popped up by targeted chemo treatments. He finally died after a brief stay in the hospital. It was kidney failure, caused by the cancer. That was just a year and a half ago. My mother needed time to recuperate. She didn't need to worry about me.

She made me my favorite dinner, rockfish. An open bottle of my favorite Sauvignon Blanc was on the counter. She poured two glasses. She continued to dig into my life.

"I'm your mother, I know that things aren't right with you. You seem distracted. What's wrong? Is it still about Cam?"

"Wow, am I that transparent?" I asked, sipping my wine while she finished tossing the salad.

"It's not about Cam. An issue has come up about D.L."

"I read about her murder in the paper. I was going to call you but thought better of it."

"Why?"

"Because you get wrought up when you talk about her."

I laughed. "Here I am tiptoeing around you, and you are tiptoeing around me. It's funny."

She didn't smile and looked at me quizzically.

"Well, I'm not going to talk about any issues in my life because you've had enough grief in your life to last a long time."

"You'd be surprised how tough I am," she said, looking me in the eyes. She was smiling. "Where do you think you got your spunk? But if you don't want to talk, that's fine. You've always had your life under control and I'm so proud of you for it. Sometimes, Suzanne seemed so lost and I didn't know what to do because you and Lynn never lost your direction."

OMG. If she only knew how much pressure that put on me! I can't fail after that. But what if I do?

The next morning, I ran to the boardwalk and back to look around town. Then I showered, changed and walked to my mother's shop. She offered and I accepted a wardrobe "touch-up", as she called it. She did this with such diplomacy and love that I couldn't take offense at her efforts to make me, if not trendy, at least passable. She floated around her shop pulling out a blouse here, a jacket there and adding colorful and striking accessories, like a belt or a scarf. No need to tell her that scarves flummoxed me, that I could never get them to stay in place. She already knew that by looking. But I kept trying.

After my makeover, we went to lunch at our favorite seafood place across the street. She greeted several friends and customers as we walked to our table. We chatted a few minutes with one of her friendly competitors before we sat down to our favorite — crab cakes and slaw. It was good to be home and to see friendly faces. I felt momentary relief. After lunch, my mother went back to her shop and I walked back to her house. My phone rang. I looked at the number. It didn't look familiar, but I answered anyway. It was Graciela and she was in tears.

"What's the matter?" I asked.

"My boy. He ran away."

"Oh, no! Do you have any idea where he went?"

"Jes, we found. At parquet. Crying."

I felt horrible because I had not followed through yet with the Pro Bono group.

"Graciela, I will research this afternoon. I think that a bilingual attorney will help you with school, but I will also ask her about counseling. Don't worry, I will be back in touch with you as soon as possible. When can I call you?"

"Call me tomorrow." She was emphatic. She was a smart, tough cookie.

I researched the D.C. Bar Pro Bono website which led me to a bilingual Advice and Referral clinic and at least got a name and a phone number. It sounded as if they would discuss the problem and either send Graciela to an attorney or a social worker. I would call Graciela tomorrow on the way home, on country roads, not the Beltway. And I would follow-up with a call to the attorney on Monday morning. Poor Graciela. Poor Matias.

In the evening, I met up with some of my hometown friends at a new upscale restaurant on the ocean block. As I drove up, I listened to the ocean: that consistent, familiar sound of the surf brought contentment, a reminder of my peaceful childhood. I should come home more often, it gives me the relaxation I need.

Sometimes I envied my school friends. Some of them came back to town after college years ago, to step into the family business. Others ran their own businesses, had families and lived what seemed to me easy small-town lives. They were doing nothing dramatic, but they appeared to be happy or at least contented.

On the other hand, I was involved in a frenetic unfolding drama whether I wanted it or not. I didn't and I really didn't want to talk about my life. Our conversation was about old times and there were stories about their kids, acting in plays, excelling (or not) at sports and school. I was glad to listen. Whenever they inquired about my life in D.C., I said life was busy, good and I was having fun, nothing more. We did not talk about Cam, although they met him several times and liked him. When I announced that we were over, Sue Ann, my (and April's) good high school friend, sighed and said, "Are you sure? You were such a good pair." It was hard not to be envious of them and their lifestyle of marriage, children and employment in a non-type A town.

"Hey, I forgot to mention this." said Sue Ann, "Did you hear about Mr. Sanders?"

"What about him?" I asked. Lou Sanders was April's dad. He was the last person to see her before she drove away in the rain. Mr. Sanders had left April's mother and moved in with a male friend who had been his secret lover for five years before.

That was back in the days when coming out was still surprising to our little community. The separation really affected April. She was mortified. She had been reclusive for a while, not wanting to talk about it or have people talk about her. April and I had many heart-to-hearts after he left the house and people began to gossip.

"Mr. Sanders died last month. In hospice, he became agitated about April's death. He mumbled over and over, as he slid in and out of con-sciousness, that her death was his fault, that she would still be alive if he... But he never got the words out to tell the hospice worker before he died."

"Does anyone have an idea what he was trying to say?" I asked, feeling a visceral reluctance to relive the anguish of my friend's death and at the same time, an eagerness to have her death explained, to erase my fear that she had impulsively swerved off the road.

"From what we hear he only talked about it in public once, shortly after the accident with his partner at a party, after several drinks. The partner moved him to the porch to let him talk. But several people overheard him sobbing. His partner doesn't want to talk about it now, said that it was Lou's secret and not his to tell."

"Wow. It must be an awful secret. On the other hand, it might be healing for her family and friends, us, to know." I felt unsettled, like there might be a resolution to the mystery of April's violent death. It's out there but we might never know it.

"Yeah, I know," Sue Ann said. "I always wondered what really happened." The group conversation switched back to the ordinary, about their activities and gossip about our classmates who were not there.

My mother had waited up for me. "Well, dear, tell me all about it."

"Mom, you know everything that goes on in this town! Why didn't you tell me about Mr. Sanders?"

My mother rarely loses her composure, but she shook her head as if to rid it of some dreadful thought.

"Leyla, he was dying and on sedatives. I don't think he knew what he was saying."

"But his partner verified that he had felt responsible and told his friends that Mr. Sanders had talked about it, described it."

"But Lou had been drinking then."

"Mother, it must be something that he said to her."

My mother looked sorrowfully at me and said, "I know you still want an explanation for her death, even after all these years. But I don't think we'll ever know for sure what really happened that night."

I realized that whatever I was feeling about this news might be exaggerated by the state of my life and that it was fruitless or even hurtful to shift it to my mother. But I made a note to myself to try to find out Mr. Sanders' secret. What was his boyfriend's name again? I would ask around. I'd email Sue Ann. What I needed right now: another mystery.

I changed the tone with my mother. We chatted about my friends and their lives, as they described them. She was delighted to hear the details about them and their children. Looking at her face, I felt a twinge of guilt for me and my younger sister Suzanne denying her more grandchildren. Grandchildren who lived closer to her. My younger sister in New York was single too, living an all-consuming life on Wall Street. She told us of 24-hour office routines with a catnap or two on a couch or the floor to get through a project. I had not seen her since Christmas. We rarely talked. Too busy.

After a walk to town and breakfast the next morning with my mother, I drove home on Sunday afternoon, dreading the bleak week ahead. My mother's parting words were, "Don't worry, dear. You have never failed in the past." To my sorry state, that felt more like an admonition than an encouragement.

Anyway, that would be tested soon: I knew that the FBI would contact me for a further discussion. I had to get through it, as I'd gotten through law school, the bar exam and as an associate. "Just do it and get past it." I told myself. It did not feel any better. I put the key in my apartment door. It was quiet and I was alone, again, with my fears.

# CHAPTER 8: The Phone Call.

O f course, it came. It was inevitable. I could tell from the number on my phone that it was the agent. It was only one week later, and Ida had come after me to set up a date for completing the interview.

"I'm hiring an attorney and she'll be back in touch with you as soon as possible," I said.

Then I called my Managing Partner who now sounded a little more serious. He counseled me, "You probably want to appear as helpful to the investigation."

It seemed to me that he was telling me not to take the Fifth. He was not comforting to me. Neither was Jesse, who appeared to be detached from my plight and, I suspected, just slightly amused by it. But I was getting paranoid. "Well, D.L. continues to come after you even from the grave," Jesse said lightly. "After all the years of her threats, it looks like she is finally putting you through the paces."

"Thanks for the support," I sniped. "I knew I could rely on you to have my back." He just laughed, and I fumed. He had an odd sense of humor.

The firm hired my attorney, Gail Davis, whom I'd researched. In our initial conversation on the phone I described my predicament. I was trying to keep my tone professional but barely held it together. I was used to being the grown-up in the room, the inquisitor, not the other way around.

Gail came highly recommended from one of my best friends in law school. Gail Davis also was a graduate from our law school and a colleague of another law school friend who practiced criminal defense in a neighboring jurisdiction. She practiced chiefly in the District of Columbia. I arranged an interview with her for the next day.

The firm notified our insurance carrier. The managing partner informed

me of the notice in a gruff voicemail. I was feeling sick. Now all of my partners, or at least the management committee, knew about me. I felt like an
outlaw, putting the firm at risk, dragging it down. This made it clear to
me that the investigation could really affect not only my law practice but
also my law firm. On one piece of gossip, my life was turned upside down.
Why?

When I arrived at Gail's office, I was escorted to a plain conference
room by her assistant. Gail was a solo practitioner and her offices were
fittingly not flamboyant. I'd emailed her some representative documents
that I'd filed at the Administration which involved some of my strongest
arguments with D.L. Outside of the Administration, the things that D.L.
had stated in her papers could have constituted slander or libel, but within
the Administration, those things easily could be written—particularly by
someone who was attempting to be her own lawyer. In layman's terms,
there is a privilege that has been applied to statements made in administrative proceedings. She could call me whatever and whenever she wanted
there. I could do nothing about it.

While the documents revealed the enmity between me and Phillips,
nothing that I said—even in the most extreme cases—resembled a threat
of death from me or even slander. I was so at a loss for this interest in me
by the FBI that I had reason to believe I'd stumbled into an incriminating
evidence trap when discussing D.L.'s death without a lawyer. Who would
possibly have guessed that I'd be the least bit suspect in a case involving
a person I hadn't even seen in years? Why would the agent possibly think
that I had anything to do with this murder?

Gail Davis came into the room and introduced herself. She was a
no-nonsense, attractive brunette, long hair pulled back in a ponytail and
very buttoned down in a dark pantsuit and heels, court attire. She got
down to the immediate business, my criminal defense. A criminal defense
attorney for me! I was probably an anomaly in Gail's practice.

"So how did you get yourself in this mess?"

"Well, I'm not sure that I did it completely by myself." I tried to explain
D.L.'s idiosyncrasies and her effect on not only me but on other unfortu-
nate attorneys.

"I sometimes think that someone may by stacking the deck against
me."

The first thing Gail stressed was that there was only an "interest" by the
FBI agent in me, that my fears were not supportable. "No one has accused
you of anything and we should try to be helpful in the investigation in

order to allay any more suspicion," she said. She was going to be with me during the completion of the interview to stop it, if it ventured into accusations and to see if I wanted or needed any kind of immunity. From what, I wondered. She made me feel less apprehensive but still unsettled.

"Why do you suppose they're interested in me?" I asked. "I wasn't even in town the day of the murder. I can produce at least one witness to say that I was 100 miles away. I didn't even know that D.L. was going to be at the Administration and I had no interest in her comings and goings. How could the agent be interested at all in me?"

"Well," Gail said, "I think that she doesn't know any of your whereabouts as fact, but someone told her that you had mentioned a hitman."

"My God!" I exploded. "I wouldn't have any idea how to even contact a hitman. And what if the so-called hitman turned out to be an undercover cop? You hear about that all the time. No, I'm too smart to try anything like that."

"You told me that you travel out of the country occasionally," my attorney said. "The FBI probably knows that. You could've come across someone in your travels who might be helpful to you."

Gail was referring to my past visits to the Caribbean with Cam, which I had listed on my client form. We had made it a practice to take 4-day weekends twice a year from Washington to enjoy the sun away the dismal, dark days of Washington's "wintry mix." Although this weather lasted from the end of December to the middle of March, which seemed interminable, at least we got out of town for a little while. The idea that I would scout for a hitman while I was on a sunny vacation with my lover was unfathomable to my mind. As an aside, I wondered, with a pang, whether Cam and his new girlfriend had taken any tropical trips.

"I guess you're just playing devil's advocate," I sighed. "But it's really depressing because that's exactly what the agent would say, wouldn't she? The big question is, why are we even discussing such preposterous speculations?" I've never done anything in my life that was suspect, and now the spotlight was focused on me in the worst of ways.

"The agent raised a hitman," Gail said, "and we need to strategize about how to deal with it. You need to be cooperative. I will object if they wander into an area where they may be setting you up."

We ended our meeting with a phone call to Ida Cramer from Gail. The call went to voicemail and Gail reported that she had been hired by me. She asked Ida to return her call to set up the interview. I left Gail's office with the familiar feeling of dread.

The next morning, the call light was lit on my phone when I arrived at work. Of course, Ida had called Gail back late yesterday. Our interview would be next Tuesday. That gave me a few days to anticipate and stew about Ida's questions.

Tuesday morning, Gail and I were there bright and early, waiting for Ida and her sidekick to appear. They shuffled in and opened their files. The interview commenced.

The Transcript.

IDA CRAMER: On the record, we are here, Ms. James, with your attorney Gail Davis to complete the interview in the investigation of the death of D.L. Phillips. We interrupted our interview when we were discussing a possible comment by you to one of your peers about hiring a hitman in connection with Ms. Phillips.

GAIL DAVIS: We object to the wording of your statement, "comment by you about hiring a hitman in connection with Ms. Phillips." (Gail, with her glasses perched on her nose, was looking at the previous interview transcript.) It is out of context and, from the prior transcript, it was a question from you. You said to my client, "Did you ever tell anyone that someone should hire a hitman?" It was not a discussion with Ms. James.

Ida Cramer went on, without a beat.

IDA CRAMER: We interrupted our interview when I questioned you about a possible comment by you to one of your peers about hiring a hitman in connection with the death of Ms. Phillips.

ME: Yes, we did interrupt the interview. The question was preposterous.

IDA CRAMER: Was there such a comment?

ME: I said in the transcript that I had joked that, "I used to think that someone should hire a hitman, but now I think that D.L just needs a more exciting love life."

GAIL DAVIS: Further, we would not characterize it as a "comment." My client was remembering a joke from a conversation with a peer. We are trying to be helpful here, but you appear to have another agenda. I will let my client answer that question, but I may need to instruct her that she has the right to remain silent. I will invoke that at any time.

IDA CRAMER: Understood. Was there such a comment?

ME: First, if I made any reference to a hitman, as I said, it was in jest. What kind of a legitimate lawyer would ever seriously say such a thing? Second, I never said that I personally would hire a hitman. I was joking, and your informant did not give you the full context of the joke. Again, I said specifically that I used to think that someone should hire a hitman, but now I think that D.L. Phillips just needed a more exciting love life. The peer said, by the way, that that wasn't possible since D.L. would need simultaneous multiple exciting love affairs. Were you told that?

IDA CRAMER: What would you say, if I told you that we believe that there could be a hitman involved with Ms. Phillips' death?

ME: Can the FBI give an interviewee that kind of confidential information? Really? But since you asked, I would think that this sort of thing just couldn't happen in a federal building with a person who is not a regular visitor and who was scheduled for a meeting that only got delayed at the last minute. It could not happen under those circumstances. It was just too random.

IDA CRAMER: I did not say that it has been determined that there was a hitman. I just hypothesized that we believe that there could have been a hitman.

ME: And why do you believe that?

IDA CRAMER: The manner of the killing.

ME: Then, that leaves me out. I know nothing about killing in any manner.

IDA CRAMER: I said of the killing, not of the hiring.

ME: Hiring a hitman is outside of my area of expertise.

IDA CRAMER: Well, there was a note with an address on it at the crimescene—perhaps dropped by the killer—that had your DNA on it.

GAIL DAVIS: Let's stop right here. You said that my client's DNA is on a slip of paper with an address on it at the crime scene? First, how did you get my client's DNA to determine that and second, whose address was on the note?

IDA CRAMER: It appears that your client and her family all took DNA tests. These tests were uploaded to a genealogy website and that is where we found Leyla's DNA, after we tested the paper at the scene. And we are not at liberty to tell you whose address was on the paper.

Ida Cramer sat back with a self-satisfied demeanor as if she was the queen of sleuths. I was angry. Apparently, my lawyer was a little miffed, too. It was true that my family took the DNA tests because my sister Lynn had taken it first before she got pregnant. She found that such genetic testing can discover gene variants associated with the MS, which ran in my father's family. She didn't have the gene variant but we wondered who else was carrying it. Suzanne and I also took the test, and I didn't know what happened to the results after the testing. To think that the FBI actually used my voluntary testing for a family disease to finger me as a murder suspect was appalling. I had heard that DNA could be swiped anywhere. Presto, chango: evidence against a suspect.

GAIL DAVIS: This is a violation of my client's rights. I suggest that we end this interview because I am advising her to remain silent. If she agrees, we are finished here.

ME: I agree.

IDA CRAMER: A word of warning. Do not destroy any evidence. We may issue a subpoena for it. We may also refer this matter to a prosecutor for a grand jury.

GAIL DAVIS: We will take that under advisement.

# CHAPTER 9: What Next?

Gail and I were quiet on the walk back to her office. I expressed surprise that there wasn't a prosecutor involved already. "But then, Ida wants to play around with me for a while." I shrugged. "Her little game." Gail said nothing.

This investigation was not going in any direction that would have an immediate favorable outcome for me. In fact, if we kept going down this path, I would be either before a grand jury shortly or hear that the grand jury had indicted me. The FBI would have me set up for prosecution and Gail would counsel me the same way that I did in my practice, preaching caution to her client. The goal was to let the law take the lead and not be proactive. But I knew something from my practice and from observation: if an agency has a victim in its teeth, it never lets go easily and apologizes. It's a matter of expediency over accuracy, especially in a high-profile case like this.

I was sure the FBI was getting pressure from multiple higher authorities to solve the murder and shut down threatened Congressional inquiries. I was in the process of being swept along in the guise of letting things "settle down." I have seen "settling down" in my cases and others, and it was never a pretty sight. The settling down process could have me in court being accused of hiring a hitman and, ultimately, killing D.L.

True to form, Gail told me not to worry—rationality and the law would win the day. I did not believe that for one moment. I let her go on saying that there was no firm evidence about me and my role in the death of D.L., that many other lawyers were in the same situation I was, and so on. I did not believe any of it. I had seen my client taken to court by D.L. where we stayed for years, writing briefs, responding to amended briefs, going to hearings in the trial court, answering appeals to the court of appeals and, yes, even to the Supreme Court. The case was dismissed, finally, after four years, but the resources and expense were outrageous. I needed to save myself because I did not trust the law—no disrespect to Gail, my lawyer—to save me, without affecting my livelihood, draining my resources and my wellbeing. The physics of law is that if a case is in motion, it will stay in (slow) motion or have me waiting, squirming and indirectly paying legal fees, through the process, no matter what the facts might be. Ultimately, I might win but my life, livelihood and financial resources would be sucked dry by that time. I had to do something to save myself. But what?

Per instructions from the firm, I set up a conference call with the managing partner. His secretary told me that the firm ethics attorney would also be on the conference call. It would be held the next morning at 10:00 AM Eastern. I was to provide notes on the FBI interview for them prior to the call. Jesse was also to be on the call.

I had the distinct feeling that the firm was now taking a sterner approach to this proceeding than they had in the past. Now that the insurance company had come on board, the informal process that had existed in all my other dealings with the firm had taken a turn. I thought everything is going to be papered from here on: the firm is in full defensive mode. I was the loose cannon, in their eyes, and I wondered how long that was going to last before something more dire would develop in my status at the firm.

I sat at my desk, writing my recollections of the FBI interview. I became even more disheartened. I had no doubt that Ida was coming at me. And I had done exactly what Ray Locke had asked me not to do: asserted the right to silence. It did not matter that the questioning was overreaching, I had refused to answer the questions.

It took me two hours to put my memo together for the home office. I forwarded it to Gail and asked her to take a quick look before I emailed it to Texas.

I then settled down to returning client calls and reviewing email. An hour later, Gail called me.

"You are painting a pretty gloomy picture in your memo. Do you want to give the home office such a negative view of the proceeding?"

"Well, you were there. How do you perceive it?"

"You are one of twenty-plus people that the FBI is interviewing."

"Yes, but it appears that I'm the only one the FBI is practically accusing of hiring a hitman!"

"That's just a tactic. You aren't used to a proceeding like this. You're more at ease in civil proceedings."

"But here, my practice, my livelihood, resources and my life are on the line."

"Wait," Gail interjected. "Stop catastrophizing. Listen to me and get ahold of yourself. I will do a little editing from a more objective perspective. I'll get it back to you shortly."

A half hour later, I receive my lawyer's sunny view of the ordeal that I had just survived. It didn't appear that we were in the same interview. Nevertheless, I added one or two edits and I sent it off to the managing partner and the ethics lawyer.

I finished up and headed home. Over dinner, I read a book to get my mind off the morning meeting. When that didn't work, I watched "This is Us." Usually, the show holds my attention, but this time it didn't. I needed something to distract myself.

I called my mother. "Just checking in to say thank you for the weekend."

"It's always good to hear from you, dear. I am glad that you got away from your job for a change. You need more time away from the desk. More down time. You are always welcome here."

"So, what's going on, Mom?"

"Well, I have someone dropping by in about fifteen minutes."

"Oh, okay. Who is it?" I asked, thinking it was one of her friends that I knew.

"He's Drew Osborne, a member of the club. We are on a committee for the Holiday party this year."

"Do I know him?" I persisted.

"No, I don't think so. He and his wife moved to town full-time about three years ago."

Good, I thought. He is married. I am protective of my mother. "And then his wife died about the same time as your father."

I tensed, then immediately scolded myself. My mother has a right to her life. I cannot interfere.

"OK, Mom, I'll let you go."

"Oh, I'm ready, so I can talk." In the background, I heard the doorbell. "Oh, he's early," she said in a fluttery voice.

"Have a nice time. Maybe I'll come home for the party this year."

"Do, darling. I will talk to you soon."

"Oh, and Mom, please let me know if you hear more about Mr. Sanders."

"If I hear anything, I will let you know. Bye, darling." She hung up the phone and disappeared into a scenario that was playing out in my mind. "You," I said to myself, "are just feeling sorry for yourself and a little jealous of a man in your mother's life. Stop it." At least it was distracting, and I did not want her to get hurt—again.

Somehow, I got through the night, cobbling together five and a half hours. I went running at 6:00 AM and was out the door for work at 8:00. When I arrived, I picked up on a pleading, which needed to be filed tomorrow and had gone unattended yesterday following my interview. I started in and worked until Jesse came into my office at 9:30.

"Well, what's the plan?" he said.

"I sent them a memo detailing the interview yesterday, so I'm thinking that we will start from there."

"I would like to have seen it before it went to the home office," he said.

"You weren't around. I left a voicemail for you, so I worked with Gail on it. Here's a copy."

"There is always email," he said. He is better to track on the phone than on email, which could go unanswered for a day. But I wasn't going to argue at this moment. He was in a pissy mood.

Irritated because he had not shown much interest in what was happening until now, I handed him a copy that was on my desk. He pulled up a chair and read the memo on the edge of my desk.

"See now, I would have given a more objective view. This memo presents too positive a picture. Remember, you were being interviewed for the second time by the FBI. It was not just a friendly chat."

"Believe me, my draft was a very negative report. Gail edited it to add more objectivity, she said. She doesn't seem to accept that this is perilous to me."

"And to the firm," Jesse asserted.

Wow, I thought, this conference call is going to be a real test for me. I will have three men taking jabs at me. Just like when I was an associate, not as partners like they are. No one will be on my side and I will be labelled hysterical because of my reaction to D.L.'s aggression.

"I understand fully," I said evenly. "The firm and to me personally."

"Not to mention our practice," said Jesse.

The phone rang and it was a Texas number. I put it on speaker and said, "Leyla James."

"Hi, Leyla, it's Ray and Eliot."

"Hi, Ray and Eliot. Jesse is in my office with me."

"Hi, Jesse. How is everything in Washington these days?" Ray appeared to be in a decent mood anyway.

"Well, you know that depends on when the next scandal is scheduled to hit."

The men in Texas laughed.

"Yeah," Ray said. "Washington is not for the faint of heart. Give me Texas any day."

"Speaking of which, I am just looking at Leyla's memo," Jesse said. "Have you had a chance to look at it?" I was livid. It was my memo and I can speak for it. What is he doing taking the lead on this? He hadn't shown much interest recently. Is this a sell-out?

"We saw it," said Eliot. Did I detect judgment in his voice?

"This really shouldn't have happened," Eliot continued. "Don't you two collaborate on this case?"

"Well," Jesse said. "I have let Leyla fight it out with D.L. in the past couple of years."

"There really should have been some oversight," Eliot said. It was becoming clear—Eliot was the bad cop and I was the perpetrator. Jesse had taken a few hits, but generally I was the source of irritation for the firm.

"How do you expect this to go, Leyla?" I was relieved that he aimed that question at me, otherwise Jesse might have jumped in.

"According to my lawyer, this is just part of an initial interview process. There are around ten lawyers being interviewed, all of whom had ongoing litigation with D.L. My lawyer said that there was no reason for concern."

Actually, eight practicing lawyers, the other two were principals in litigating companies.

"But," Eliot said, "the FBI spoke to you twice and you had to retain counsel."

"Actually, all the lawyers have retained counsel," I said. "We just did it later because we agreed initially that it wasn't necessary. It was during my first interview, that I realized that the rest of lawyers were correct in getting representation."

"Well," Eliot said. "Why did we decide that it wasn't necessary when all the other participants were lawyering up?"

"I think that the feeling was that this interview was ludicrous. What I had been involved in at the Administration was just litigation."

Ray was not affirming that thought, although he had originally called it ridiculous. Jesse was silent, although I expected him to say that he was always concerned. No one spoke for a minute.

Eliot cleared his throat, "Well, we are involved in this now and the insurance company is watching. From now on, you and Jesse need to work closer together. It's clear that two people have to review any document going out of the office. We will keep things as status quo for the time being, with that exception, and hope that nothing more serious happens with the FBI. If it does, we'll examine our options. Keep us up to date with what the FBI is doing. We expect regular memos on this. And keep a low profile."

"Yes, of course," I said. Jesse said nothing.

With that admonition, the Texas team signed off, pleading other pressing matters. The whole debacle took 15 minutes.

"Well," Jesse said, "that was pretty clear. There better not be any further activity or the firm might step in to protect itself, especially if any publicity comes out about your involvement."

My career passed before my eyes. They would examine their options—possibly either a layoff or firing me. I am on an out-of-control ride, and someone else seemed to be driving. If I didn't get a handle on this and take control, I would be out of a job, shunned by the legal community and headed toward arrest for murder on the basis of an offhand jest. Not a dazzling finale to my legal career.

# CHAPTER 10: Wherein I Try to Take Control.

At this point, I needed to figure out what to do next. I had to keep on living my life, putting one foot in front of the other. I needed to keep showing up at work, I needed to keep helping my clients and continue to make money, especially now. But I continued fretting. And I kept waking up in the middle of the night from horrible nightmares of chases and people with guns.

Often now, I research aspects of my case on the internet. I research about DNA and about how MY DNA could have possibly shown up at the murder scene and how in the world there was a murder scene at the Administration where security was supposed to be infallible.

I began to wonder if the alleged hitman was an Administration employee. That would answer the question of getting in and out of the building without notice and getting a murder weapon past security—possibly a knife from a kitchen or any kind of sharp tool used by the staff? D.L. was stabbed, according to the news accounts and rumors from Graciela's friends on the custodial staff, a sort of talk therapy that turned into gossip. I needed to follow up with Graciela.

I also wondered how I could find out about recent hires. I wondered how this person knew that Phillips was coming to the Administration for a meeting. I wondered who wanted her dead and I wondered if and how my apparent adversary, fit into the picture.

Assuming my theory was correct, I tried to find out what lawyers also had adverse relationships with D.L. Phillips. I searched the Administration database for controversies involving her. This was a luxury that I did not have when I first began to practice law. Then, there was no easy access to the Administration's records. Now, information was there immediately on the internet. Small things to be thankful for: that and copying machines and FEDEX. It took me several long days to make a list of proceedings in which Phillips played a part. Most of these were controversial and went on for years without the Administration staff reining her in. She was a bully to everyone, not just me. I made a list of people (lawyers, Administration licensees, vendors) who were battling her at the Administration. It was long. She filed supplement after supplement, appeal after appeal when she lost, and no one at the Administration reprimanded her or penalized her. There was nothing in the database that indicated any positive relationship between D.L. and any of my peers' clients—no joint filings, no filings in support of D.L.'s pleadings, nothing. On the other hand, it would be note-worthy, even shocking, if anyone did file in support of D.L. and vice versa. That would have caused a torrent of gossip in our legal community.

There were also several license auction proceedings in which Phillips made voluminous filings. The issue was usually involving some other participant's right to participate. Phillips was likely the plaintiff. No one wanted to get sucked into that kind of quagmire by a proactive attack. These proceedings went back at least 10 years, and most were still pending at the second of the three levels of appeal. I suspected that the issue and the proceeding had to be something recent. I could not imagine someone fighting D.L. for ten years and then finally killing her, although, the FBI imagined that scenario about me.

Whatever it was, the proceeding was likely to still be in the decision process and there was some concern about the legitimacy of the application or of a bidding credit by at least two participants in it. I concentrated on recent auction activity in which a company co-owned by D.L. had partic-ipated and had won 100 licenses. The permits for these licenses had just been granted by the Administration in mid-March.

I spent a Saturday in the office scrutinizing everything on the Admin-istration website about that auction, all the releases, comments and orders. I could find no issues either with the Phillips' application or any of the other applicants. Phillips had stated in the application that she had no bid-ding arrangements with any other applicants, in response to the standard Administration question.

But one thing was unusual in this auction. Her company was new, not one of the other companies my client was involved with that D.L. had created and always used. There was also a 49% owner, a woman I had never heard of. That was unusual for D.L., having an ownership agreement with another woman. Also, the simple ownership interested me. Generally, D.L.'s business structures were convoluted and had to be diagrammed to even get a basic understanding of what she was attempting to do. I had tried that once, only to discover that one such structure was the subject of a court proceeding with her partner, whose interest had been deftly and surreptitiously diluted.

The other unusual issues in the auction were the type of licenses being auctioned and the large amount of money she had put down. These licenses were not ones that D.L. Phillips had ever shown any interest in, and the amount of money paid upfront indicated, at least to my past experience with her, that this venture might not be self-funded because there was too much money involved. The licenses that Phillips had bid for and got involved in were what the industry calls "work horse" radio frequencies, used to control the movement of fleets like garbage trucks and bus systems. Phillips in the past filled the Administration databases with filings on her futuristic system of the integrated automation for houses, cars, and cities, operating together, complete with diagrams and engineering studies. It appeared to me, a nonengineer, that the nature of these auction frequencies could not be integrated into such a system.

To verify my opinion, the next day I called a communications engineering friend, Bill Steen. Bill and I knew each other from the time I was hired by my law partner Jesse. Jesse and Bill were good friends and worked together often on cases throughout the years. Early in my tenure as associate, Jesse opted out of going to certain client association meetings in Las Vegas. He only attended the high-roller conferences and I was sent to the smaller ones. Bill attended them also. The meetings were male dominated and very uncomfortable for me. I felt like an oddity or a hooker, not very welcome.

Once, after the end of an event and waiting for a client, I stood at the bottom of an escalator watching the exit from the main hall. I saw not one woman in the departing crowd. So, Bill was always a friendly face, although he had made an awkward pass at me at one point and I made an awkward refusal. We had been treated to various socializing events that evening and then went on to see a show. After the show, we walked to the hotel and he asked whether I wanted to come to his room. I laughed and said, "To see the etchings? I don't think that I should do that." I was not sure if he was sober, but he looked crestfallen. Any such liaison would have been out of the question. Like Jesse, Bill and I had an informal information reciprocal agreement. We would advise him, gratis, on a legal problem that he might have with his client. In exchange, we were not reluctant to ask his engineering opinion.

"So, Bill, what's with Specialized Service licenses these days? What are they good for? Anything besides bus or truck fleet control?" I asked, after we exchanged pleasantries and benign disparagement of the business climate.

Always the engineer, he gave me a roundabout answer, giving me a history lesson, then added, "A year or so ago, Neil Patrick, a guy in my radio club, thought that this spectrum might be the new cellular. There was a lot of discussion about how that might work. But I think it was just wishful thinking by some speculators. So no, I don't see any other use for those licenses."

I knew Neil Patrick. He was a think-outside-the-box engineer. He could have talked up the radio frequencies to speculators, who wanted to be first in line with alternative uses: the smartest guys in the room. Neil was happy to provide his pricey consulting services. On the other hand, Bill was a traditionalist and, to his own mind, more realistic.

Nevertheless, his confirmation of my first impression was gratifying: these frequencies could not be used for anything more than their work horse designation, without elaborate engineering and regulatory work-arounds. Even the Administration acknowledged their basic capabilities on the auction fact sheet. Typically, the auction description gives a "flexible use" statement on the spectrum to be auctioned, with a short description of possible future uses. This auction statement was brief and agreed with Bill's analysis. It appeared there was not much, if any, futuristic ability in this band for the present. So why did D.L. spend so much money throughout the country on these inflexible frequencies? Did she fall for Neil Patrick's spiel?

When I took a closer look at the application documents, I saw that although it looked as though Phillips had prepared and filed it herself at the Administration, there was an alternate bidder on the list of possible bidders that I recognized. He was or at least had been at one time employed as a paralegal in the Gallagher firm. I knew that paralegal from the time when Leon and I had a client issue that he had made very complicated. It was likely an Administration error, but I got a letter addressed to me, with one of Leon's clients listed on the envelope. Leon's immediate issue was client confidentiality. I thought it was clear cut, it was a staff error. But Leon felt that it was necessary to check with the D.C. Bar counsel to resolve the issue of who should open the letter. This was way too anal for me but Leon forged ahead, following the absolute letter of the law. We were both on the phone with bar counsel, who appeared to be semi-interested but said we should resolve the issue ourselves. I offered to give the letter to Leon since I knew that it was a routine notification. The paralegal, Keith Olson, came with Leon to retrieve the envelope from my office. It was at that meeting when Leon introduced me in glowing terms to Keith. I was surprised by this enthusiasm given Leon's impassive nature. Keith appeared to be a decent, earnest guy, trying to impress his boss.

Keith's listing on the application was perplexing because it gave what looked like a home address. Why would an employee, or at least a former employee of his firm, be listed as an alternate bidder? I wondered whether the firm could be involved in some way with Phillips. Did it have another client that could be involved with Phillips and did that client possibly not trust D.L.? But no, a further document revealed that Keith Olson was employed by D.L. There went my hopes in another dead end. Besides which, if all my perceptions were valid, Leon would never stray off the path of virtue. He was the classic straight arrow.

I spent my Sunday afternoon searching the Administration website, inputting Keith Olson's name. Several proceedings came up, but one in particular interested me. It was a long past hearing proceeding on the debarred lawyer and Jesse's old friend, Carlton Edwards, who had committed fraud at the Administration. At that time, Jesse and I had talked endlessly about Edwards. Of course, Jesse had said, "When he says that he is just an old Southern boy, you need to watch your wallet." Jesse was himself an old Southern boy and knew the characteristics. Edwards was barred from dealings at the Administration. End of inquiry.

It appeared from the website that Leon had gotten himself quite a client, though, guaranteed to need intense help. I took a timeout to question my sanity. Maybe I was becoming delusional, or maybe I was just frantic to find a way out for me.

From the extent of the documents, I ventured that Leon was making huge cash contributions to his firm over a period of several years while the hearing proceeding was being litigated. If Edwards was still a client, that meant that he probably kept current with his billing. Another branch office of the firm also represented Edwards in one state court proceeding. Leon was probably the billing partner on that proceeding, too. It was useless for me to speculate on where the money to pay the bills came from; Edwards probably had resources from his many deals, here and abroad, including the mysterious Andrei Ceban, that might provide him with cash. I reminded myself that all of this might just be speculation. And I reminded myself that Leon was as pure as snow.

I thought that I should bounce all of this off someone, but at this point I wasn't sure who I could talk with. Jesse was out. The truth is what I learned right off in law school—I needed more facts not conjecture. I can hear my professor bellowing after a student offered his opinion on a hypothetical case, "Need more facts!" But where do I get them?

I had several huge questions that could not be researched on the internet but needed to be resolved before I could be free from suspicion. Why was Phillips killed? If there was a killer and it was an Administration employee, how could I find that out? How did it happen that the meeting with Administration staff and Phillips was delayed long enough to move Phillips to another location to be murdered? What was the device on the table at the crime scene described by Graciela to her friends and then to other Administration staffers? And how did it figure in the murder? Was it intentionally left to throw investigators off track?

Finally, as Ida Cramer asked in my interview, how did my DNA get on the slip of paper and of what significance was the address? I could only assume that this was done to implicate me. I sat staring at my computer on that Saturday evening and, at last, had an idea that both thrilled and terrified me.

# CHAPTER 11: The Government Employee Database.

My ex-lover Cam, who worked at the State Department as an assistant to the Secretary, told me there was a public but obscure site on the internet that listed all government employees without security clearances, by agency and hire date. He had learned this from a friend at the Office of Personnel Management when he was researching a State employee's background.

Hoping that the database still existed, now that privacy was becoming of much more concern, I went online and spent three hours on the personnel management site. I tried 20 different searches to find it. I got nothing. At least nothing that I, a non-government employee, could find. Maybe it was blocked now and there was no more public access. More speculation.

I hesitated to call Cam, because we were not on speaking terms and he was involved, obviously, with someone else. Why we broke up is complicated: both of us spent many hours and intense focus on our work. It gradually caused friction and arguments between us. Maybe I am too independent for a relationship and/or maybe he demanded more than I could give. And it wasn't as if he didn't travel for days with the Secretary on a moment's notice. Everything is unclear to me except for the fact that I was still examining what went wrong.

Sometimes we were both stubborn and unwilling to negotiate. In my off hours, I wanted to get out of town. He wasn't always ready to hit the road just after a trip to Brussels, and he sometimes liked to hang out in D.C. to decompress. I liked to try new restaurants; he liked the same Thai food. He liked action movies, I like films "with substance" and on and on.

It added up to unmet needs and lack of trying to please the other.

One time in particular highlighted our relationship issues. At the end of one day, my very important California client called my cell phone with an emergency. I was on my way out of the office and sat in the reception area for an hour trying to resolve the issue. Cam and I were going to dinner to celebrate his promotion to one of the top positions in the Policy Planning Staff at State. He had made reservations and I couldn't call or text him while I was on my phone to tell him about my delay. When I hung up, I called him. No answer. I went to the restaurant. I was told that the reservation had been cancelled. When I got home, he wasn't there. I waited for him and at 11, he came home, responding abruptly when I asked, that he had gone to the movies.

"Why am I always the one who gets sacrificed for your clients," he complained.

"You don't understand about practicing law in a firm," I said. "The money depends on the work you do. It is not like the government where you get a paycheck regardless." That was the wrong thing to say to an ambitious and high-reaching federal worker, like Cam. I regretted that I said it although I thought that it was somewhat true. Law firms operate on the "what have you done for me lately" principle. To retain my position, I needed to respond to the clients' needs when they needed me and to get paid for it. Sometimes that didn't even work, thinking of my too-recent encounter with the firm's managing partner and ethics lawyer. That night, Cam and I called a truce but it was one more strain leading to our demise. Our gig was good for about three years and then it wasn't.

I hadn't talked to Cam in six months. He called a couple weeks after he moved out, to retrieve a tennis racket lost in the back of a closet. When he dropped by, I still felt that electric attraction to him. I always thought he was good looking, way good looking. I know, it is superficial but that was the first thing that caught me. He is also fit. I remembered the good times and felt the pain of regret that it was over. At that time, I assumed he was already involved with someone else. Things were active in Washington, D.C., especially with someone like Cam. Our ending had not been good. Too many "you" statements, a therapist told me. "You never wanted to..." and "You never asked me what I wanted to do." He was abrupt in our conversation at my front door that day and barely looked at me as I handed him the racket. He was gone in a nanosecond. It hurt. I am still getting over it. And it didn't help to see his recent picture with his new flame on a mutual friend's Facebook.

I remembered our trip to St. John over the long Presidents Day weekend last year. One night, we went to a club in Coral Bay and sat outside with our drinks. The trade winds rustled the palm trees lining the patio and a trio played jazz in the background. Later, we wandered down to the beach in front of our hotel and lay down in the lounge chair at the end of the beach. The surf was lapping. "Nice," he said, kissing me on the back of my neck.

"Mmmm. Nice and easy..." I breathed the words from a booty song into his ear and his hands went down my back to my thighs.

But that moment was in the past. I sighed. I thought that any relationship or communication with him was done. In fact, I was thinking that any relationship with any man was done for me.

But now, my business and personal life relied on his knowledge. I couldn't let my stubbornness or pride stop me. I was shaking when I called him. I got his voicemail.

"Hi, Cam, this is Leyla. I have a big problem and I am asking for your help. Last year, you told me there was a database of government employees, online, and I need to get access to it." My voice broke and I let out an inadvertent sob. "Please. My life depends on it." I hung up.

It was six-thirty on Sunday. I had gone without lunch and I decided I should eat dinner. I had barely anything in my refrigerator—that too was a friction point with Cam. I always forgot or didn't care to get groceries. He complained about always having to shop, and he wanted me to share the burden, sometimes demanding it. That irritated me. I just wasn't focused on food—except at a restaurant when someone else cooked.

I found some wilted spring mix in a package and a limp piece of broccoli in a bottom drawer of the refrigerator. I also had frozen salmon in the freezer. Some gourmet dinner. I put the salmon and broccoli in my steamer. I poured a glass of wine and went to the computer for another search. Nothing. I drank my wine and ate my dinner. Cam did not call. I did not sleep. What's new?

The next morning in the office, I was on the phone with a client and his vice president when my second line rang. This conference call was not going to end soon, so the line rolled over to voicemail. A half hour later and off the call, I played it. It was Cam. He sounded slightly friendlier than the last time we spoke, but not exactly warm. He told me to call him at his office and he would walk me through the process. He wanted to know about my problem. I think that it was my sob that intrigued him. I almost never cried. I didn't cry when we broke up and he left. I never cried when we fought. When I have issues at work, I just bluster. I do not cry.

I shut my office door and called him back. When he picked up the phone, I just started crying. I could not stop. "I have a huge legal problem," I sobbed. "I haven't told anyone except my managing partner, my law partner and my attorney." That was true. In those conversations, I had to maintain my professional self, not my emotional self. I did not want to expose myself to other nonprofessional people in my life until I could keep myself under control. But this was a relief and the dam of emotions had burst.

I told him everything between sobs, "There was a murder at the Administration. The woman who was killed and I had a very bad relationship."

"Yes," he said, "I read about it. I remember her."

"It turns out there was some evidence at the scene that seems to link me to the murder. I have been interviewed by the FBI. They called me in again, and my lawyer and I left protesting the interrogation, with a threat from the FBI. I think someone is trying to implicate me further." I paused and cried, "It is such a disaster and it could ruin my life."

He listened and when he spoke, he sounded stunned. "I think we need to talk about this in person, Leyla. When will you be home tonight?"

"I have a meeting at 4:00 PM at another law office in town, if I can keep myself together for that. But I can be home by 6."

He was at my house at six. He held out his arms and I went into them, holding onto him. We went into my apartment and sat on the couch. I was sobbing and shaking and telling him again about the murder, the FBI interviews, my lawyer, my fear of being slowly bled to death by the legal system, and now my desperate search to extract myself from what seemed like a snare trap. At the end of my story, Cam again put his arms around me, and this time I felt that it was not a consoling embrace.

"Wait." I said, bluntly, slightly shifting. "I heard that you are dating someone. I don't think that we should do this if you are with someone else now."

Cam went silent. I had no idea what would happen next, whether he would get up in a huff and leave. I did not know what he was thinking but he soon told me.

"Well, yes, I am seeing someone now. I don't know whether it is friendship or romance, it's too soon. We have a good time." He left things dangling. It was so hard to hear but I had asked for it.

"But that is beside the point in this situation." That was also cutting to me because it wasn't beside the point to me. Certainly I wasn't going to sleep with him under those circumstances, but I needed his help.

I sighed. "Yeah, I need a friend now. We've known each other for three and a half years and have been through a lot together, my dad's death for one. I trust you. And I need your expertise but also as a sounding board. Will you help me?"

"Of course, I will," he said. "I'd never let someone I care about be in a situation like this without helping."

"Well, I'm glad to hear that you care about me," I said. "When we ended, I was sure that you simply hated me, that we'd never see each other again."

"I hated the way we were living, not you. We needed a break."

That gave me a little ray of hope, but I reminded myself that I was too fragile to make any evaluations of our dialogue. Anything that felt kind right now was a new dimension to me. I'd been through some big, bad events lately.

We talked about my situation for a while. I told him that I felt as if the momentum was pushing me into a lose-lose situation and that I'd made up my mind to take control by doing some investigation on my own. I was skeptical about my attorney's approach, the typical wait-and-see protocol, but I couldn't wait for the noose. I had to save myself, my law practice, and my financial life.

Cam listened and nodded his head. He took a piece of paper out of his pocket and gave it to me. It was the website URL that was still open to the public and instructions on how to get to the Administration personnel database. He told me that the list included grade and date of hire and termination of the federal personnel without security clearances. I doubted that my target would have a security clearance. The list was exactly what I needed.

I looked him straight in the eyes and said, "You have no idea what this means to me. Your help. I feel as though I am fighting everyone and I'm scared." He searched my face the same way my mother had looked at me when I came into her house on my last visit. What was that look? His eyes stopped on my lips. My heart skipped. Sometimes in the past he had said that he loved the seductive curl of my lower lip. I smiled.

He got up abruptly, ready to leave. As he headed to the door, he told me to be in touch and let him know if I needed help. To be honest, I felt let down. I don't know what I expected. My thoughts went immediately to the probability that he had a date and was in a hurry to meet his whatever. I told myself to be thankful for his help, to see him again and to feel the same tingle that I had felt so often before. It will take time, I thought, and maybe I can get him back before his "friend" steps into his heart and his bed, if she had not done that already.

The next morning, I took the note with me to the office. In the afternoon, during the business lull over the lunch hour, I shut my door and found the massive database. It was divided into agencies and location, making my job much easier. The list was also arranged chronologically according to the worker's start date; the most recent hires were listed at the top. At least something in my search was getting easier. Maybe, just maybe, my luck was going to change.

I started by looking for newly hired Administration staff, probably male. However, the list didn't include gender. I'd need to guess. I was also assuming that a hired killer wouldn't stick around the Administration after the hit.

There appeared to be five male hires in late February: two had left by mid-April. One was on the janitorial staff and the other was an IT employee. Their names were Tyrone Brown, an intern in IT in the personnel section, and Jimmi Stanley on the janitorial staff. There were three female hires in March and all of them were still at the Administration. There was no other information. No addresses or other contact information available.

I went online to try to get that information from other sources. There must have been 20 Tyrone Browns in D.C. alone, more in Maryland and Virginia. There was nothing for Jimmi Stanley. There were James Stanleys or Jim Stanleys or J. Stanley, but no Jimmi. Nothing even in West Virginia or Pennsylvania either. He had either moved, had used a variation of the first name or a fictitious name, impossible to find in the phone book. Useless.

I texted Cam, asking him if there was any other public contact information with home addresses for federal employees on the database.

To my surprise, he responded late in the afternoon that he talked to his friend at OPM, and said he would show me what he'd discovered that night. I asked him to dinner. Two things to anticipate. I would stop at the supermarket on the way home. He stopped, too. We met at my front door with enough food for three meals. It was good to know that we both had learned some lessons.

We worked together in the kitchen, shifting around each other in my small kitchen while chopping and shredding, dumping vegetables in the wok. We made a great spicy hot Asian meal of stir fry and brown rice. He opened a bottle of dry white wine. Like old times, I thought, then reminded myself to watch out.

We chatted about what each of us had done in the past six months. He was very low key about his activities, talking mainly about work, and of course I assumed the worse, for me, about his social life.

"Well, not much action for me," I said. "I've been knee deep in this stuff for a couple months."

Of course, he noticed that I was not at the gym.

"I couldn't take seeing you there and having you be angry at me," I explained.

He nodded, "It would've hurt."

I looked at his dark eyes and could see a slight hint of hurt. Again, I wondered what had happened that brought us to the edge. Our egos, maybe? There wasn't much win-win going on, toward the end. Stop, Leyla, he's dating someone else.

He told me that he'd gone up to visit a college roommate in New York for a party shortly after he moved out and that it wasn't fun. I thought back on our own trip to New York to stay with his roommate last year and what a great time we had on the Five-Boro Bike Tour. We rode 40 miles and had a huge party that Saturday night, dancing and drinking wine with his friends from UVA. We had such an awesome time last year," I laughed. "It was so much fun to ride through New York without cars and people everywhere."

"You weren't there this year. There was a downpour," he pointed out, looking at me. I covered my mouth to avoid any temptation. I'm thinking that I'm playing with fire. But I could never understand his fascination with my mouth: it wasn't at all interesting to me and it often lacked lipstick. I ate it off.

"Good point," I said. "I'm an idiot."

"I'm not so smart myself, "he said. We laughed.

"Well anyway, I wasn't having much fun," I confessed. "If I ever have to suffer through that much gloom again, I will seriously re-evaluate my life."

"What would you do?"

"I don't know. Quit my job, move to the tropics. Maybe."

"That's not like a Type A," he said.

"Well, sometimes it's good to not be so Type A." He raised his eyebrows at me.

"What?" I said, laughing.

Then, we talked about my search for Tyrone Brown, an IT intern, and Jimmi Stanley, the custodian. After dinner, Cam downloaded two huge databases. An hour later, we located the contact information from an obscure site. "They really keep this hidden," I said. According to Cam, this information was still in the public domain—for the time being. And I had no reason to doubt him. He knew his way around data.

We found addresses for both Tyrone Brown and Jimmi Stanley. No telephone numbers. Brown was in Prince Georges County in Maryland; and Stanley was in Southeast D.C.

"I'll look for them this weekend," I said.

"I'll go with you. I don't want you to go looking for a hitman by yourself," Cam asserted.

This time, I knew that he was trying to protect me. Not to dominate me. "Thanks," I said. "You realize, in the past, I would have been offended by your offer." I would have rebuffed him because I thought accepting would make me look weak. I welcomed not being so independent this time. I hadn't known what I would find when I got total independence.

"I appreciate the help. I'm no PI." We laughed.

"I'm not either," he said. "We'll learn together."

# CHAPTER 12: Dead Ends.

On Saturday morning, Cam picked me up after he worked out in the gym. We set out to Prince Georges County first. The County was to the east of the District. The traffic was backed-up randomly at choke points on the Beltway and it took an hour to drive from downtown D.C. to Central Avenue in PG County. "It's amazing that at ten on a weekend morning, there is rush hour traffic," I groused. "We've hit every single red light between my house and the Beltway."

The GPS took us to Tyrone Brown's neighborhood. We drove around until we finally found the house, a two-story, half-shingle and half-brick townhouse in a development near the District line. The neighborhood was one of those constructed when people started moving out to the County from the District, chasing better schools, newer homes, and lower crime rates. But crime followed the migration despite efforts to prevent it.

Cam drove slowly by the townhouse. We saw two small boys playing in the front yard with plastic fire trucks, one boy was slightly taller than the other and stood instructing the shorter one on using his truck. I had never aspired to invade someone else's privacy. I knew how I would react if someone knocked on my door asking personal questions. I felt awkward knocking on the door of a stranger and asking whether this Tyrone Brown had begun work for the Administration in February and had quit in April. But I had to know this to save my professional and financial life. I had to do it, reservations or not. I took a deep breath and straightened my shoulders. I left Cam in the car and went up to the front door. A young pretty woman answered the door. She looked harassed.

"I am so sorry to bother you," I apologized, smiling. I handed her my card. "I am not selling anything. I just have one or two quick questions, not a survey, and I will leave you alone. I am looking for the Tyrone Brown who was on the Radio Frequency Administration staff from February to April of this year. He might know someone that I am trying to find," I said. This was not entirely false, just a little misleading since I was looking for Mr. Brown himself as a possible killer.

She relaxed and then smiled back. "Tyrone isn't at the Administration anymore. He applied to finish his college degree after he completed his Air Force service last fall. He took the job while he was waiting for acceptance. He is going to Maryland now.

"Tyrone told me that he would continue at the Administration while he was in school," She continued. "But I told him to quit and focus on his degree, that I would take care of us for a while. If you give me your phone number, I will have him call you."

"Could I have his number? I can call him," I said boldly. She gave it to me. Apparently, I looked honest.

From what his wife had volunteered, Tyrone didn't appear to be moonlighting as a hitman. He seemed like a normal, hard working person who had quit the Administration to become more educated and prosperous.

This was a happy story, and it looked like it would have a happy ending. I thanked her for her help and walked back to the car, smiling.

"I don't think he's our guy. I told Cam. "He just got out of the Air Force and is going to Maryland to finish his degree."

Cam laughed. "Not your hitman then."

"I like your laugh." I smiled. "And I like you, too. Thanks for your help." He looked genuinely happy. It was pretty easy to be grateful, I reminded myself.

In Southeast D.C., however, I lost that smile. We found no house for Jimmi Stanley. The address was a dirty vacant lot, with discarded liquor bottles, take-out containers and cardboard boxes that were possibly beds for the homeless. We drove up the street. It was a seedy neighborhood. Whoever lived here probably was never employed by the Administration even on a short-time basis. We drove to the same address in Southwest. We found no such address there, although the neighborhood was tidier, with 70s urban renewal townhouses and apartments. It was pretty sterile in my book but safer at least.

"Well, what now?" I asked Cam. "I have no idea what to do. But I think that Jimmi Stanley might be a lead if we could find him." We sat in the car and said nothing. Once again, it appeared to be the end of road in my search for vindication.

"Wait," Cam finally said, "there is a guy down the hall from me who used to be a D.C. cop. I don't know where he works now, but I talk to him the hall. He's friendly. I could ask him."

"Don't tell him about me," I urged. "I don't want him to know about me until after we find out if he can help."

"No, I'll just say it's a friend who needs to find a guy and he got a wrong address." That sounded right to me. So, we decided to see if that worked. We stopped by a curb and Cam called his neighbor.

It did not work so well. Cam's neighbor, Len Reynolds, was reluctant to use any of his old sources, and Cam agreed that he shouldn't. But Len said that he did have a good friend, Dave Samuels, also an ex-cop and just off the force last year, who did some investigative work. He gave Cam Dave's number. He told Cam that he had worked with Dave and that he was a great guy, a good and diligent cop. He and Dave had known each other for ten years and went to hockey and baseball games together when they had a chance. Cam got off the phone and wrote down Dave's number. A whole new direction for me. He started up the car and we headed to my house. It was almost 1PM.

"Shall we get some lunch?" he asked. "I have a little time this afternoon, before I need to go."

"Great!" I said. "Port of Piraeus?"

That he needed to go was not lost on me, but I kept my questions to myself. We chatted with the restaurant's owner who was presiding over the tables that were filled with nearby West End residents. My Greek salad was great, as usual. Cam told me that he was going with the Secretary to Strasbourg for a conference the following week, leaving on Wednesday and returning on Saturday. He said that he was preparing the documents for the meeting and was working on getting the briefing papers together. He had an exciting job.

"Sounds fabulous," I said. "You are doing great at State."

"Well, I really like the Secretary. We are on the same wavelength and work well together."

"I'm truly happy for you!"

"He's starting to include me in events sometimes."

"Really good. I mean, the chance to meet with interesting folks and make contacts."

"The reception last week was for the French Minister of State. It was in one of the Diplomatic Reception rooms that look out toward the Lincoln Memorial and the Potomac. It was great."

I nodded my head approvingly. I wondered if he took a guest.

We finished our lunch. Cam looked at his phone and said, "I've got to run."

He dropped me off at my apartment and patted me on the arm. "I know that it will work out for you. Hang in there."

I went in my apartment, befuddled. He didn't mention any follow-up. On Monday, after a solitary weekend mainly at work (my own fault), I called Dave Samuels. First, I asked him for confidentiality. Getting his promise, I gave him a summary of my dilemma.

I heard a sigh on the other end of the phone.

"Yeah, I know," I said. "Anyway, it appears that someone has already told the agents about my problems with the victim. That person seems to have told the FBI that I said something in jest about hiring a hitman. I fear that the FBI agent either wants or needs to believe that person for political reasons."

I went on. "This murder on federal property needs to be solved immediately. It's embarrassing to the officials that it happened in the Administration where security is supposed to be stringent. A former employee at the Administration might have some information. I tried to locate him, but the address on the Administration personnel file is an empty lot in SE. We need to find him."

Dave Samuels sounded like a smart, knowledgeable person. There was a little arrogance there but he agreed to help me and his price was right.

I met him on Monday night after work at his office, a walk-up on P Street NW, second floor. He met me at the door. He was tall and well built. He had a square jaw and wary eyes. I'm not sure that I would have liked to have been stopped by him for speeding. He seemed no nonsense. There were a couple of chairs, a file cabinet, and a desk in his sparse office. There were no pictures on the wall and only a computer and two screens on his desk. I wondered if I was one of his first paying customers. After a handshake and short pleasantries, we got started.

"The former employee is Jimmi Stanley. He worked at the Federal Radio Administration beginning in February this year and left mid-April," I said. "I have an address for him that I had been given but it must have been wrong."

"You probably wrote it down wrong," he said.

Nice start to the relationship, I thought, but I needed his help, so I kept this put down to myself. I did not want to start out by giving lessons on sexism to a man who might be able to help me get out of this trap.

Dave got up and went around to his computer at his desk. The back of the screens faced me so I couldn't see the databases or any other information. "You're right, his address is a vacant lot." He sounded less cocky.

"So, do you think his real name is Jimmi Stanley?" I asked. "And if it isn't, how could he get a job at a federal administration? Also, how can we find out if that name is an alias?"

"Lots of questions," he said sounding slightly annoyed. I was not sure if that was because of my questions or his unwillingness to have a helper in his investigative work. "It could be a similar name or a false ID. If it is a false ID, we have to figure out why."

"I know why," I said. "He could be a killer for hire."

"Can't be," he snorted. "In a federal agency, a hitman? No way." He was brusque, too, and I was a paying customer!

"Well, that was one way the murder could have happened," I said.

"My sources told me that there is a suspect in that murder."

"Who?" I asked.

"I heard it was a female lawyer who mixed it up with her."

It was the word on the street? Who had put that word out there? I got a chill.

"Let me put it this way," I said. "You were likely hearing gossip about me, your client. That is why I am trying to find Jimmi Stanley. He could be the killer. It wasn't me, and I didn't hire anyone to kill her."

"OK," he sighed, "let's see what we can find out about Mr. Stanley." I thought I detected a touch of skepticism. Was it about Stanley or my innocence? I was paranoid.

Dave was silent at his desk for more than a half hour, appearing to shift from one database to another. I assumed that he was doing what his trade allowed him to do. I didn't ask about the process or what he was viewing. I didn't really want to know. He did investigations; I practiced law—when I was not trying to avoid a criminal investigation.

"Excuse me, for one second," he said at last. He was at least being polite, and I was surprised at the change of tone. He now sounded as if he had become interested in something. He went into the next room, which must have been the bathroom. This was not a huge office. I heard him talking on the phone. He mentioned the name, Jimmi Stanley. Then he asked, "What? Uh huh Lana Stanford?" He was quiet for several minutes and must have gotten a positive response. He came back into the room.

"Jimmi Stanley is also known as Lana Stanford," he said. "She has been convicted of armed robbery and is currently involved in the Warriors

Gang, mainly operating in D.C. but with some activity in Baltimore, drugs and other stuff. She also might have been involved in rival gang shootings. She was never convicted of those, but she isn't someone that you—" he gave me a look "—should go looking for to discuss her employment at the federal government."

I was stunned. "Jimmi Stanley/Lana Stanford is a woman?"

"Yes. You think all criminals are men?"

"But I don't understand this at all."

"This could explain your problem. Jimmi has a relationship with a man who is also part of the leadership of the Warriors."

"Okay. What kind of a relationship?" I asked.

"They know each other from way back in the same neighborhood, and that's where they started their activity together. They just worked their way up from petty to big-time crimes."

"Are you saying that she's a lover of the leader of the pack?"

"That's what I hear," Dave said, grimly. "I don't know that for sure. I'm told she's a looker."

That was cringe-worthy, but I blew by it. "But who is going to talk to her, if I don't?"

"First we are going to positively identify that she is our person. You mentioned Tyrone Brown in PG County. Maybe he could identify her from her mug shot or she might have changed her appearance, who knows? I'll try to find out." I gave Dave Tyrone Brown's phone number.

The next day, Dave drove out to Prince Georges County to talk to Tyrone. Later, he called me at work. "Tyrone wasn't absolutely sure from the picture, but said that the weight and height were about right. He did say there was a follow-up government check on Stanley that he was aware of and he was part of the IT personnel search project. The follow-up left some questions about Stanley's past work experience, but that appeared to be reconciled because Stanley stayed on. She had received a very good reference from some employer.

"I wonder what employer that was," I asked, sarcastically.

"Brown said that he didn't remember, but the decision makers thought that it was very good source. That gave her the job."

Stanley left the Administration a couple of weeks later, anyway. Tyrone also said that Stanley was a disturbing person. Stanley had been asked to come up to personnel for the follow-up check. She was close mouthed and appeared to be suspicious of everyone. According to Dave, Tyrone said that he heard she didn't speak to many people and she always seemed pre-occupied on the job. The other employees avoided her.

"So, Stanley left after the Phillips' murder?"

"Yeah, she left on April 14."

"I wonder what her work schedule was and where she was assigned."

"Tyrone said that Stanley worked where needed but sometimes on the janitorial staff in the North Building when it was being used for meetings," Dave responded.

"Okay. So, she was familiar with the building and that conference room. What next?" I asked.

"We figure out where Stanley was on that Friday afternoon. Tyrone gave me a name of another Administration janitor, Karl Jacobs, who worked the same shift as Stanley. Tyrone said that Karl was a good guy, trying to work himself up at the Administration, taking courses at UDC and staying away from the neighborhood he came from. Maybe we can find out something from him: did Stanley go missing about three that Friday afternoon and when did she re-surface? Things could get dark."

"Like, what are you thinking?"

"If she did disappear and resurface, who was she working for and why was murder necessary? Also, why is someone trying to implicate you? And if Jimmi was actually a hitman, was there some way you could be tied into it?"

"The FBI said they found a note with my DNA on it, at the scene."

"DNA can be transferred from one object to another," Dave scoffed. "All anyone needs is a sample of your DNA to put on the note. That evidence can be discredited. They know it and they just brought it up to intimidate you."

"I don't practice criminal law," I said.

"That's clear," said Dave, abruptly.

"Oh, and there is one other thing. The custodian who discovered the body and I have communicated. I knew her from the health club where she worked part-time. When I saw her at the Administration, I spoke with her about the murder. The conversation ended with her asking me to find someone to help her son who is bullied at school. She doesn't speak English very well. I found a contact for her, and I thought that I would follow-up with her. I could ask her about Jimmi, too. Okay?"

He nodded and went off to talk with the other Administration staffer who had been with Stanley on March 28.

I called Graciela. First, I wanted to know whether the contact had helped her and Matias. I also wanted to know what she knew about Jimmi

Stanley. I left a voicemail. She called me back at the end of the day.

She told me that she had met with the advisor and that she had arranged a meeting with the school principal. The advisor spoke Spanish and would accompany Graciela to the school.

"Did you like the advisor?" I asked. "Did she tell you her thoughts on the school enforcing bullying rules?"

"Jes, she is simpatico. Not unusual, bullying."

"When are you going?" I asked.

The appointment was set for the next day.

"By the way," I said. "Do you know Jimmi Stanley?"

"Jes," she said. "Not nice."

"Did she ever talk with you?" I asked.

"Not to wetbacks," she said.

"Is that what she called you?" I asked, horrified.

"Jes. Horrible."

"I'm so sorry, Graciela! If you can think of anything at all that Jimmi Stanley did that was suspicious, please let me know."

"Sospechoso?"

"Yes," I said. "Sospechoso."

The next day, Dave called. He said that he had met with Karl Jacobs and that he was a heavy set, former wrestler who had developed an intense dislike for Jimmi Stanley in the short time that Jimmi was at the Administration. Jacobs willingly discussed her and her activities. She was insulting to him and to his co-workers, as though she felt she was superior to the rest of the custodians.

"And," Dave said, "according to Karl Jacobs, Stanley disappeared in the early afternoon of March 28. She came back with her cleaning equipment around the close of business. Jacobs said that Stanley seemed flushed and more out of sorts than usual. Stanley stored her cart and rushed off, not acknowledging her several-hour absence, and not talking to anyone. Jacobs told me that no one complained because they usually avoided her. Worse, he said that they all disliked her, and the feeling was mutual. He also said that Stanley had had a visitor at the Administration on Monday of that week."

"How did he know that?" I asked.

"A guard came up to get Stanley and told her that a woman had come to see her. The woman was waiting at the guard's desk in the lobby. Stanley asked the guard who she was. The guard said Louise Richards. Stanley shrugged and did not appear to be surprised."

"What was D.L.'s assistant doing visiting Stanley at the Administration?" I said to Dave. "If Stanley was there for the purpose of murdering her boss, why would her loyal assistant be assisting the murderer?"

"Maybe D.L. or Louise was involved in the remote device effort, too. Maybe she was giving the instructions on the timing or removing the remote device. The Administration had just granted the applications to D.L.'s company and so there was no concern on that point anymore. But that is speculation. Jimmi is probably the only one who can answer that," he said. "The problem now is that we would have to hound her and bring her out because there is already at least one easy target for the FBI and the prosecutor: you. Why get one's hands dirty when there's a sitting duck right in front of you?"

Well, it seemed that Dave and I shared the same view: that I was on the road to conviction if everything remained status quo. We had to change that. "Stanley is not the only person," I said. "Louise Richards would know why she came to see Stanley at the Administration."

Dave and I looked at each other. How to debrief Louise Richards? "Well, I guess that would be up to me since I've dealt with her in the past and at least she knows who I am." I said. We parted with me being assigned to the task of contacting Louise. Dave would wait to search out Jimmi.

I went back to the office and tried to put my desk back in order. Contacted clients who had called me and searched for Louise Richard's contact information. I found D.L.'s number. It was still a working number and I was told to leave a message. I asked Louise to give me a call.

The next day, my attorney Gail called. I was in my office, trying to review a radio tower lease agreement for a client, but I'd just been distracted by Jesse, who had just dropped by my office. We were talking about the investigation. Since Jesse and Gail knew each other, I put her on speaker phone and closed my door.

Gail said, "Just thought that I would let you know there's apparently going to be a grand jury within the next ten days to see if there's enough evidence for a criminal indictment in the Phillips murder."

"I was afraid that would happen," said Jesse, eyeing me. I was silent but seething at his negativity.

Although this was supposed to be secret, word had leaked out. At this point, this was one more piece of evidence of a symbiotic relationship between whoever had started the rumors and the FBI. This was a notorious practice in D.C. known as leaking. Not good for me since it seemed that the information about me was being fed to the investigators and, in turn, someone was getting and leaking information. For what purpose I wasn't sure. It did cause me hyper vigilance as well as hypertension.

According to Gail's sources, there was also a leak about a letter from Louise Richards to the FBI, contents unknown. "You know, this is the second time in two days, Louise Richards has been mentioned," I said. "First, I heard that she showed up at the Administration on the Monday of the week of D.L.'s murder, to talk to one of the cleaners. And now I hear that she has written a letter to the FBI. I need to find out how she is involved."

I then filled Gail in on what was happening with my own private investigation. She didn't like to hear anything about it and didn't hide her resistance to my activities. "Leyla, I don't think that this will help you." In fact, when I first told her a week ago, she had argued against it forcefully. "Do not do this, Leyla, the FBI could say that you are interfering with the investigation."

Up to this point, Jesse had not said much, but now he agreed with Gail. "This is an amateur attempt to investigate. It won't uncover anything, and it will only irritate the FBI."

I was adamant. To me, it was being pro-active in my own defense or I would end up in jail. No one else was helping me and I said, "What investigation? Someone is trying to get my name out there as the leading suspect, and I'm not running into anyone who is investigating anything or any other person outside of the FBI building. I have to defend myself."

My opinion of "Justice" was becoming dimmer with each day as I felt the push toward an indictment. I was a hot suspect. My antagonist was seeing to that. I would be in jail in the foreseeable future, and Jimmi Stanley, and whoever hired her, would be free.

One thing was obvious from my discussion was Gail: I hadn't been called as a witness in the grand jury. That could mean a couple of things. Either the prosecutor wasn't interested in my testimony or I was the target and as such, I would likely not be called to testify. I highly doubted the former and feared the latter. It appeared to me that I was being set up because at least one witness wanted to link me to the crime.

After Gail's call and Jesse had gone, I called Dave and told him the news. "Gail says that there is a rumor a grand jury will be held on the Phillips murder within ten days. She also told me that there was a letter from Louise Richards to the FBI. We need to find out about Louise's involvement and locate Stanley. We need to work fast or I'll soon be indicted and headed for an ordeal that could end my life as I know it, and my livelihood."

The next person I called was Cam. "I'm so sorry to keep bothering you, but you're the only member of my support team!" I told his voicemail what was up. He called me back in an hour.

"You aren't catching any breaks on this," he said.

"Not to mention that there's a letter floating around that was sent to the FBI by Louise Richards, D.L.'s assistant," I said. "I have no idea what it says but it could be bad for me."

"Would any of your law friends know about that letter and what's in it?" he asked. It was so wonderful to talk with someone who was on my side and would at least offer suggestions instead of telling me how wrong it was for me to defend myself. Gail and Jesse refused to bless my self-help, and Dave was not hired to be emotionally supportive to me.

Cam and I had put the past aside more easily than I would've guessed. We had resumed our easy comradery. "I could ask Adam Ross or maybe Jean McInerny," I said.

"It's worth a shot," he said.

I told Cam that Dave was on it and would get back to me. He signed off by telling me that we should think about what could be done to help Dave.

I wished him a bon voyage. He said the trip was going to be briefer than the Secretary had planned, just three days. They were leaving on Thursday and back on Saturday. He would call when he got back. He asked me to text him if things got out of control.

I laughed, "They are already out of control!"

# CHAPTER 13: Louise Richards.

I took a deep breath and called Jean McInerny. I felt as though I was begging for her help and it was not a good feeling. She was away from her desk and I left a voicemail for her. I hoped that I hadn't become such a leper that even my good friends would hesitate to call me or not answer if they saw my phone number on their phone.

Then I called Adam Ross. He answered his phone. Answering the phone was one difference between serving inside and outside clients. But my Administration staff friends say that often it's better to serve outside clients than the many layers of inside clients who want to take their time to affect a decision, if only for ego's sake. Greener grass, I guess.

"Hi, Adam," I said. "It's Leyla."

Adam was cordial. "I haven't heard from you in a while."

"I've been busy being harassed."

"Yah, I heard."

"I have some words of wisdom for you," I said. "Never crack a joke to someone who doesn't have a sense of humor."

"Yeah." At least, Adam sounded sympathetic.

"This is getting pretty tedious. But I have a question. I heard a rumor that Louise Richards, D.L.'s assistant, sent a letter to the FBI. Have you heard anything about that?"

"No." Adam paused longer than he should have. What's up with that? I wondered. Why the hesitation. "But I wouldn't be surprised."

"What does that mean?"

"Well, behind that crunchy laid-back façade, there was a rift between D.L. and Louise. They got along OK when Darius was around, but after he died, the relationship went to hell. My assistant Miriam heard it all from

Louise."

"Don't tell me, I know," I said. "Let's see, D.L. would forget to pay Louise, and when she was reminded, she couldn't remember what the financial arrangement had been if there was one. Or she might even argue there wasn't one. That must have been tough on a single mother."

"Louise was livid, according to Miriam. They belong to the legal assistants association and see each other frequently at meetings. Louise downloaded to Miriam a few months before D.L. was killed."

"No surprise. I wonder who might know about the letter," I said. "Also, confidentially, Louise showed up at the Administration the week of D.L.'s murder to talk with a custodian."

"That's pretty interesting. How do you know that?" Adam replied.

"One of the Administration staffers said so."

"How did you find out about that?"

Something about that question bothered me. Was he maybe too eager to find out my source? It was more than a gossip thing.

"Oh, someone at lunch mentioned it," I said.

He paused. "Do you want me to talk with Miriam? Maybe I could get more information."

"Possibly a copy of the letter? But please don't tell her that I want to know!"

"No worries. Your name will not be mentioned. I'll give you a call in a couple days."

I was grateful for Adam's friendship. I had known him when he was on the Administration staff in the hearing division. Jesse and I represented a client who had applied to be a radio broadcast station licensee. That was long ago when the Administration had hearings on such things. It was a sort of Kabuki Theater, with broadcasters making deals with minorities and women to file applications for radio stations, and the Administration giving them credits for being minorities, women or local owners. Lawyers paraded around with their applicants at the hearings, asking silly questions. Deals were made behind the scenes and it often ended up with settlement agreements. But that process could go on for years, especially in bigger markets, with appeals and travels to the court of appeals. Now, the Administration just holds an auction. The days of hearings before Administrative Law Judges are long gone, with the one hearing formerly starring D.L. being the exception. Adam had been one of the lawyers in our long-ago hearing proceeding and we developed a rapport, mainly through our mutual disdain for the process, which was rightly and finally abandoned.

He was a nice solid guy, always upbeat, a dad-type guy. And he was savvy. He was lured away from the Administration five or so years ago into a law practice as solid as he is.

His apparent friendliness was a bonus to me. But I didn't download my emotional torment on him. I did not want my personal anguish to get around to my peers. I needed to present the image that I was holding up under pressure. Anyway, now my worry was that there wasn't very much time to sleuth out Louise's malice and her letter.

Maybe Dave could find out some background on Louise. I called him. He told me that he had already tried to research Louise. There wasn't much information out there on her. She was from Montana and came to Washington fifteen years ago. She was hired by Darius as a legal assistant/secretary about the same time. She rented a townhouse in Fairfax County, Virginia. There were no records on her, but he had found a birth certificate for her thirteen-year-old daughter. The certificate only had Louise's name as the mother. No father's name listed. So much for my typecast assumption about Louise, the widow. I am not sure where I got that.

I told him that Louise and D.L. were having issues at the time of D.L.'s death. The relationship went bad after D.L.'s father died. The feud involved D.L.'s reluctance or neglect to pay Louise. We both knew enough about D.L. that no comment was necessary.

"Why would the relationship go downhill after Darius died?" I wondered. "Was he protecting her for some reason? Was D.L. upset about Darius's treatment of Louise? If so, why? And if the situation was bad, why did Louise stay?" These were all questions that might lead to interesting answers. But we had so little time. In the meantime, Dave said that he would try to track Stanley.

In early afternoon, Jesse sauntered into my office with a copy of an email sent out by the newspaper that afternoon. There was a header on one of the stories stating, "Several lawyers questioned by FBI in Radio Frequency Administration murder." Thank God no names were listed in the article. But this could be just the beginning.

"I think that you might want to send this to Ray," he suggested.

"Well, it doesn't list any names," I responded, irritated.

"It's just to let him know that something is out there. There will probably be a follow-up story."

"Please tell me why my dilemma is so important to you? I think that I should be able to decide why and when I contact Ray."

"You don't want to withhold information from the firm. We need to anticipate when the next shoe will drop. They asked us to work together on this." Jesse was unflappable, patiently explaining legal ethics to someone without legal experience who didn't quite understand. It infuriated me. He was pressuring me, and this would only lead to more pressure from the firm's board.

I did not respond. He dropped the email on my desk and sauntered out.

Another thing to fret about.

I turned to business, which had been neglected in my turmoil. I needed to keep billing those hours. For a few hours, I tried to forget all the negative events swirling around me. Soon it was 7:00 PM and I closed my office. I went home without hearing from Adam or Jean.

Eating my solitary dinner, I contemplated Louise's trip to the Administration to see Stanley. Was she the messenger for D.L. or did she have another role in this drama? Need more information, the law school mantra.

Late the next morning, Adam called me with further information about Louise's background. He told me about the single motherhood. I knew that already from Dave, but kept it to myself.

"One thing of interest," he said. "Miriam, my legal assistant, said that Louise told her D.L. had a problem with her father's relationship with Louise. D.L. complained to Darius when he was alive that he treated Louise with deference, not as a hired employee. According to Miriam, Louise assumed that to mean that he stopped D.L. from mistreating Louise while he was alive. The mistreatment began soon after Darius died."

"Why did she stay?" I asked. "There are many refugees from the Phillips office in D.C. law firms."

"Well, one thing happened a month or so before D.L. became involved in the auction. A former messenger for Leon Gallagher's firm was hired by D.L.

The guy, Keith Olson, was a messenger, gofer, IT guy. Louise struck up a relationship with him. He tried to buffer between D.L. and Louise. He helped keep the office from becoming a hell for her."

"That still leaves us with the question of why Darius treated Louise with kindness when that wasn't his usual modus operandi. I mean, Louise is a nice person and smart, according to my client who met her one time, but those qualities didn't seem to matter with other employees to either father or daughter."

"Maybe it had something to do with her daughter?" Adam questioned.

"O-ka-a-a-y. What do you know about that?"

"Well," he confessed, "Miriam said that at a happy hour for the association, Louise implied that her daughter might have a connection to Darius."

"She doesn't seem like his type. She is sort of 70s and he was Las Vegas."

"Maybe looks deceive," he said. "I know nothing about Darius or what attracts people. All I know is what the gossip is."

"If all that is true," I said, "maybe that is why Louise stayed on at the firm and became involved in the D.L. transaction. I'm just not sure why she would expose herself by visiting Stanley at the Administration or write a letter to the FBI, for that matter."

"We lawyers are great at speculating," he said. "What if she had something big to gain if she acted as go between with Stanley for both D.L. and for—say, Keith?"

"A double agent? That does not sound like Louise Richards to me."

"Well, if you have a child to support and you were provided for in Darius's will: that might have some impact on your life view. You would stick around to see it through and make sure it happens. The will hasn't been settled yet because D.L. 'procrastinated', as usual."

"How do you know all this?"

"Remember, Miriam and Louise are really good friends."

"Adam, I don't know how to thank you. This is so important to me!"

Adam laughed, "Well, if I'm ever on my way to being tried for murder, I will expect you to help me, too."

"I will of course, but you would never be put in that situation. You don't crack jokes about hitmen. And, by the way, did Miriam know anything about the letter to the FBI."

"She said she would mention it when she talks to Louise and see what happens. Take care. When I hear anything, I will let you know."

He had given me much more than I could have wished for.

While pondering my new information, Graciela called. We talked about her meeting with the school principal and her adviser. She was happy. She said they were switching Matias to a class with three other Hispanic children.

"How does Matias feel about school now?" I asked.

"Bueno! Happy now. But Stanley, I tell you. Stanley with guy on bike. In front of building, she yelling."

"What did he look like?"

What she described to me matched Keith Olson as he was when I saw him at my law firm. A little shaggy, but good looking and cyclist build.

"What happened?"

"Just standing outside. She yelling, he mad. At end, he rode away fast." Something else to ponder.

By the end of the day, I still had not heard from Jean. That bothered me.

# CHAPTER 14: Dave Investigates.

I had no idea what we were going to do to locate Stanley—this villain—and what we were going to do with her if we found her. We couldn't tie her up and drop her off at the FBI or the prosecutor's office. Apparently, neither the FBI nor the prosecutor knew that Jimmi Stanley or Lana Stanford even existed. And I don't think they cared. They had me in its sights, and someone was guiding them into thinking that I did the hiring. They were waiting for me to confess, I believe. That would never happen.

Would it be better to find and put pressure on my snitch? I had no idea what I would say to whoever it was, except to accuse that person of trying to frame me. Frame me! That sounded like a phrase out of The Maltese Falcon. All we needed now was Humphrey Bogart.

I had become vulnerable to the bad behavior of a gangland thug. And our motley team was supposed to capture her! I knew that I was not equipped for that. I had to rely on Dave and his expertise. And as he warned, this could get dark, way too dark for me.

Now, we were operating against the clock and that could lead to a lot of different mistakes, mistakes that could get one or both of us hurt or maybe killed. I woke up in the middle of the night after a dream full of chases by faceless enemies. I wondered what the hell I was doing. I had no more expertise in capturing a supposed killer than my doorman, if I'd had one. Maybe my doorman would have more. I am a lawyer who practices telecommunications law. I don't know anything about how to do this.

But if I didn't do something, I would be shoved into a huge mess that I might get out of, but not without spending lots of money and ruining my career. I had to do this. Dave could help me—as a former cop, he knows about this stuff.

The clock said 2:00 AM, my favorite time to wake up in a panic. Now I would lie awake in this dark room, looking at the shadows from the streetlights on the walls and contemplating a dismal future. I pushed back the comforter and got up. I went to the medicine cabinet and got some melatonin. It never works for me. I don't know why I even bother. When I am up, I am up. I'd better take a book to the living room and try to get back to sleep there. That was a helpful hint I read in a health magazine. The point was to not stay in bed thinking. Sometimes reading worked, sometimes it didn't.

I picked up my phone, another no-no from the sleep experts who advocate putting electronics away for the night. I noticed there was a text from Cam! He told me that his neighbor, Len Reynolds, was with Dave in the emergency room. Dave had been shot. Len didn't have my number, so he texted Cam.

My God! Like another scene out of a movie.

I have never even touched a gun, and now the man I was paying to protect me had been shot. I guessed that it was our friend Jimmi or one of her friends. They weren't kidding around. We should fear for our lives: she, and whoever she hung around with, had a lot to lose if we found her. That strengthened Dave's view that Stanley was not approachable by me and now, for that matter, by Dave alone. We were going to need more muscle.

I texted Cam back and asked for Len's number. Cam called me.

"Well, it's good that we couldn't locate her when we were looking," he said.

"Yeah, she doesn't mess around. How is Dave? Did you talk to Len at all?"

"I did. Len said that Dave was asking about Stanley in a NE bar, a Warriors hangout. No one knew Stanley, they said. They said that they didn't know Stanford either. When he left the bar, Len said, he was on his way to his car. He saw someone move in the alley as he was opening his car door. Before he could defend himself or even get behind the open door, he was shot at from the alley. The shot grazed his left side, significant enough not to be called superficial."

"You think it was a warning to stay away by someone who knew how to place bullets?"

"I don't know," said Cam. "There is something about this shooting that got Len agitated, maybe an ex-cop reaction, maybe a friend's response, maybe because he had recommended Dave to you, and now he feels responsible. Anyway, Len jumped on board with you, volunteering to help.

If Dave recovers quickly, at least there will be two guys defending you."

"But I am wondering if I have enough time. And how can I get involved with this, other than paying them?"

"I don't think that you should be involved in any other way. Just keep paying them to do what they're good at, and don't do anything foolish, like running after a thug," Cam added.

"I'm sorry that you got involved, that Len contacted you at two in the morning."

"It's ok. I wasn't sleeping very well anyway. There is a lot going on in the office and I was just semi-asleep."

"Well, try to go back to sleep," I said. "Goodnight."

"Goodnight. Ummm, why were you up?"

"Lots going on with me, too, and this is another setback in my life adventure."

"Don't worry, things will be ok," he said.

"I'll take your word for it," I laughed. "Goodnight."

"Go back to sleep." He hung up.

I met with Len the next day. He was a big muscular guy, very intense. He was eager to help his friend and me, in that order. He said, "To be honest, I did not think this job was for real. Now, I know that someone is out there with something to hide. From what Dave said, you have a credible case."

I kept my thoughts to myself, as I do often when communicating with male clients or lawyers, who sometimes pick up my points and then feed them back to me as their own. But the important thing was that Dave, and now Len, had come around to my side and trusted me. I was elated.

Len told me that he had gotten a call earlier that day from one of his police friends. "It wasn't a surprise," he admitted. According to Len, they are like fraternity brothers and they had access to all the reports and gossip, especially about a friend. Len's friend asked about Dave's investigation.

"Off the record, Dave thought someone in the Warriors might have had something to do with the Radio Frequency Administration murder. Of course, my friend knew there was the issue of the murder investigation being conducted by the FBI."

"But still," I said to Len, "if one of your own gets hit, isn't there anything you, as a friend, could do?"

Len did not respond. I hoped so, but it would be rough. I knew nothing about how the police worked, and if and when they respected each other's turf or if there is special dispensation from the norm if one's buddy from another police force is hit. All Len's friend had told him was, "Keep us in the loop." He would, for what it was worth. My reservations about this involvement persisted, but I didn't ask about the details because I didn't want to know. I would welcome any help we got. I gave Len the background on my case.

"It was one of my confidants, I don't know who, because I said it to several people when we talked about D.L." Telling my tale once again. "Anyway, that person told the investigator about a joke I made about D.L. and a hitman several years ago. The FBI took it seriously. There is an imperative to find the murderer as quickly as possible: it's an embarrassment to the Administration. I'm just guessing my supposed friend embellished on our discussion, to the FBI. From what I could gather from the investigator, that person elaborated on it by stating that D.L. and I had vendettas against each other. That's not quite true but the combination of gossip could prove fatal to me. The FBI agent had written examples of my Administration filings given to her. The examples were in the agent's file folder when she was questioning me."

"That is thin stuff," Len said. "And why would he do that?"

"Well, I am guessing that that person might have ties, in some way, to D.L. Phillips' company in a recent spectrum auction, for which permits have just been approved. My theory is that someone let her hang on until the process was complete and then they had her offed. If that theory were true, it would be necessary to put the blame on someone, maybe a lawyer who had well-known filing brawls with D.L. That would be me. Then, it was a process of spreading the word to the investigators."

"So, you think that these two parties were working together? Phillips doing what her cohort wanted but that person somehow wanted to stay in the background?"

"That's my guess. It's done, occasionally."

"Maybe the culprit thinks Phillips went off the plan?"

"Maybe Phillips wanted more money," I said, "and she was waiting until after she was sure that the Administration had approved everything. Then she went off the reservation and demanded more money. That is so D.L. and it would not surprise me."

"So, you think that this person had Phillips killed after the permits had been granted. What happens to them now?"

"Well, they are still only permits. They have to be constructed within a certain timeframe, but they are in the company name, which still exists even if one owner doesn't. There is another owner, 49% who should now own 100%. They will just have to make a simple filing to reflect that they are the sole owner. That shouldn't be a problem as long as they aren't a felon or an alien. In fact, and I'm really guessing here," I said, "that change will be so easy that it makes me wonder if the murder wasn't planned earlier, like when the concept was envisioned. But I don't know the identity of the remaining owner. I was surprised to see her listed because D.L. never operated that way. She could have a tie to the rascal, too."

"So, to recap: your theory is that the perp hired Stanley?"

"Well, someone hired Stanley. I know that I didn't".

"An attorney?"

"No way. I don't think so for a couple of reasons. I don't think that even the money man, whoever he is or how rich he is, would ask an attorney to get his hands dirty like that, simply because he could lose the attorney and it could possibly bite him. And frankly, I can't believe that any of my peers would get involved with anything like an assassination. That is too insane. But I do think that the client could have asked him or her to make sure to get someone implicated and I was the lucky one. I would really like to know the address on the note at the crime scene and what that unidentified device was and what it was doing on the conference room table."

"I'm brainstorming here. Could that object be Phillips' assurance that no one at the FCC discussed the ownership in her company or raised any sensitive issues? Could it have been planted in someone's office?"

"Of course, it was! Sam Watson's office. Sam is the one who monitors those types of details, particularly Phillips' details. He seems to be the go-to man at the Administration for D.L., and it isn't because they are friends: it's to keep the Administration from being wrapped around the axle. By now, he knows what she's capable of. Wow! But I wonder how it was planted and when. Also, why did Stanley leave it with Phillips?"

"Perhaps to show that Phillips knew about it and she was in on the auction plan? Or maybe to implicate the Administration staff by hinting that someone had confronted Phillips with a bug that she'd planted, and killed her in a rage?"

"There are too many unknowns. We need to find Stanley," Len said. "I am going to pick up where Dave left off, until he is ready to come back."

I conveyed my concern by wincing. "You have to promise me that you will be careful. I don't want another shooting victim in this mess."

Len shrugged, showing to me that he was ready to do what was necessary for his friend, Dave. Dave had promised to be back in action as soon as he could persuade his doctor. He was seeing her the next day. I didn't know how you could speed up recovery from a gunshot wound.

"We're also trying to talk with Louise Richards," I said. "She was D.L.'s assistant, who fell out with her after D.L.'s father died, probably for financial reasons. She not only visited Stanley at the Administration the week of D.L.'s murder but she sent a letter to the FBI regarding the investigation. I would bet there was something about me in that letter. I am trying to find out what."

# CHAPTER 15: More Conversation with the FBI.

My lawyer Gail called again that afternoon. I was in the middle of a hectic day and had no patience with one more agenda item, particularly having to do with the FBI. I was about to explode, but I kept myself under tight control.

"Ida Cramer called and has some additional questions for you," Gail said. I cringed. I was "invited" to have a further conversation with the investigators the next morning. I could guess what that was going to be: questions on my self-defense activities. Obviously, they were watching me and apparently were perturbed that I had taken measures to attempt to help myself to staunch the march forward in my prosecution.

Gail and I met in Cramer's conference room. She was more formidable (and dowdier) than usual. She was not happy with my activities I knew, but I did not care. If no one else was going to take control of my protection, I would. I am not a passive person and that wouldn't change, even for the FBI.

The Transcript

IDA CRAMER: We are here once again, Ms. James, this time to discuss some information that we have received about your recent activities that might interfere with the FBI investigation of the death of D.L. Phillips.

GAIL DAVIS: What recent activities are you referring to?

IDA CRAMER: Enlisting individuals to investigate the murder of D.L. Phillips and to interfere with the FBI investigation.

GAIL DAVIS: We object to the wording, "interfere."

IDA CRAMER: How would you characterize it?

ME: Self-defense.

IDA CRAMER: Self-defense from whom?

ME: The only person, to my knowledge that the FBI seriously appears to be investigating, is me. There is no word on the street that you are looking for the real murderer. You are calling me in on a regular basis, and from that I understand, I am the only one being seriously investigated.

Gail frowned at me, an effort to get me to keep my mouth shut. Ida ignored my comments.

IDA CRAMER: Again, self-defense from whom?

ME: It seems obvious to me and it should be to you also.

GAIL DAVIS: I will let my client answer that question specifically if she wishes, but I may have the need to instruct her that she has the right to refuse to answer any question on the grounds that it could incriminate her. I will invoke that at any time.

IDA CRAMER: Understood.

ME: Gail, we need to invoke it now.

GAIL DAVIS: I suggest that we end this interview because my client is advising me that she wishes to remain silent.

IDA CRAMER: We may refer this matter to a prosecutor for a grand jury.

GAIL DAVIS: Isn't there a grand jury set for this matter this week?

IDA CRAMER: Not on an obstruction of justice charge.

Gail and I left the office in silence. I got into her car and exhaled. "So, I pissed her off?"

"No," Gail said, "you pissed off the FBI. They don't like local cops looking over their shoulders."

"I did not put my guy up to that. The local police have an interest in this: one of their own got shot and that upsets them."

"Yes, but who started the wheels rolling?"

"OK, OK. I accept the blame, but I should just sit still and let 'justice' happen? Let the law take care of me and my pocketbook? What is the likelihood of that? I've seen how long the law takes to get done and undone. I cannot just sit back because someone wants me to—how do they say it in the movies—take the fall? I refuse to be passive, just sit and wait until the FBI comes for me and puts me in prison, after a brief kangaroo court. I have to be an aggressive person because my life as I know it is at risk and this scene is moving fast forward. I need to save my own life because nobody else seems to want to. And yes, my defense wheels are in motion and because of what happened, they are not going to stop, if I can help it."

Gail and I parted at her office, and I continued back to mine. I called Len and told him about the interview. "The bottom line is that Ida threatened me with an obstruction of justice charge because she said I was interfering with the investigation."

Len blew up. "Interfering with what investigation? Here we have those guys thinking that they're going to put it all on you. They aren't even looking for the killer. They aren't investigating anything hard. They are sitting on their asses and talking with lawyers, clients and "safe" Administration staff. As far as I can figure, they haven't even looked at the janitorial staff. They don't want to get their hands dirty when they can nab an innocent who's an easy target. They're thinking they'll get the total picture when they squeeze that person: you."

"Tell me how you really feel," I said, sighing. But I was glad that Len had become a strong advocate, even though indirectly. I had had it for the day. I'd returned to my office to unwind—by doing client work. Then, the phone rang.

It was Dave. He was in pain but the fact that he was on the phone gave me hope. "I'm so happy to hear from you!" I said, relieved just to hear his voice.

"Not half as happy as I am. Apparently, Ms. Stanley doesn't like people talking about her. It makes her and her special friends really nervous."

"Well, what's the next move?"

"Len and I and some friends are going to look for her."

"Are you healed enough to go out there again? What did your doctor say?"

"She said that she doesn't like it, but that she knows what I'll do."

"You really should follow her orders."

"I'm fine," he insisted.

I sighed. "Be careful. Who are your friends?"

"Some off duties. Cops can take outside jobs, I've heard."

"Well, if it makes you feel any worse, my FBI interrogator seems to think we're interfering with the Bureau's operations. Obstruction of justice."

"That's good about the FBI," he said, echoing Len. "I don't see them trying to find the hired hand. I see them interrogating you and other lawyers and some select Administration staff. They aren't on the beat. They are sitting in their offices thinking that they have a winning case in you."

"Thanks for your support. You sound like Len. But we need to find Stanley and get her to talk about who paid for the hit, which will be even harder." We ended by setting up a phone call in two days with Len, Dave, and me to strategize.

I got up to get a cup of coffee. When I returned to my desk, there was a voice mail message from Adam Ross on my phone. He said that he had a copy of Louise's letter to the FBI.

I called him immediately. He told me that Louise had sent Miriam a copy of her letter to the FBI and now Adam was reading it to me. In the letter, she told the FBI that D.L. had Sam Watson's office bugged. She said that she hadn't known about the bugging until D.L. asked her to meet with an employee of the Administration, a custodian by the name of Jimmi Stanley, to request that she remove the device from Watson's office and to return it. The letter was written the Tuesday after D.L.'s death on Friday and was clearly intended to cast D.L. in a bad light.

A wave of relief surged over me. There was nothing about me in that letter at all.

When Louise wrote that letter, she had no reason to hold back. It looked as if she was acting on her own. D.L. was dead. She was fed up and had been mistreated by D.L, not getting paid and was concerned that her daughter, a rightful heir, would be cut off from Darius' will. But also, she was being asked by D.L. to participate in an indirect way with an illegal bugging of a Federal employee's office. She wanted no part of it and although she did go to the Administration and talk with Jimmi Stanley, she told her that her contact would be waiting for an Administration meeting on Friday at 3 on the main building's third floor and for her to give the device to her there, right before 3. The contact had red hair. This was all in the letter.

"I am confused," I said to Adam. "If Louise had sent the letter right after D.L.'s death, why had the FBI not looked into this Jimmi Stanley or this illegal activity on D.L.'s part after they received it? Why had there been no investigation of the circumstances around the device at the murder scene? I'm not sure I am getting the whole picture here." I shook my head, honestly at a loss. "I understand Louise's effort to exonerate herself if the FBI ever investigated the bugging of Sam's office, but I don't understand the FBI's inaction on it. Wouldn't they wonder about this custodian at the Administration and her involvement with D.L. and her possible meeting with her at the Administration on the Friday afternoon before her murder? Here is a fabulous piece of evidence that has been disregarded."

"Maybe it wasn't credible evidence to the FBI in light of the big picture," Adam suggested.

"The big picture? Isn't an Administration employee participating in the bugging of the office by a woman who is then murdered an important part of the big picture?"

"Yeah, I don't know. But you're sort of subjectively involved."

Well, that certainly wasn't very supportive. Maybe I was leaning on him too much and he wanted to distant himself. OK. I get that.

"I guess I should call my lawyer about this," I said. "It smells terrible, but I don't think that I will get much reaction from her."

"What's the problem?" Adam asked.

"She thinks that I should wait and see what happens with the FBI. I think I'd be stupid to wait for the ax to fall."

"Well, good luck," said Adam. "If I hear anything more, I'll let you know."

"You are a good friend." I hung up with Adam, thanking him profusely.

I called Gail and told her about the letter. In fact, I forwarded the letter via email from Adam. "I think it's really suspicious that the FBI never did any investigation into Louise's letter. Here was a clear lead and they dropped the ball. Why was that?"

Gail sounded less than impressed. "First of all, we don't know if they did any investigation — they may have. And second, it sounds like a self-serving letter to me. Louise was just covering her behind."

"But," I said, "the letter discusses the custodian at the Administration who was involved somehow with D.L. and who left her job after D.L.'s murder. I wonder if the FBI even looked for her." Gail, like Adam, was not ready to add any more fuel to my self-preservation plan. We closed off our conversation.

Frustrated, I called Dave and repeated my story. I sent him Louise's letter and we commiserated over the apparent disinterest by the FBI in the letter. The custodian's name did not even appear on the FBI interview list. What was that all about?

I asked him to hold off searching for Stanley while we sorted out this new development. Instead, I asked him to look into Ida Cramer: her background, her education, her friends and her family. I wondered again if it was possible that she was bending to some kind of force, someone pressuring her to move the investigation in a way that would benefit them. Were there other figures involved in this scenario that we didn't yet know about? I did not see her jeopardizing her standing by hanging out with thugs or convicted felons. But I could see her being influenced by a good friend, relative or law classmate. Dave said he would try, but he did not sound very happy to do it. I understood. The FBI is not your friend, no matter who you are.

That night, I texted Cam, my IT genius who was now in Brussels, with a short question on a wide internet search. He called me a short while later. It was early morning his time. We caught up and I apologized yet again. Questions popped out of me: how could I investigate an FBI investigator? It was so intimidating. Where did she go to school? Who did she know that might influence her search? I needed to know everything about her.

For starters, Cam suggested that I input her name into browsers and see what came up. Of course, I should try that, but I was dubious about the result. I thought that FBI employees like Ida might be search proof. I told Cam that I had a onetime neighbor who was an FBI agent and she (or someone) deactivated the built-in alarm system which was supposed to protect the whole complex. I have no idea what her substitute system was, but it appeared to me that it was to protect her phone line from any kind of monitoring. I told him that another neighbor across the hall worked for the Defense Intelligence Agency and had her apartment heavily alarmed, again not by the standard alarm system. My neighbor did not tell me about the DIA but a security clearance investigator, showing me his government badge, came to my door and asked me a lot of questions about her. So, if even the designated alarm systems aren't protection enough for the government intelligence people, what were the chances for a personal profile showing up for public scrutiny on the internet?

"Good luck with that." I thought for a moment. "And Cam, if I do investigate the investigators, what might happen to me? I have already been put on notice for obstruction. Would the next charge be harassment?" I needed to think about everything thoroughly before I actually did it. We hung up and I tried an advanced search. Nothing on Ida Cramer came up. Of course.

# CHAPTER 16: An Old Friend with an Old Problem.

When I arrived in my office the next morning, my message light was on. It was my friend Jean, apologizing for not getting back to me sooner. She said she had been selected for a big project for one of the Administration commissioners a week ago and had just come down from 14-hour days, including the weekend. She asked me to give her a call that morning and left her cell phone number. A good sign. I had been afraid when she hadn't called back now that I was persona non grata with her and maybe the Administration.

I got a coffee from the kitchen, said good morning to Dot, my assistant, and went into my office. I shut the door and dialed Jean's number. She answered on the third ring.

"Hi, Leyla," she said, "I have been thinking about you. I really want to talk with you."

"I really want to talk with you, too."

"Let's have lunch," she said. "How about 12:30 today at the Cascade Cafe in the National Gallery?"

"I'll see you there."

The Cafe was halfway between my firm and Jean's office at the Administration. I decided to walk because it was a mild sunny day in D.C., after two soggy dark days of rain. I was buoyed by the thought that I might get some information from Jean that would help my case. I arrived first and got a table by the waterfall behind the glass wall in the Cafe. I waited for Jean, full of hope.

When she came up to the table, I was shocked. She looked bad. She had a bluish smudge on her cheek barely hidden under heavy make-up, and she appeared bedraggled. She did not look at all like the put-together Jean of the past. The last time I saw her was three months ago at a group meeting and she was fine. I wondered what on earth had happened since then. All thoughts of information extraction disappeared. Neither of us made a move toward the service line.

"Oh, Jean," I said. "What happened?"

"Dick and I are splitting. We are fighting about everything: money, the house, the kids, even the car."

"Is he being abusive?" I asked, looking at her face.

She nodded but held back and did not say anything. She was upset.

"Can I do anything to help?" I asked.

"I need money," she said bluntly. "Dick drained our accounts and moved the money. My lawyer is fighting it, but I don't have any money for anything now. My last paycheck was deposited last week and right after that Dick shifted most of the money to a new account in his name. My parents can't help me financially, and Dick knows that. He is relying on my helplessness to get his way."

I was speechless. I immediately thought about the ethics of giving her money. She is a government official, and I am a lawyer practicing before her agency. What if I gave her money and someone found out? I assumed someone would, with all eyes on me these days. Even if there was no ethical problem, because it wouldn't be a bribe or the information did not pertain to any Administration business, the FBI might make something of it.

Still, I wanted to help Jean. She was my fellow sufferer through the dark days at the firm when we were brand new lawyers. We had been sisters in misery and cried on each other's shoulders about various ogre partners at the firm. When she had her two babies, she left private practice to work at the Administration. We continued to see each other through the years. In fact, Cam and I went out to dinner with them a year or so ago, and they seemed happy enough. I was shocked to hear that Dick would cut her and their kids off from not only his money but hers. That was just plain cruel.

"Jean, I can loan you or give you some money. How much do you need?"

"I need five thousand until the next pay day at the end of the month. I didn't want to ask you, but you are the only person I knew I could go to for help, who would keep it quiet. It would be a loan. My lawyer will work it out. I trust him. This has been a nightmare."

"What happened?"

"It turns out that it's the old story: he had an affair with someone in his office. I knew it, I just knew it." She stopped and drew a breath. "I didn't know who it was, but I knew it happened and that it was ongoing. He never traveled much on his job before and then he started taking mid-week 'job site' visits. They were visits to high-end hotels in D.C. for the evening and morning. Then he would be back in the office mid-morning. He lied to me when I asked and said I was simply imagining things."

Her eyes teared up and she blew her nose. "The same old story: there was something wrong with me that I didn't trust him. But he didn't get to the credit card statement as fast as I did one month, when I was working from home because Dylan was sick. When I confronted him, he acknowledged the affair but said it was over. It wasn't and I knew that, too. He had no more out of town visits, but his nights out with the boys occurred a little too often and ran a little too late. When I told him that I was done with the pretense, he promised me that it was over. Again, it wasn't. Another confrontation and this time he told me what he had done, which was to drain out the accounts, to give him some leverage. Those were our accounts, and he acts like he doesn't care about me or the kids. He just wants to have his way and he's being a bully."

My plan to press Jean for information about Ida was forgotten. I sat and listened to her and watched her keep herself somewhat under control. I thought she was being courageous. But I admit it, I was still shocked about her marriage and her request for money.

"Leyla, I wish I didn't have to ask you for—" She sighed. "I have to pay my lawyer."

"Yeah, I know," I said. "I have a lawyer, too. Sometimes I feel that she is trying to help me get convicted. I'm kidding, but it's frustrating. I think the FBI actually believes that I had something to do with D.L.'s murder, and she's not helping. So I understand."

She told me that she'd heard about the FBI investigation. "I am so sorry to put this on you when you are under such pressure."

"But I want to help you!" I said. "Maybe you could just tell me just one thing." Then I asked her my question, "Do you know anything at all about the lead investigator, Ida Cramer?"

Jean went silent for a minute, then lowered her voice. "I will tell you what I—and a few other Administration staffers—know about Ida. She went to law school with several of our friends."

"Okay, thanks."

"It's the least I can do," she said. "Here's the thing—Ida Cramer and

Adam Ross went to law school together. There are others, a bunch of them in telecom. Lydia King, remember her, and Leon Gallagher, too." Jean said. "At one point, people thought they might have been a thing, but it appears that they both moved on. Leon, of course, got married. She didn't. They remained friends. I'm thinking that she might have worked at his firm right after law school for a brief stint in telecom law. Word is, she didn't like it, and the firm didn't like her. She is very controlling. Everything has to be her way and she can be downright mean. None of the Administration staff that interfaced with her could deal with her unreasonable demands. Remember, practitioners are supposed to be supplicants." We laughed at her joke. But I, as a practitioner, often felt like a supplicant. "After three years, she went to the FBI, with Leon's highest recommendations. I think that he was glad to see her go."

We laughed again and changed the subject, continuing to chat about Jean's problems and how her children were responding. I felt so sorry for her. She had everything, I thought, and now she was going through such pain. We talked briefly about her projects and my practice while we were grabbing some lunch. We finished eating quickly and hugged each other goodbye. She went her way with my check, and I had some information. Maybe not worth

$5,000, but at least I had a lead or two. I would have to keep on searching. I thought I would check in with Adam about Ida.

When I came into the reception area, Monique the receptionist told me that Jesse was looking for me. I stopped in his office and he was on the phone. He motioned me in, and I sat in the chair in front of his desk.

"Yes," he said. "She is right here." He put his phone on speaker.

"Hi, Leyla," Ray greeted me. Oh oh, I thought, this could be trouble. "Hi, Ray. How are you doing?"

"The question is how are you?"

"I'm ok. I had another conversation with the FBI yesterday, and I sent a memo on it to Eliot."

"Yeah, Eliot shared it with me." He paused. "Tell me, do you think that you should be investigating your own case?"

I wondered whether Jesse had prompted him to ask that question. "Well, I would prefer not to need to, but no one is offering me much assistance."

"Isn't your lawyer assisting you?" he asked.

"She is doing all the lawyerly things and following procedure. My problem is that I didn't do anything wrong. Yet I feel I'm being led into this incriminating maze that will soon overwhelm me, if I don't help myself."

"But aren't you provoking the FBI?" he asked. "I fear that if you continue to do this, it will result in bad press to the firm."

Jesse was observing me with a bland expression, as if our years of working together deserved no allegiance at all. I wondered if he had initiated the conversation with the managing partner.

"Are you asking me to stop defending myself," I asked.

"Of course not. I just don't want to have the firm getting involved. Can you tone it down? I don't want you to have to take a leave, so just cool it."

"How am I supposed to do that?" I asked.

"Have your PI do all the work. Don't be so visibly involved."

"I'll see what I can do," I said, thinking that this might come to a head soon and then I might be without a job, with a little help from my longtime law partner.

"That's all we are asking for now, Leyla. Play nice with the FBI."

We said our goodbyes after I promised to keep them up to date. Ray hung up.

"Did Ray call you?" I asked Jesse. "No, I called him."

"Why?"

"Because I thought he should know what is going on."

"Without asking me," I said.

"They told us to work together," he responded.

"For God's Sake, Jesse. You need to let me know what you are doing that directly affects me. What is happening here? We used to be respectful of each other, and now you're going behind my back and making things worse. Nothing that I am doing has affected our clients or the firm. I feel betrayed."

"They wanted to be kept informed," he said flatly. There was no apology. "Well, don't do this again without telling me," I said. I got up from the chair and left his office.

Then, I got down to billable hours. At least that might keep the managing partner from bouncing me, for the time being. Four hours later, I closed it down and headed home.

# CHAPTER 17: More Info.

The next morning, I was on the phone with Adam first thing. Thankfully, he picked up. I began by talking about our mutual clients' proceeding and our effort to get it off from the hold caused by D.L.'s death. I didn't want him to detect the urgency of getting information on Ida.

"I emailed Tom yesterday," I said, referring to an Administrative staffer. "I asked him when we were going to see some movement on the Tuscan case. Since all the papers were in, I told him that I thought a decision could be made. He's hesitant. He is waiting for D.L.'s representative to respond to his call."

"Did her rep send out a notice to the Administration?" Adam asked.

"Yup. He sent it out a couple weeks after the murder. Didn't you get a copy? He's supposed to send it to all the parties."

"Hmm. I don't remember getting anything. I'll ask Miriam. I wonder what he's going to be like."

"Judging from his correspondence with me on another issue between my client and D.L.'s office, I am thinking that there will only be a slight change in tenor. I don't believe he has any telecom experience, so I don't know how that will work. I thought that he notified the FCC just to make sure nothing went astray."

"Great!" he said with a sigh. "More fun."

"Think of it this way. It simply cannot be as bad as before."

"I just want Tom to clean up the mess."

"Let's hope. By the way, what do you know about Ida Cramer? Did you go to law school with her?"

Adam paused. "Yes, we were in the same class."

"What's she like?"

"She's tough," he said. "What do you mean?"

"Well, once she grabs ahold of something, she doesn't let go. She makes up her mind and there is no going back for her."

"That's her business m.o. What's she like as a person? Does she have a significant other, kids, a dog?"

"Not sure of a significant other. She keeps pretty much to herself. She does live in Georgetown, in a townhouse, and drives a Jeep."

"That's different, I would never have guessed."

"Yeah, it doesn't fit with her image."

I kept my thoughts to myself about her image. "Do you Georgetowners get together often?"

"As a group, not much anymore. Most of us don't live in the District now and have families that take up our lives. Not much time to pub-crawl, like the old days."

"Does she see any of the old crowd at all that you know of?"

"I've heard they do some hiking and a little biking occasionally."

"Hence, the Jeep. Who does she hike with?"

"Annie Sims, sometimes. Maybe Gene Lopez. I think that I heard that Leon has gone a couple of times with his son. I don't know how any of them have the time."

"Annie Sims works in the Chairman's office, right? Isn't she the liaison with the GC's office on the D.L. situation? I don't remember Gene. Is he in telecom?"

"Yes, Annie works for the Chairman. He's taken a hit on the murder. He wants it solved. Gene works for the Wired Trade Group. He's had a few tangles with D.L. Minor tussles, compared to yours, but still notable."

My other line rang. I signed off, saying that I had a conference call scheduled. I didn't. I did get some interesting tidbits from Adam.

In keeping with my promise to the managing partner, I passed along the names of these people to Dave to investigate. For the time being, I was going to stick to law and the clients. Unfortunately, that did not last for long.

Late morning, I left the office to run an errand down the street. I had to drop off a file I'd borrowed from a friend at another firm. I could've had a messenger deliver it, but it was a sunny day and I needed to be outdoors. I walked to my friend's office.

We chatted about the case, which involved several parties, including one of mine. The clients were involved in a complicated telecom transaction that also involved an investment banker who thought he was a telecom expert after two conference calls. I thanked her and walked back in the sunshine, looking in restaurant windows at the food displays. I was hungry. One of these days, I would buy a giant Panini and totally eat all of it, followed by a soft ice cream cone. But for now, I'd stick to my boring salad. I needed to stay awake this afternoon.

Returning to my office with my salad retrieved from the refrigerator, I saw that my message light was on. I wondered what other "good" news was waiting for me. It was Louise, of all people. She said that she needed to talk with me, right away.

I returned her call at D.L.'s office number. Louise answered the phone and I identified myself. We had never been introduced, but I am sure my name had been "bandied" about the office in an unfavorable way many times. When she spoke, her tone was cool. "I understand you were talking with Dan Ross about me. I'm wondering why you are interested in my business. I thought that I would ask you directly."

"Louise," I said, "someone mentioned to me that you had written a letter to the FBI about a bugging device at the Administration. I wanted to find out more about it. I asked Adam Ross. Did the FBI ever acknowledge that the letter was received?"

"I guess you heard about the letter from Miriam." She sounded exasperated.

"Well, no," I said. "I heard it indirectly because I've been interviewed by the FBI on D.L.'s case. Because of that, one of my friends mentioned your letter to me."

"I haven't heard anything from the FBI about that letter," she said. "I wanted them to know that I had nothing to do with D.L.'s actions, in case they investigated the device. But, so far, no response."

"Well, there is another way. You could get that letter out to the public," I said. "You could send copies to the Administration's General Counsel and the commissioners."

"Yes, I thought of doing that. That's why Miriam and I had an argument. I mentioned to her that I was putting letters together and she told me not to. She said it would be a bad idea. That her boss, Adam Ross, said it could cause problems for me."

"That's interesting. Did he say why?" I asked. Very interesting indeed! "Yes, he said that it might interfere with the FBI's investigation."

"Well," I said. "That might be a good thing for you. Right now, they're not paying any attention to your evidence that an Administration custodian was involved. It may be important information. But more important, it should exonerate you, if anyone investigates the bugging of an Administration staff member."

"That's what I thought. In fact, I had all the letters set to go when Miriam told me not to do it."

"But don't you think it would help your case?" I said. "You also might want to send a copy to the Chairman of the Senate Committee on Commerce, Science and Transportation. That might help focus the Administration's attention."

"That's a great idea. D.L. did that one time, when the staff was not moving an issue along fast enough. It did get some action!" I vaguely remembered that episode. That drove the Administration staff crazy and put Sam Watson in a bad light.

"That's good, Louise. Is there anything that I can do to help you? I would hate to see you involved in D.L.'s death in any way."

"Thank you! But no," she said. "I will make up another letter to the Senate and then mail all of them right away. Thank you for calling me back."

"It is for the best," I said. Whew.

I wondered why Adam had tried to stop Louise from making her letter public. The fact that he would discourage Louise from getting her information out to the Administration was puzzling. After all, it did affect the security not to mention hiring practices of the agency. It was something that the Administration needed to know, but the fact that he was basically dissuading Louise from telling her story was puzzling to me.

On a hunch, I called Jean. She answered her cell phone. I asked her how things were going and whether Dick was behaving. "My lawyer is getting him reined in," she said. "He told Dick's lawyer that this bank account tactic would not help him with the child custody."

"I am so glad he's getting religion," I said. "I just hate to have him hurt you. I cannot believe that the nice person I thought I knew is behaving this badly!"

"I appreciate your standing by me," she said. "How are your problems these days?"

"Not good, but there may be a way you can help me."

"Anything," she said.

"Do you know who else went to law school with Adam Ross, Annie Sims, Ida and Leon?"

"Keith Olson."

"Keith Olson? He's a go-fer!"

"I didn't say that he finished law school. But he was part of the same class for a year and a half."

"Wow. What happened?"

"No idea. He just tuned in and dropped out, as they say."

"That's very interesting. He's living an alternative lifestyle now. Anyway, another question: Is Adam friendly with Ida?"

Jean let out a guffaw, "Not at all. They never got along. He told me that she was a harpy in school and she's never changed. I doubt they've spoken to each other in ten years."

"That too is very interesting," I said. "Thank you for the info. Keep in touch, Jean. Let me know how everything is going."

"I will. And if you have time, let's get together again soon. I need all the support I can get." she said.

"Of course, any time you want. Just let me know when you're available and I will be, too." She had been there for me when Cam and I broke up. I needed to return the favor.

I suppose it was a little better that Adam and Ida weren't buddies, but someone was pulling strings behind my back. Adam knew nothing of anyone's involvement in my investigation until now, obviously, or he wouldn't have helped me with background on Louise. I wonder who got to him. Maybe Adam owed something to somebody. Or someone knew something about his past and had threatened to reveal it to the world if he continued to "conspire" with me on my self-protection investigation.

I decided to verify Louise's understanding by directly asking him.

"Hi, Adam," I said to his voicemail the next morning. "When you get a chance would you please give me a call? I have a question about whether you knew that Louise wanted to get her letter out into the public domain. Thanks, Adam, and I really appreciate all your help."

My day began its crazy cycle. Soon I was dealing with little fires, convoluted emails and an interminable conference call that could have been resolved efficiently in 15 minutes but took an hour because there were three lawyers involved. Before I knew it, it was 1:00 PM, and I still hadn't heard from Adam. He was usually so responsive. That bothered me a bit. I got up to fetch my salad from the kitchen.

When I came back to my office, there was a message from Adam. He was evasive about what he knew about Louise. He just said that Miriam and Louise had a misunderstanding and they weren't speaking right now. So, he didn't know. End of voice mail. Dial tone.

I was now sure that something had changed between me and Adam. I could understand that he might not feel comfortable speaking for Louise, especially if Miriam and Louise had a misunderstanding. But, listening to his message, I felt a new coolness in his tone. He had seemed sympathetic to me before. So why the sudden change? I wondered whether someone in his law school group had gotten to him. Not Ida, for sure. Maybe Annie Sims, because of her position in the Chairman's office? Gene Lopez seemed to have no business reason to muzzle Adam. Leon, although really ambitious, was just too conservative to have been part of a nefarious plot.

I didn't have a clue. But it was obvious that I was missing something.

# CHAPTER 18: Jimmi Stanley Surfaces.

Two days later, Louise called me at the office. "I just got a call from the General Counsel's office. Seth Hayes, the GC, wants me to come and talk with him tomorrow morning. I am not sure whether I should be pleased or afraid. Do you think I should bring a lawyer with me?"

I didn't know. Louise wasn't an attorney, and that was of some concern because she had basically confessed to having knowledge of the bugging of a federal official. It was indirect knowledge, but the way the case was going against me, this might be a sword over Louise's head and could be used as a threat. Her defense would be that she told the FBI almost immediately after she knew.

"Louise, let me talk to my attorney and see what she thinks. My area of expertise ends at telecom law."

Gail wasn't happy that Louise had gone public and asked me why I was involved. "Tell her not to mention your name," she warned.

"Louise told me that she thought about releasing the letter after she didn't hear from the FBI and she asked me what I thought."

"Why were you talking to Louise?" she asked.

"Because I wanted to know if she'd heard anything from the FBI since I was being investigated." I was defensive. "She said that she hadn't."

"Anyway," said Gail. "I think it's best for Louise to begin the process by going alone and not setting the stage for an adversarial proceeding." She was in favor of Louise seeing what happened at the meeting, which I feared might not end well. I was concerned for Louise. I knew that she was a smart woman, after all she had survived the Phillips family. I thought that she wouldn't knowingly say anything against her own interest. Gail's point about not launching into an adversarial proceeding at the beginning was well taken, but I still was suspicious. I explained that to Louise.

"Louise, I am worried about you," I said. "Take it from me, please don't say anything more than what you said in the letter. Hopefully, it will be a friendly meeting. I'm assuming that you don't know any more than what you mentioned in the letter: that D.L. had asked you to meet the custodian at the Administration; that you knew nothing about the bugging and had no deeper knowledge of any other details—like Jimmi Stanley—other than what you wrote in the letter."

Louise paused and my heart fell. "Well, a month or so before Darius died, he got a call from someone with a similar voice. She did not identify herself. Darius was out and she said that she would call back. I'm not sure that she ever did. I didn't answer if she did call."

I did not exactly advocate omitting that piece of information but did suggest that she had no knowledge that it was in fact Stanley and stressed that she had actually seen and talked to Stanley only once, at the Administration. I even wondered out loud if this detail was relevant to her discussion at the Administration. She said that it probably was not, to my relief.

Then, she said that she would be able to take care of herself in a meeting if it meant not getting into a legal hassle right off. "What was in the letter is all I know. I never met Jimmi Stanley in the past and I did not know before that day that someone had Watson's office bugged. I don't even know whether D.L. knew it before or whether she had just found out about it. She just wanted it removed immediately but I never mentioned her name to Stanley. I just told her that her contact would be at the Administration on Friday afternoon and that she had red hair."

I wished her luck and asked her to call me after the meeting. I said that we could decide then if she needed representation. I had in mind, my attorney Gail. Although I was at times upset with her, I felt that she knew the terrain and she was an effective advocate for her client before authorities. She just didn't like me operating on my own.

In the meantime, I had questions about whether D.L. herself had plotted the bugging or whether a mysterious someone else had made the arrangements or at least the suggestion. That seemed more likely because arranging for a bug herself put her outside of a very narrow line she had drawn for herself. One thing I knew for sure: D.L. would not have paid for this operation. She wasn't about to pay for anything like that, if she could help it.

The next afternoon, Louise called me. She said she was vaguely uneasy after the meeting. She reported that there was another Administration lawyer, Chris Smyth, in the meeting with her and Seth Hayes.

"That's what they do, Louise. Don't worry about that. They always have someone else in the meeting. You never know what a visitor might say about the meeting afterwards if there is only one staff member present."

I didn't recognize Chris's name. He must have been one of those Washington, D.C. whiz kids, floating in from an Ivy League school to get another line on his impressive resume before heading to a prestigious law firm. In any event, the two Administration lawyers went over the letter with her and asked whether there was any additional information that she wanted to add. "I told them, that I knew nothing about the bugging until about an hour before I was sent to the Administration, that I took a cab there and went to the reception desk. I said that I told the officer at the desk that it was important I talked to Jimmi Stanley and that my employer had been unable to reach her in any other way. I asked that she come down for just five minutes, which was all I needed. Ms. Stanley came down. She was suspicious of me and looked aggravated. I told her that my contact had sent me and had asked that she remove "the gadget". I told her that my contact would be at the Administration on Friday afternoon a little before 3:00 PM in the third-floor conference room and for Jimmi to give her the device then. After that, I left the Administration."

"Did they ask about any other details, like why D.L. didn't go herself?"

"Yes, they asked me that," Louise said. "I told them she said that she had an important meeting to attend and the trip to the Administration couldn't wait. So, I was sent instead."

"What were they like? Were they suspicious of you? Were they friendly? Were they interested in the letter? Did they tell you anything more about the reaction at the Administration to it?"

"They were very interested in the letter. They said that it was important that I had come forward and so quickly after D.L.'s murder. They said that the Administration needed to know when it appeared that an employee was involved in something illegal. They seemed somewhat friendly, definitely not hostile. When I told them I'd never gotten a response from the FBI, they looked at each other. Of course, they knew that, but that look was hard for me to figure out. It was like a knowing but peeved look. I did not know who they were peeved at. I don't think that it was me because they treated me politely."

"I guess that was unsettling," I said sympathetically.

"Well, it was like there was another agenda in the meeting that I didn't know about. I think I did all right. I told the truth about what I knew but nothing else. I don't think they asked me any trick questions. When I left, I didn't feel that there was any unfinished business. I don't think that anyone else will need to talk to me about the letter again."

Louise was wrong about that. She got a call the next morning.

"Ms. Richards, I hear you talked with the Radio Frequency Administration about me. Is that right, Ms. Richards?"

Somehow, Louise knew she was talking to Jimmi Stanley. "Well, I talked with Mr. Hayes at the Administration yesterday about the bugging."

"But you talked about me, too, didn't you?"

"Only that I delivered a message from my employer to you at the Administration."

"Ms. Richards, you know that you could get me in trouble there, don't you?"

"I...I...had no idea. I figured that they would've talked to you already anyway."

"Why would they do that, if they didn't know anything about me?"

"I thought that in their investigation, they would locate the staff on duty that day and talk with them, like they did with the cleaner who found the body. I thought they knew who was on duty that day. You could have explained it yourself, however you wanted. I was just telling my side."

"Well, your side of the story makes trouble for me, understand? Now they'll come looking for me. If they do, you and your daughter are going to pay."

At the click of the phone, Louise immediately called me, crying, "Jimmi Stanley just called me. She threatened me and my daughter if the FBI comes looking for her. What do I do, Leyla?" We ran through the whole conversation. I heard her fear.

"Oh, Louise," I said. "I am so sorry. I have hired someone to help me out in all this. Let me talk to him and see what he thinks. Are you safe at home? Do you have someplace else you can stay if you need to?"

"I don't have another place to go," she sobbed. "What if she takes Ginny?"

What if she hurts her? I'm afraid."

Although I had a client project that needed writing that afternoon, I'd postpone it until later that night. This was more important. "Come to my office," I said. "We will talk about it."

Part of the problem was that I was feeling guilty after I had so enthusiastically supported her release of the letter to the Administration and congress. Now, I could see a huge downside. I am sure that the mastermind of all this had something to do with Stanley's knowledge of the Administration meeting. How that person found out, I don't know, but it seemed that he had moles everywhere. Who was it? Dave was supposed to be checking the other names. But I sensed the threat was closing in. And I now needed a way to get Louise out of this mess.

When I hung up, I called Dave. "OK, so Stanley just surfaced. She called Louise Richards at D.L.'s office and threatened her for sending copies of her FBI letter to the Administration. She already knew, from someone on the inside obviously, that Louise had gone to the Administration to talk with the General Counsel about the letter and she said that Louise and her daughter would be in trouble if anyone came after her. Louise is distraught. She is on her way over to my office now. What can we do? Do you know anything more about the possible villains that I gave you to investigate?"

"Come over to my office," Dave said. "We'll talk about everything. Most importantly, I just don't like the idea of Louise being unprotected when that gangster is out on the streets. And even if she might not be out there, her buddies could be sent to do the deed."

"You would know, my friend," I said.

"Nothing like getting shot to tell you the kind of thug you're after."

"I know you are joking, but maybe we should not mention that to Louise. She is a nervous wreck as it is."

"I think she needs to get out of town," Dave said.

"She says that she doesn't have any place to go. Besides, I think her daughter is in school."

"She needs to find another place to live for a while and get her daughter into school there. She shouldn't be here. She can't have much work left to do with D.L.'s projects now. If she does, she can telecommute. I just don't think she should stay in the D.C. area right now."

"How long does she have to be gone?" I asked. I was starting to get an idea.

"Until we pick up Jimmi Stanley and we wrap up this case. However long it takes us."

Just then, there was a knock on my door and my assistant Dot stuck her head in. "Louise Richards is here," she whispered.

"Alright, Dave. She's here in my office and we will walk over to your place right now. Be there in five."

Louise and I were quiet on our walk to Dave's office. Louise was always low key but now she was non-communicative. Whatever fears she had from the authorities, be it the FBI or the Administration, were now dwarfed by the terror of pursuit by a possible killer stalking her and her child. When we reached Dave's office, she was looking for a life raft.

# CHAPTER 19: A Safe House?

Dave's office was as spare and uninviting as ever, but at least I knew now that he was a steady diligent guy and our interests were his interests. He had called Len in the meantime. Len said that he would drop by. He wanted to know more about Stanley, too. I introduced Louise to Dave and explained that Dave was investigating D.L.'s murder for me because of the FBI's interest in me.

Louise was upset and launched into a description of the phone call, just as Len came through the door. The office was beginning to feel crowded. We had just enough chairs for all of us.

"She had that stern voice that I remember from our meeting," Louise said. "She's such a nasty b word. But I'm really surprised that the FBI hasn't even talked to her because she was working the day of the murder, at least that's what she had planned when I talked to her on that Monday. She said that she'd be there on Friday and would give the contact the device." She shuddered. "I wanted to have nothing to do with her or it. And now, she says that she is coming after me if the FBI comes after her"

"What exactly did she say?" asked Dave.

Louise repeated the entire conversation with Stanley, exactly as she'd earlier told me. Then finished with, "Before she hung up, Stanley said in a quivering voice, if the FBI came looking for her, my daughter and I were going to pay."

Dave looked grim and he had every right. One shot was enough to tell him that Louise and her daughter would be in peril.

"Leyla tells me that you don't have another place to go, outside of the D.C. area. Is that right?" Louise nodded her head yes.

"Your parents?"

"No, they live in Montana and we don't communicate, or get along. They don't think I'm living an 'acceptable' life, especially since I had Ginny. They belong to a kind of cult. My sister lives there too but I don't want to ask her for help. My brother lives in LA but just gets by. And I just don't have the money to pay my rent plus another place."

"I think that I may have an idea," I said. "It is really important for you and your daughter to leave town. It's not safe."

Len agreed that Louise and Ginny couldn't continue to live in Fairfax while Jimmi and her friends were around. The question was—how fast could she relocate and would it be fast enough?

I knew that the mastermind of this plan would keep the action going and as long as he did, we couldn't be unguarded. Then, my mind went to Ginny's whereabouts.

"Where is Ginny now?" I asked. Three faces looked at me with dismay.

"She's at my neighbor's house. She goes there after school, and I pick her up on the way home."

"Does anyone else know the arrangement?" I asked.

"Not that I know of," Louise said, looking anxious.

"Maybe you could give her a call?"

Louise's phone was out, she looked at her directory, mentioned the name and she was dialing. Dave was writing the name on a pad. Someone answered and Louise said, "Hi, Nancy, sorry to bother you but I was just wondering if Ginny was there."

The response caused Louise's face to turn gray. "What was happening after school? I didn't know she had a project that she was working on. She didn't tell me."

Dave, Len and I sat without breathing, listening to Louise, "But I don't understand, she always comes to your house or lets me know where she will be if she isn't. When did she call you?" She paused. "Did she say when she was coming home?" Louise's voice was wavering. "I wonder why she didn't call me about this." She paused again. "Yes, I know that she is a teenager but just barely and I want to know where she is." Pause. "No, I'm not being overprotected. It is just that something has come up and I need to know where she is. Please have her call me as soon as you hear from her." She hung up.

"We can't jump to conclusions." Dave said. "We don't know where she is."

"Maybe you and I should take a ride out to her school," said Dave. Louise nodded her head yes. She picked up her purse and her coat to leave.

Dave followed her. He held the door open for me and for Len. "I'll let you know what's up," he said as he propelled Louise out to his car.

"Don't worry," I said to her. "We'll make sure that everything is OK, and we will get you away from Stanley. I have an idea."

"Hi, Mom," I said, as I walked back to my office. "How much work would it take to clean up the guest apartment over the garage?" I smiled, as she responded. "Not long." Among her many qualities is her ability to never be flustered.

"Why?" she asked.

My mother and dad had so many summer visitors each year that 20 years ago they built an apartment over the garage. It wasn't large: it had two small bedrooms, one bathroom and a combination kitchen, dining, living room that ran the length of the apartment. There was a small balcony in the front, with only a view of the side of the yard, but it was nice in the summertime.

When my sisters and I left, it wasn't used much, maybe twice a year, but it still was comfortable if just a little outdated.

"There is a woman who has a big problem right now and we think that she needs to leave Washington quickly. She has a 13-year-old daughter. They may need some protection."

"A daughter?" My mother's voice perked up, as if she would be delighted to have another young girl around the house. "When do they need to come?" I could imagine the wheels in her head organizing the cleaning of the apartment as we spoke on the phone.

"As soon as possible," I said.

"OK." She was game for anything that came along. I was delighted.

"Now, I want to tell you who the woman is." I said. "She was D.L.'s assistant for 15 years."

My mother laughed. "This is going to be a long story. When can you come down?"

I promised that I would visit as soon as I could. "I will call you tomorrow morning," I said.

"Oh, by the way," my mother added before I could hang up. "There is a rumor going around that Lou's partner has finally discussed Mr. Sanders' dying words."

"What did he say?"

"I have no idea. I don't travel in his circle. Dee came into the shop and was really upset. She said that she heard that Lou's partner said that Lou felt that April's death was his fault."

"Wow. I'll check around with my friends and see what they've heard. Does that sound like he thought she did it on purpose?" That really disturbed me. It revived the sickening feeling that I could have done or said something to help April. I ended the conversation, promising that I would get back in touch soon. What else?

"Are you kidding me?" Cam emailed that night, responding to my question about my plan. He knew my mother, so I thought I could ask him. "Strike that: I meant do you think that putting Louise and her daughter at your mother's house is a good plan? There is a possibility that your mother could become collateral damage. If the killer stalks Louise and discovers where she is... Stanley and her gang likely will have ways of finding her, don't you think?"

"Good point. Dave said that he would call me when they find Ginny and I will ask him what he thinks of the idea. If he thinks that my mother would be in danger, then I will figure out some other plan."

Argument avoided. We were both trying to be mature. In the past, I would have been headstrong and stuck to my idea, but now I could see that I was being impulsive and putting my own mother in possible danger. But what's the point, I thought. Cam has a girlfriend and there may be no hope for rekindling us. Sigh.

Dave did call. The red alert had ended: Ginny was at school, working on a last-minute project and had forgotten to tell Louise. But the danger of allowing Louise and Ginny to stay at their house was immediate. I mentioned my mother's apartment to Dave but expressed my concerns over her safety.

"Let's think about it," he said. "It might not be a bad idea, maybe not her apartment, but she might know another one in town. Louise could stop her mail at home and at the office, then have it picked up at the post office. If she has any deliveries, she can stop those. There would be no way to trace her from that. She could change her phone settings. But she will be two states away. We locked them in for the night and told Louise not to go anywhere or let anyone in. But the sooner they're out of there, the better for everyone. I'll talk with Len about your idea and let you know what we think in the morning."

Len was in favor of moving Louise and Ginny immediately. He wanted them packed up and relocated the next day. He didn't want Jimmi Stanley to have any easy access to them. But Cam's warning was still in my head and I wondered whether it was up to me to provide a safe house for a woman I barely knew.

On the other hand, I did set her up by persuading her to send her letter to the Administration. That had caused her problems and I felt responsible. I mentioned all of that to Dave.

"Well, I am sure that it is NOT your responsibility. She had already sent the letter to the FBI and you didn't hear about it until weeks later. It really is her problem, not yours."

"Yes, but now that I know she is in danger, I can't sit still and let something happen to her. That wouldn't be right."

"We'll sort it out tomorrow," Dave said. "A friend of mine is keeping an eye on her house tonight."

Moot point. In the morning, Dave left a cryptic shocking message for me that Louise and her daughter had disappeared overnight. He did not tell me how he knew. And when I called him back, the phone rolled over into mail. Now, it was a question of whether we should be concerned or get involved. The disappearance could be voluntary or not and I did not have any right to know whether she found a shelter on her own or whether Jimmi Stanley had made good on her threat. I still felt responsible, but I was helpless.

Dave said that he would stay on it, but it was a low priority when the FBI was after me and we had to find Ms. Stanley to try to wring the truth out of her.

I was uncertain. I didn't have Louise's neighbor's phone number. I knew that I couldn't file a missing person's report myself since I barely knew the woman. Still the thought of a possible unreported abduction or murder was unacceptable to me. I couldn't call Adam Ross now because of his new restraint in communicating with me. I knew no one other than Miriam who was a confidant of Louise and they weren't speaking. I was at a loss.

I called my mother and broke the news that Louise and her daughter had disappeared. She sounded shocked and sorry that they wouldn't be staying with her. She was concerned. I had no more information to give her: it was a dead end.

"I feel sorry for the poor thing and her child. I would've liked to help." She sighed, then paused and said, "Oh, I do have some news, Leyla. Lou Sanders' partner works on the Thyme restaurant. Drew reminded me that we saw him there one time."

Err, I thought, she dropped his name like they were a thing. I hoped he was a nice guy. I wanted her happy, but...

"Drew knows Gray from the Art League. They both take woodworking art classes. Gray is a nice guy according to Drew. Apparently, he went through a bad time when Lou Sanders died. He just has started to come out of it, by working part-time and taking classes at the Art League. Lou's death was a shock to everyone."

"Do you think that he would talk to you about April?" I asked.

My mother hesitated. "I'm not sure, Leyla. He might if you were there and would tell him how close you were to April." Her voice trailed off. I felt anxious about approaching him, part of me wanted to know and part of me had gotten used to the unknown, even feared what he would say.

"Well, maybe, we could catch him at the restaurant and ask to talk with him about April." I said, half-heartedly.

"We could do that." My mother said. "I know that her death was devastating to you."

"I felt guilty. That I was alive and she wasn't and that maybe I could have helped."

"Let's think about it," my mother said, and we signed off.

# CHAPTER 20: Ida Strikes Again.

Dave left me a quick voicemail. I could tell he was relieved that I was out of the caretaker role. He had come around to Cam's belief that there would be nothing but trouble if anyone found out—for good or for evil—that Louise and Ginny were hiding out in my mother's house. He told me that he would talk to me more later. I guess I was relieved too, but I didn't want Louise and Ginny dead and I feared the worst from Stanley. On the other hand, I did not want my mother dead either.

The next morning, Gail called me at the office. Now when I hear her voice, I feel dread. But actually, this time the news was not all bad. The grand jury had been postponed. However, Ida wanted to see me again. This was the fourth time. I wondered if all the witnesses on the list had been as thoroughly vetted as I had. I wondered if this was even acceptable protocol. Four times! "Can she keep doing this to me?" Judging from the silence from Gail, it was a "duh" question.

"Why, this time?" I was resigned.

"She wants to know about your relationship to Louise Richards. And she mentioned something about an Administration lawyer, Jean McInerny."

"Oh, God. She wants to badger me," I snapped. "What is the situation with Jean McInerny?"

"She's having problems in her marriage, her husband cut off the accounts and she needed money."

"Leyla, you gave money to an Administration staffer! What were you thinking?"

"She's a longtime friend and she desperately needed money. It was a loan. She didn't have anyone else to go to. She has nothing to do with the murder, at all!"

"Everyone is suspect. Good grief! Could that have been a set-up?"

"With Jean? Absolutely not!"

"Well, we will find out all about it tomorrow. We need to go and try to be friendly."

"When does she want to see us?" I sighed.

"Tomorrow morning at 9:30."

"Yikes, she doesn't waste any time, does she? Well, if I have to go, at least we might get some idea of where Louise and her daughter are."

We ended the conversation and I went back to my work. I thought of the interview intermittently throughout the day. I needed a plan of attack. Perhaps I would question Ida about her relationship with any law school friends. What would be the downside to that, besides being on her enemies list? I was there already, so that wasn't a problem. She wouldn't want it rumored that she was running a biased investigation. That would be bad for her reputation. I ran that by Cam that night. He was back from Brussels, in his office catching up. At least, he didn't fly right back into his lover's arms, I thought as we talked.

Cam is not a boat rocker, but he could see the draining effect of this investigation on me and was willing to consider anything that might move things along. "Can you ask that question in a nebulous way?"

"Like, is there a friend of yours outside of the FBI who is helping you with this investigation?"

Cam agreed. "Something like that, without mentioning names."

"Then, where do I go with it, if she denies it?"

"You could say," Cam suggested, "a friend mentioned that she knew some telecom lawyers and Ida were very good friends."

"And then she would say that just because she was friends with telecom lawyers, did not make it a conspiracy," I offered, in a nah, nah, nah voice.

Cam laughed, referencing a recent pop song, "Ce'Cile! You there, Babe."

I burst out laughing. "That is one of the reasons why I like you! Way too quirky for a State guy."

He was silent for a minute. I probably should not have said that.

I jumped in, "Anyway, she wouldn't say a conspiracy. I could say it."

"Nope," he said. "Not smart. You could say that the telecom lawyer leaked the news about Louise's FBI letter to a mutual friend, and you wondered how he knew about it."

"Yes!" I enthused. "That would bring up the letter even if it wasn't on Ida's agenda. Then I could muse about rumors of it being sent to the

Administration, about a custodian who had some interaction with the murder victim."

"I would like to be a fly on the wall just to see Ida's face. But be your discrete self." Cam laughed.

"You know I'm not that discrete. This could be kind of fun."

Gail and I arrived in the pouring rain, a little late after searching for a cab. We were ushered into the conference room, dripping. The conference room was very cold. We were wet and shivering. Ida and her sidekick Randall were waiting for us. Ida appeared more irritable than usual.

The Transcript

IDA CRAMER: We are here once again, Ms. James, to have further discussions about your recent activities that might interfere with the FBI investigation of the death of D.L. Phillips.

GAIL DAVIS: What recent activities are you referring to now?

IDA CRAMER: Enlisting more individuals to investigate the death of D.L. Phillips and to interfere with the FBI investigation.

GAIL DAVIS: We object again to the wording, "interfere."

IDA CRAMER: How would you characterize it?

ME: The same as the last interview, self-defense. I have a question for you, though. Are there friends of yours outside of the FBI who are helping you with this investigation?

Ida Cramer took a quick look sideways at Randall who was sitting up and looking directly at her. Her face had heightened color.

IDA CRAMER: I don't know what you are talking about.

ME: A friend mentioned that she had heard at least one telecom lawyer and you were very good friends and share ideas.

IDA CRAMER: Ms. James, just because I am a friend of some telecom lawyers, does not mean that I am getting help from outside the agency.

ME: I have been told that one of the telecom lawyers originally leaked the news about Louise Richard's letter to the FBI and then about an Administration meeting dealing with Louise Richard's letter to someone with an interest in the investigation. I wonder how that particular lawyer knew about them. The letter apparently discussed a D.L. transaction with an Administration custodian. I also understand that the Administration was never notified of the letter until the person who wrote it recently sent copies to the General Counsel and the Commissioners.

IDA CRAMER: Ms. James, you are disrupting this interview process. You are repeating rumors and gossip and speculating about things that just are not true.

ME: I have seen the letter. Gail and I have a copy of the letter. I have spoken to the writer of that letter who told me that she never received a response from the FBI about the letter.

Ida Cramer's face was now quite flushed. She seemed to be holding herself in check, preventing herself from having one of her notorious melt-downs. I was rather enjoying it. Evan Randall was spellbound. Gail was staring at me.

IDA CRAMER: We get letters from crackpots all the time. After a while, one develops an instinct about what is true and what is demented. She is just covering herself in the investigation.

ME: She did not seem demented to me. I don't think that the G.C., Seth Hayes, thought so either. She had a meeting with him, as you are probably aware. Did you ever talk with the writer?

Ida's hands were trembling; she quickly hid them beneath the table. Her face had gone from flushed to plum-red and she sat rigidly immobile in her seat. Her voice was ice cold. She was staring at me with hate in her eyes.

IDA CRAMER: This is none of your business, Ms. James! I am not here to be questioned by you. I am here to interrogate you.

I started to laugh.

ME: I thought that this was an interview, now we finally learn that it actually is an interrogation.

Ida gathered up her files and stalked out of the conference room. Evan stared at her retreating back.

GAIL DAVIS: I assume the interview is over unless you, Mr. Randall, would like to pick up on the questioning.

EVAN RANDALL: I have no questions.

ME: I do have one question. Louise Richards and her daughter Ginny are missing. I understand she was threatened by Jimmi Stanley, the Admin-istration custodian mentioned in her letter to the FBI. Does the FBI know her whereabouts? I'm worried about her.

EVAN RANDALL: I don't know who Louise Richards and her daugh-ter are. I haven't even heard those names before. I know nothing about the letter to the FBI from Ms. Richards or an Administration custodian, Jimmi Stanley. As I said, I have no further questions for Ms. James.

GAIL DAVIS: I suggest that we end this interview then

Gail and I left the building. The rain was still pouring down. With umbrellas up, we waved for a cab to pick us up. Finally, one stopped, and we got in. Gail looked at me with a hint of a smile—or was it a grimace? "Let's see what happens now."

I got back to my office and my message light was on. It was Adam. I was surprised to hear from him, after the brush-off I had gotten. He left a message saying that Miriam had heard that Louise and her daughter Ginny had gone missing and for me to call him. I wondered, why all of a sudden he wanted information from me. Had someone put him up to calling me? If so, maybe somehow Louise was involved in the D.L. situation and she had gone AWOL. But that was confusing to me because it might mean that she already knew Stanley was the killer. The mastermind might keep things and people compartmentalized. This speculation was beyond my pay grade. I had no idea.

I dialed Adam back and the call rolled over to voicemail. "Hi, Adam. It's Leyla. I am responding to yours. Give me a call."

I went back to my growing pile of work. I was pleased that I had made my billable hour quota and then some, so far this year, despite all the time and angst spent on the D.L. matter. At least, the main office couldn't fault me on that. I was more than forthcoming with my recent status reports to the firm management and no one was raising concerns, to the best of my knowledge. Jesse asked about the matter regularly but seemed disinterested when I didn't have anything major or upsetting to report. I decided that I would hold off in disclosing today's discussion with Ida. It seemed unlikely that her stalking out of a meeting would make the evening news.

Dave called several hours later. I told him about the FBI interview.

"Ida had a meltdown and said that she was the one who was supposed to be interrogating me. I laughed and told her that I thought that it was an interview, at which point she stormed out of the room. Evan Randall, her sidekick, just looked confused and claimed he knew zilch about Louise Richards or Louise's letter to the FBI. How's that?"

Dave took it in. "Cramer definitely wanted that letter kept under wraps. Makes me wonder why it was leaked."

"Well," I ventured, "I had thought that someone leaked it originally to scare me before I knew the contents. But maybe someone else did it just because it made for good gossip. Maybe it was Louise herself. I know that she told another legal assistant about the letter. She might have told others. And she had a strong motivation to clear her name and distance herself from any of D.L.'s activities. The FBI wasn't responding. So, it could be that Louise got it out herself and I was wrong about a leaker."

"No way of knowing, I guess," Dave said. "But I have more information for you on Louise Richards and her daughter." He said that he had contacted a Fairfax County cop the day before yesterday who he had worked a case with and asked him to check on Louise Richards and her daughter. The cop drove by her house for two nights: the first night, the car was in the driveway and lights were on. The following night, all the lights were off, the car was gone and a note on the door asked that all packages be brought next door. He also said there was no missing persons information on them. They had only been gone two days, not long enough for the school to get involved. The cop promised that he would stay in touch with Dave about it.

Dave also had met with the undercover guy who agreed to help us in our search for Stanley. The trick would be to entice Stanley to claim the payment for the removal of the bug and for the undercover guys to facilitate that payment by the introduction to Stanley. The guy knows Stanley. He said that she is a real con artist who could wring a dollar out of anyone. He wasn't surprised that Stanley might be involved in a murder. Stanley had no reservations about taking other people's money or their lives. It was all the same. The undercover did say that Stanley was like a snake, that she would slither away before she was caught.

"I told him that we needed to be snake charmers then. We needed to woo her with the sound of money so that we could get her to perform and then we could put her in a basket."

"Dave, that is downright poetic." I laughed.

# CHAPTER 21: More from Ida.

Gail called early that evening. She said that she had received yet another call from Ida. Ida came on a little aggressive to her about my "misconduct" in the interview and about possibly trying to influence a witness (Louise), but it didn't sound as if she would pursue it. The charge of my influencing Louise's testimony was laughable. Just because I talked to her! But my guess was that Ida did not want the background on outside legal involvement or the letter to the FBI from Louise discussed in any forum at any length. She might lose control of the case if others in her office became aware of it.

"Well," I retorted, "she is living in a dream world if she thinks her coworkers don't know about the letter. Now, Randle knows it. As soon as the GC got the letter, I would think that he would have been in touch with her supervisor. Then there's the reaction from the Chairman of the Senate Committee. I assume that since the letter describes the custodian as being involved with at least the bugging of the office, the GC would be furious that he wasn't informed by Ida."

Gail seemed to be less sure that the letter had caused a stir at the FBI. "Ida apparently has been given a lot of leeway in the way she conducts the investigation. If she thinks the letter was bogus or on the fringe, she can rightfully ignore it. At least that was what she said to me. She added some phrase like 'having long tenure', and that she 'has earned the trust.'"

I was incensed. "Does she think that Louise made up a story about meeting with Jimmi Stanley? What about the bug? Did she invent that story, too?"

"Ida said that Louise could not substantiate anything. That the bug is part of the evidence and there was no direct evidence that D.L. or the custodian had anything to do with it."

"Huh," I said. "What about the bug being found in the conference room with D.L.'s body?"

"Not to get you fired up, Leyla, but Ida said she believes that Louise made it up after the fact to make sure that, on the record, she has no connection with either the bug or with the murder."

"That doesn't make sense," I retorted. "Who would assume that Louise had anything to do with it at all?"

"Ida has heard the rumors about D.L.'s father and Louise's problems with D.L. after the death of Darius. She seems to think that Louise wanted to put distance between her and any inference of involvement in the crime."

"Right," I sighed. "Ida can cleverly explain Louise's evidence away, but when it comes to me, she is willing to accept any faint whiff as evidence that I could be involved."

"That's the strange thing," Gail agreed. "It doesn't sound to me as if she is considering a grand jury anymore. She did say that there was an agent conducting a search for Jimmi Stanley at this point. And she mentioned that she was aware Louise and her daughter had gone missing. She said, 'We're looking into that.' Whatever that means. But she didn't bring up your loan to Jean this time. That issue seems to have dropped off the map."

"So, basically, why did she call you? Is this common procedure, for the FBI investigator to schmooze up the attorney for a witness—er, suspect—and give that attorney information on the investigation?"

"My opinion? To cover her behind. She was seriously losing it when she left the conference room. Both of us witnessed it. As did her assistant. I got the distinct feeling that even she knew that it was unprofessional. Now she's spinning it that she was merely being forceful in dealing with a stubborn interviewee and she needed to get you to behave."

I snorted. "She can dress it up the way she wants but she never answered the questions I asked."

"That's the point she was making. Her position is that she did not have to respond, according to her world view. She was asking the questions and you weren't."

"Well, at least she is looking into Louise's disappearance. Did she possibly make any comments about that?"

"Nope."

"OK. Did she say that we are going to have the pleasure of seeing her again?"

"She left that open. But she left me with the impression that you were still on her list, but lower down."

"Well, I guess Jimmi must be feeling a little pressure at this point. If the FBI and the Administration have been forced to acknowledge her, you'd think that she will at least be brought in for questioning."

"You'd think. Well, I just wanted to let you know how the spin is going in case anyone tells you that they heard you 'misbehaved' at the FBI."

"Ha, no one is talking to me these days anyway," I said, and almost added—and I don't give a damn.

The next day, on the call with Dave and Len, I told them the latest information on Ida. "As I told you, Dave, Ida has been a good friend of several Administration lawyers since law school. One was responsible for her first job and gave her a great recommendation for her second job. She is beholden to him. I think she has disregarded evidence that was inconsistent with their theory. She's getting instructions from someone. Did you have any luck researching Ida's four Georgetown friends?"

"Not much more than what you told me," Dave said. "So, what do we do next?"

"Well, the way I see it, we have a several tasks. The FBI letter is already before the Administration and the Senate Committee on Commerce, Science and Transportation. That might speed up the investigation."

"Seems right to me," Len agreed.

"But the problem is the glacial approach to their problem solving," I said. "By the time they catch up to Jimmi, my trial, if there is one, will be over."

"For sure, we cannot wait for the wheels of government to grind away," Dave said with a sigh.

Len agreed, "We need to move our investigation along. I think we should keep trying to find Stanley, if only so we can point her out to the authorities."

"Be careful," I said. "Look what happened the last time."

"Dave and I and our friends will be on the lookout for her. We'll be careful." Len was emphatic. "Dave shouldn't have gone alone."

"Also, I am wondering how we can shine a bigger light on Ida's relationship with her lawyer friends and the effect that it might have on the investigation," I said. "I'll think about that. Maybe I'll call Adam again to see if I can drag any further information out of him, on Louise. I'd like to test out how he is responding to me this time. But I agree, Stanley may be the key to all of this. If we can somehow get her to talk and—"

"We have some ideas," Dave said.

"Just please don't give me any details," I jumped in. "I don't want to know anything. You do what you do, and I'll just practice law. Wake me up when it's all over."

We signed off. I went back to work to stay in the good graces of the firm. Adam returned my call the next morning, and we began by discussing Louise and her daughter's disappearance. "Miriam talked to Louise's neighbor, who knew nothing about Louise leaving town, only that the lights were out. There was no activity but she saw the note on the door asking that packages be brought to her house."

"What about her daughter's school?" I asked. "Did anyone check to see if the school knew she was missing?"

"I don't know. What have you heard?" He apparently wanted information from me after all. I suspected he wouldn't have called me back otherwise. It was the "I'll tell you what I know if you tell me what you know" game. I had never liked games and loathed being used.

But I was happy to inform him that the FBI staff said they were looking into it. I couldn't give him any specifics, not even who the information came from. But I suspected that he, and maybe Leon, knew that Ida was involved. It took me a while to think that Leon might be involved some way. He was friends with Ida, Adam was not.

"I did hear that you went to see the FBI again and things did not go so well."

"You know, it is amazing how word flies around Washington. The Administration barely gets the letter and talks to Louise, when Jimmi is calling Louise to threaten her. Now the word is that I have been back to the FBI. I'd like to know who is so tightly wrapped into this investigation that they know everything about it and they spread rumors about it. I just cannot fathom the depths of this information network. What I would really like to know is who knows all this stuff as soon as it happens. Do you know, Adam?"

He went quiet. Things were not moving along as smoothly in this conversation as he had planned. Apparently, he wanted to get information from his sources to the network and his target (me) was not cooperating.

"Yes," he said in a quiet voice. "It is amazing."

"I suppose it's the Georgetown Law network."

"I guess," he said. "Look, Leyla, I don't mean to press you on this. I am concerned, like Miriam is, that something bad could happen to Louise and her daughter."

Now I didn't know what to say to him. He sounded sincere. But I no longer trusted him. He had dropped me once, and now he is back to fish for information. Maybe they wanted to know if I knew where Louise was. I had no idea what the repercussions from that information would be for Louise with this crowd. But I did know now that they didn't have Louise and her daughter under their control, at least at this moment. I was tired of trying to figure out where all the people were in this puzzle, what their motives and intentions were. There were just too many moving parts.

"I guess we need to stay tuned," I said.

My next call was from Dave. He already had organized the team to locate Stanley. His undercover buddies from the street were trying to get an idea where Stanley was hanging out. They also knew who Stanley's buddies were. They heard that Stanley spent most of her time in D.C., living at undisclosed locations. She moved around a lot. Which meant she must be feeling the pressure. In the past, she was often seen at the club Dave had visited before he was shot. Now, Stanley had dropped off that scene. The word on the street—she was still in the trade but staying out of the spotlight. She had her lover and his minions running errands for her while she was in hiding.

It seemed apparent that she was picked for the Administration job because of her chameleon-like quality of fitting into the background. It seemed to be working well now. The guys on the street wondered how she covered her assortment of tats, which would have been a dead giveaway.

But it just seemed odd to me that this woman with her background actually got a job at the Administration as a custodian. I know that she didn't have to pass a top security clearance, but with her record, it was a real puzzle how she could pass any test for employment with the federal government. She was certainly not the type to push a broom from 8-5 at a federal agency or hold any kind of regular job. In addition, it was odd that she had actually two tasks there for her "client" (or clients): to bug a place that was obviously difficult to bug or at least debug that place without setting off alarms, literally and figuratively. And to kill an agency visitor while at the agency, no less. I wondered how hard that was to plan.

Obviously, it took some expertise to install something that would not be noticed by the occupant of the office or security. And it took criminal chutzpah to lure someone into an area where their body wouldn't be discovered for days. But the mystery remained—how was she hired and by whom? Perhaps a resume was hijacked to enable her to get the custodian job, hence the change of name.

Maybe the key was the person who was paying her and the amount of money that she had been paid to do these tasks. It had to be a lot and maybe she didn't want to share. The question was why and what was it worth to kill D.L. to the mastermind of this plot. To my thinking, it could only be for one thing: the value of the licenses. It was originally worth it to include D.L. on the plot, but something happened that soured the deal with her. Stanley might have known what caused the deal to go south, or at least she would have known who knew. That person had hired her and possibly cleared the way into the job at the Administration.

Dave's undercover guys continued to ask around about Stanley. They had been on the street for three years and were known to the locals as druggies. It was likely they helped spread the word themselves. But in the time that they had been looking, the undercovers failed to discern a pattern in Stanley's moves around the city. And it was difficult to get inside Stanley's closest circles. Hoods didn't trust druggies, it seemed. They were too unpredictable. One thing Dave now knew was that the FBI was looking for Stanley, too.

We talked on the phone about that.

"What do you think the effect of an FBI interview would have on Stanley? Assuming they catch her and that she even acknowledges she had anything to do with the murder? And how do you think that it would affect me?"

"Unless she lies and says that you hired her, it should help you."

"Unless the investigator sets her up to say that I hired her."

"That sounds too complicated to lie about. You never met each other. She doesn't know anything about you. There is no connection between you two."

"That won't stop Ida." I rolled my eyes.

"Well, she'd need to concoct a lot of facts: What was the trigger point for the murder? How did you know she was a killer for hire? How did you get her hired at the Administration? How did you pay her? And how did you communicate with her, when there is no evidence of calls on your work or personal phones? Plus, it all has to be synched to reality. There's just so much fabrication necessary. I don't see how it could hold together."

"I have faith in Ida. If anyone could do it, she could." I shook my head, a sick feeling burning in my stomach. "I know her. She needs a win. She told Gail that the prosecutor would take her case. She sounded so sure of herself. If it holds up in court or not—that may be another issue. But her trickery will force me to run through my resources and, in the end, may well ruin my business."

# CHAPTER 22: Some Surprises.

The other line rang in my office. An unknown number. I signed off from Dave and pushed the button. It was Louise.

"Where the hell are you?" I demanded.

"Hiding. I can't tell you where."

"Why didn't you call me?"

"I am calling you. Now. I wanted to let you know that I am OK. I knew you'd be worrying about us and you were trying to help me find a place for us to hide. Ginny is with me."

I let out a long weary breath. "I am delighted to hear that. Does anyone else know?"

"Yes, the person who came with us."

"Who is that?"

"A friend who has access to a cabin in the woods."

"Do you know where Stanley is?"

"I heard that she came around Ginny's school the day we left. She was too late, we had gone already."

"Did you know that the FBI was looking for you, too?"

"No, how did they know about my disappearance?"

"I told them. I was being interviewed and I asked them whether they knew that you left town?"

"I wish you hadn't." She sounded dismayed.

"I was worried about you and Ginny. The last thing I had heard from you was that Stanley had called and you were afraid for your lives. Do you know anything about the investigation? Did your friend tell you anything at all?"

"That's another reason why I'm calling you. My friend found out that

Stanley was looking for me. His landlord told him that a woman had come to see him, claiming she was a friend. She asked to be let in to wait for him. The landlord said no, he never let anyone into anyone's apartment unless they had a warrant or the tenant had left instructions. He offered to take a message but the woman said she would come back later. When the landlord told my friend about the visit, he knew that he—and I—were in immediate danger and we had to leave town. He called me. We packed some clothes and I picked him up at his place."

"So, Stanley thinks that your friend has something to tell the authorities, too?"

"Yes. He worked with D.L. as a Legal Assistant and go-for for the last year before she died. He was involved in the auction as an alternative bidder."

"So, the murder may have had something to do with the auction?

"Yes, of course. D.L. was part of a company that bid in an auction. She had made a deal to get a certain percentage from the sales of the frequencies. But she changed her mind and was demanding more. She threatened to expose the scheme to the Administration, if she didn't get what she wanted."

"The scheme?"

"Yes, she was fronting a man who didn't want to appear before the Administration?"

This was getting better and better, I thought. "And I wonder how she would have gotten away from that confession unscathed?"

"By saying that she had been deceived from the beginning, that she was operating through a middleman. She had already created forged documents for proof of the deception. They were in her safe. But she must have figured that she would probably never have to use them. "

"Then, the other people in the deal decided they would have to kill her to shut her up." It was beginning to make sense to me.

"That is what my friend told me."

"You two are in trouble from all directions: the hit woman and the parties to the deal. You both know too much to be kept alive."

"It looks like it," she moaned, sounding as if she was about to cry.

"How long can you stay away?"

"Until the money runs out, whenever that is."

Maybe that was the real reason for the call. I'd let them figure it out. I couldn't afford for the FBI to find out that I had supported their run from Ida's investigation. I was still worried about when she would again bring up my loan to Jean and what an uproar she would make about that.

"OK. So does your friend know anything more about the whereabouts of Ms. Stanley, or how D.L. knew about her and whether she got in touch with her."

"We don't know whether she did or not. As I told you, I think that she called one day for Darius, but I don't know whether she ever got in touch with him. I think that Stanley's name came from a lawyer at my friend's former law firm."

"Was that the Gallagher firm, by chance? And is your friend's name Keith, by any chance?"

"Yes, his name is Keith. But I have no idea who the lawyer or the law firm is."

"Is Keith alright with you telling me this?"

"Yes, if it will save our lives. He told me everything."

"Is he there? Would he say that he is OK with you talking to me? I need to hear it from him. And maybe he could tell me which lawyer mentioned Stanley's name?"

"Yes, he is standing next to me. We're in a parking lot." I could hear traffic going by. And in the distance, even busier traffic. They must be off the interstate somewhere. Pity that she probably was going to throw the phone away as soon as I rang off.

I could hear her speaking to someone. Probably relaying my message.

A man's voice came over the phone now. "It wasn't a lawyer, it actually was a client of the firm."

"The Gallagher firm?"

"Yes." Keith was very abrupt. I paused. I really wanted to ask who the client was but that involved client confidentiality. Keith got his lesson on that from Leon. I left that alone for now.

"Louise, is Ginny there with you?"

"No. She's at the cabin. She's safe."

"Good. Back to the whereabouts of Ms. Stanley."

"Keith, did you ever go to see her or talk with her on the phone?"

"I did. But I knew her as Lana Stanford, through a messenger service. I used to work there before the law firm. I knew the owner and the owner knew Stanford or Stanley. I think the owner and Stanley did other business together."

"Like?"

"Not always legal stuff."

"Do you have any idea where Stanley can be located?"

"Not now. She used to have a place near Hanover Place NE."

"Really!!" I heard that D.C. was trying to civilize that area and maybe it really had changed since I knew it, but I would not have dared to go there, alone or with anyone else, in the recent past.

"Yeah, the place was a dump. I made a delivery there one time. Not a good scene."

But, I thought, it was a place to begin. "Anything else that you want to tell me?"

"That's it and I am tossing this phone. It is a burner. I don't trust telephone conversations."

"How can I reach you?"

"Possibly through Sandy Nelson in Fairfax, if she will get involved."

The name was not Sandy Nelson. It came back to me now. It was Nancy. Louise was talking about her friend in Fairfax, who she paid to provide Ginny a place to go after school. Dave had jotted her name when Louise talked about her in his office. Louise obviously did not want me to get back to her at all. Her lying to me was unsettling. Whose side was she on?

As soon as Louise hung up, I hit speed dial. "Hi, Dave. I need to talk to you," I said to his machine. "Let's meet somewhere."

I also called my mother and told her that Louise was okay. She sounded relieved that mother and daughter were safe. "I've been thinking that maybe we could go and talk to Gray. It might help him." I had no idea how it would help him to talk about a soul-wrenching event watching your lover die, but Mother followed her kind instincts and maybe I should just accept her need to do so this time.

"When can you come down again?"

I looked at my calendar, "How about this weekend?" I really needed to get away, and yet so much was happening here. Could I really just leave the city in the middle of this mess?

"Good," she said. "I can also set up a dinner with Drew, if you want to meet him."

"Sure," I said, not feeling sure at all. There was the whole issue of whether Drew was taking Dad's place. I know that's selfish, thinking like that, and she needed to move on. She needed to be happy, dammit. I decided to meet Drew and be happy about it. "See you this weekend." I hung up.

Dave called me back 15 minutes later. We agreed to meet at a park near Dupont Circle.

"I got a call from Louise," I said once we'd walked away from other people, so we could talk. "I'm guessing that the real reason she called me was to keep her missing status out of the media. She might also have wanted money. She, her daughter and Keith Olson, a go-for for D.L. in her last year, and an alternative bidder in the auction as well as a former Georgetown law student, are hiding in a cabin somewhere. Interesting to me because Graciela, the custodian who found D.L. in the conference room, said that she saw Stanley arguing with a messenger who looked like Keith in front of the Administration building. That makes it seem as though Keith might be in on the plot. But is Louise? This is getting complicated. Was she just setting us up to prove her innocence?"

"Did she tell you where she was?" Dave asked. "Any clues?"

"Not really. And she called me on a disposable phone. My guess is that they were nowhere near the cabin, if it exists, when they called. I think that she was near an interstate, for what that's worth. Of course, she knows about cell phone signaling."

"Wouldn't help us much anyway, if she's on the move."

"Right. She said that they left town before Stanley showed up at Ginny's school and after she had gone to Keith's apartment, looking for him. Keith's landlord wouldn't let her in. It turns out that they may be running not only from Stanley but from the parties to the deal, not to mention the FBI. I gathered that from a call I got from Adam, the guy in the Georgetown network."

Dave thought for a moment as they walked. "She sound at all like she might be willing to turn herself in to the FBI, to tell them all of this?"

"No. In fact, I think she might be better off avoiding being interviewed by the FBI, which might put her in a more harmful place than if she stays missing. She didn't say that to me, but when I told her that I reported to the FBI that she was missing, she was upset with me. At this point, she and I appear to be in similar positions: we both want Stanley caught. At least I think so. She told me that Keith had heard about a scheme for D.L. to front a scam in the auction. Keith said there was an outside individual who put it together. He said he didn't know who that individual was, it could have been one of her former clients, but that guy had come up with a scheme to use D.L. and his girlfriend as co-owners to the applicant. I'm not sure how he is financially involved yet, but Keith thinks that D.L. wanted more profit and tried to renegotiate her cut. Apparently, that started the effort to have her killed. Maybe our schemer figured that once they had a revised deal, she would want to keep more. Which sounds like the way she works anyway."

"Any clue to Stanley's location?"

"Keith thinks her old apartment was near Hanover Place NE."

"OK, that's a good address," Dave laughed. "I suppose we start there."

"Right. What do your undercover guys know about that area?"

"I expect, a lot." Dave reflected. "Why are we meeting in a park, by the way?"

"I didn't ask Louise, but I thought she was concerned about a bug, maybe on my phone, and that was why she was using a burner. Or maybe she doesn't trust anyone, and I am beginning to feel the same way. Also, when I asked if there was a way to contact her, she gave me a fake name. It should have been the name she mentioned to you in your office, Nancy something, when she was calling to check up on Ginny. You wrote it down. I don't remember it. Adam's paralegal might know it, but I don't trust him anymore."

"Yeah, it's in my file. Who does she think is bugging her phone?"

"Don't know. She may just be gun shy because of her experience with the bug at the Administration. I guess she figures that the force behind this has no qualms. I don't really know who she suspects. It could be Stanley, it could be Ida, it could be anyone. She wasn't very guarded when she gave me the background information, so maybe she thinks we already know everything we talked about."

"But," Dave looked at me apprehensively, "whoever is behind this—if there is a bug on your phone—now they know what you know."

I threw up my hands in frustration. "I'm in no worse a place than I was before the call. Ida, for one, knows I am investigating the case. You were looking for Stanley when you got shot, and she should be able to guess who your client is. As you told me when we met, the word on the street is that I am involved with D.L.'s murder. What's the big deal?"

"Just be careful," he warned.

"Don't worry, I'm being careful at the office and at home."

"Do you have a gun?"

"Dave, I just can't do that. I am so not a gun owner and I'm just not interested in becoming one."

"Sorry. But I think that you should have one at home. Not forever, just for now. These people aren't the type to want to just talk sense into you. They want to get rid of you for trying to mess up their game plan and working to expose it."

"But the exposure is happening already. Louise and Keith have gone into hiding. Ida is having second thoughts about sticking with whatever plan she was following, since there is now public knowledge of an

Administration custodian who could be involved. At least, she has "postponed", maybe indefinitely, the grand jury. I am not giving up further information to Adam because I don't know where it is going and who is using it. Leon? Annie in the Chairman's office? What I do know is that things are not going as planned."

"Just be careful. I'll talk to my guys about Hanover Place. We might take a look around there tonight or tomorrow. Maybe someone in the neighborhood knows Stanley and where she is. I won't go, if you're worried about that. I learned my lesson. But my friends will know the area and the characters. And the characters will know them. We'll see what turns up."

When I got back to my office, a message from Gail waited. Ida had struck again.

# CHAPTER 23: Ida, Again?

"Well, what is it this time?" I asked Gail, when I finally got through to her. "Maybe I should just move there so she can talk to me all the time."

Gail ignored my comment. "She now wants to know more about the loan to Jean McInerny."

"OK. I knew she would circle around to that, sooner or later. But what has that got to do with her investigation?"

"She mentioned something about bribing a federal employee for information that might interfere with a government investigation.

"Did she tell you what the information was that I was supposed to have gotten that might interfere with her investigation?"

"No. She wanted to talk with you."

"Have mercy," I said. "As I told you, it was a personal issue. This is all I know. She was having marital problems. Her husband had moved most of the money from a joint account to his account. Don't ask me how he did it. She didn't know. All she knew was that bills were coming due and she had no money. She was a wreck. We went through a lot when we were both newbies at our first law firm. When Cam and I broke up, she supported me. If she needed money, I was going to loan her some."

"So, it was a loan? Any supporting documents?"

"No. She asked me at lunch, and I wrote a check."

"Does she think that it is a loan?"

"I said that it could be a loan or a gift. She told me that it would be a loan. Has Ida said otherwise?"

"No. She said that you had been talking to Jean and that Jean may have given you some information. Did she?"

"Yes. But we often gossiped about things together."

"What information did she give you?"

"She told me that I was on the witness list, but Adam also told me that. It wasn't new information. She told me that Ida went to law school at the same time with several peers that I knew, and she told me that Adam did not get along at all with Ida. But that's just gossip."

"The thing that could be a problem is that Jean gave the information about you being on the witness list, I think."

"My God. I do not want to cause any problems for Jean right now. She is respected at the Administration. She needs the money, and nothing can interfere with her job. Ida has a way of causing trouble for people and now she could cause big problems for Jean."

"I think that you need to talk to Jean about Ida. And Adam needs to know the kind of damage that his gossip group could do if Jean gets in their sights."

"What if I talk to Jean and tell her. Then, I talk to Adam and appeal to his better self. I'm not sure how much it would help if Jean called him."

"Call Jean and go from there," commanded Gail.

I called Jean and left a voicemail on her machine. I suggested that we go out for lunch or a drink after work.

Later in the afternoon, she called. "Let's meet after work. Dick has the kids tonight."

"OK, the usual place? See you at 5:45." I was now completely paranoid. In the event that someone was listening in, I didn't want them to know where we were going.

"Yep," she said. "See you there."

Jean and I met again at The Bar, right across the street from the old Administration building. We had often landed there when we were associates, before Jean got married. A lot of angst was spilled in this bar. I now had a delicate task to deal with.

I got there first. She had taken the metro. I got up from the table and gave her a hug when she came in.

"How are things?" I asked.

"They are getting better. Dick now understands we're no longer advocates for each other, so no more temper tantrums."

"That's fabulous," I said.

"Yes, and one other thing. He is making noises about giving it a second chance."

"Wow. How do you feel?" I remembered the smudge on her beautiful face.

"I miss him, but I want him to go to anger management therapy: no more hitting. And I don't think I could go through another episode with the girlfriend again. That just about killed me, knowing what was going on and having him deny it like I wasn't smart enough to pick up the clues."

"So?"

"I told him that and he said that it was over."

"Do you believe him?"

"Sort of. He's having a rough time, I think. I'm at least in our house. He's living in an efficiency and it is inconvenient to his office and to us. He's willing to go to couples therapy, too. Before when we were in the same house, he was in denial about everything and wouldn't talk to me about anything—except to discuss chores around the house. Maybe, we can work things out."

"I am delighted," I said, hating to segue into the Ida situation. "I really hope you two can work it out, if that's what you want."

We ordered drinks. White wine for me and a margarita for Jean. I 'm not a liquor person. It's often more potent and definitely more fattening. A bartender can either make you drunk or make you pay for a glass of flavored water.

"How is it going with you?"

I grimaced. "I got another call from Ida. It was threatening. It was about my relationship with you."

"What! Why?"

"She said that she'd heard I might have been trying to bribe a government official to get information that would interfere with her investigation."

"Damn her."

"Yes. What's worse is that you did tell me that I was on the witness list. She would say that it was a leak."

"My God," Jean's face turned ashen.

"I know. I feel so bad. I don't know how she found out."

"I'm sure I never told anyone about the loan, but..."

I looked at her, questioning the hesitation.

"Maybe Dick said something about the money situation to one of his partners, Bob Dunning, who seems to have become his 'therapist' throughout this whole process. He should know, having been through it twice."

Bob Dunning was another member of the telecommunications bar. God knows who he knows—Ida? Aargh.

"Does Bob usually gossip about confidential information? What kind of 'therapist' is that?"

"I don't know. Dick apparently trusts him."

"I wonder if Dick told Bob that it was a loan from me."

"Again I don't know. But I think probably not. He probably just complained that you gave me some money, which ruined his plan to bring me to my senses."

"Remind me not to tell any secrets to Bob or to talk to him ever again, for that matter. At least, you and I agree that it's a loan. Ida implied that she'd heard it was a gift for information."

"How do we solve this?"

"One of two ways," I said. "You can talk to Adam to tell him the truth and get him to stop Ida, no matter who he's working with behind the scenes, from going down that road. Or I can talk to Adam with the same message. It's up to you. If Adam listens and is able to influence whoever is behind this craziness, that would be great. If you want me to talk to Adam, I will. But one thing: I'll have to tell him about the marriage problems. I won't describe them in any way because I really don't know everything. So, I would just tell him that you needed a loan and I gave it to you. Another person one of us might talk to is Leon. He may still be friends with Ida, I'm not sure. Ida is a she-devil."

"Yeah, she is. I will try Adam."

"Are you comfortable with that?"

"Yes, of course." Then there was a look of thoughtfulness on her face. "What's up?" I said and then I was smiling, "You have something, don't you?!

"Yes. I remembered something that I discovered long ago. It was so far out of my mind that I almost forgot. All I am saying is, I don't think that Ida knows that I know something about her distant past. Something that might cause her problems. And I don't usually work like this, but she's playing the game, so we need to play it, too."

"I'll second that." I was dying to know what it was. I wondered if it had to do with Ida's brief tenure as a telecommunications lawyer or something that happened in law school. But I wouldn't pump Jean. Probably best that I didn't know. Suddenly I thought that this might be a little something breaking my way. Things might turn out just fine between Ida and me this time. Maybe I wouldn't have to visit her again.

We had our drink, caught up and gossiped a little. We hugged goodbye and I wished her well with the counseling. I really did. They were a good couple. He had been a lot stupid. Hitting her indeed!

I relayed the day's events to Cam that night via text. He gave me a thumbs-up on Jean's ploy with Ida. I'm glad he was there and rooting for me, despite a girlfriend lurking in the shadows.

Then he called me, "I just want this damn thing over soon for your sake. I'm worried about it. How is Dave doing?"

"He's good. He wants to get this done quickly, too. His undercover friends are going over to Hanover Place NE tonight or tomorrow."

"Harsh."

"I know. That's where Stanley lived. A real class act. And Dave told me to be careful. He suggested buying a gun. I'm against it."

"You know how I feel. It's just that, what happens if there is a break-in? You have an alarm, I don't know what else to do. I want you safe."

"I know." I just didn't want a gun in my house or anywhere near me.

"Take care," he said, and we hung up.

The following day, I called Gail.

"I think that we might not be bothered any more on the Jean front." I said.

Gail sighed, "I'm afraid to ask."

"I had a drink with Jean last night. I'm in full paranoid mode. I think someone might be listening to us, or maybe just to me. Not sure, mind you, but maybe." So there, I was thinking. If there is no one, then OK. But if someone wants to hear about my business, at least they know that I'm not living in any dreamland.

"Why don't you drop over to see me? I don't want to not have background for the next round with Ida."

"OK, I'll be there in 10 minutes. We'll go for coffee."

"So," I said to Gail as we walked near her office, "Jean apparently knows something about Ida's past that no one else might know. And Jean is willing to use it. Do not ask me what it is because Jean didn't tell me. My guess would be it has something to do with law school. It has to be either unlawful or very embarrassing if it were leaked, which is likely going to happen, if Ida keeps it up. Jean is going to talk to Adam today. In fact, she probably has already talked to him. I doubt that she would have ever brought this up, but people do what they have to do with bullies. I didn't want to even make any reference to misadventure by Ida on the phone."

"That's really interesting," Gail mused. "Something about law school?"

"I can't say for sure. It sounded like it was a past misdeed; one that Ida probably thought was buried. But, as I said, it is amazing what people can remember when someone threatens them. I will tell you if I hear any more. But I don't think we need to be in a big hurry to get back to Ida."

On the way back to my office, I got a call from Jean. She was evasive on the phone. Both of us being very careful in our conversation.

"Well, I made the call this morning. There was some interest about the nature of the situation. I was not disclosing a lot, but I did get the idea across that if things started happening with me, there could be consequences for a past deed by a mutual friend. The message was received and there was no room for misunderstanding in what I said."

"Did Adam say what he was going to do?"

"Obviously, speak to the third party. He sounded flustered."

"OK. That's good."

"Yeah, I thought so."

"Keep me in the loop and I will do the same."

After I hung up the phone, a spark from the conversation came to me. Was it possible that the same issue in Ida's past was also being used by someone else to hold her in line? Was she fearful of her position and that was why she hid the letter from Louise? And kept the pressure on me?

When I got home that night, I called Cam on my landline. I relayed the conversation to him. "Am I being speculative, if I raise the issue of whether Ida is being blackmailed by someone to keep the pressure on me, despite all evidence to the contrary?"

"It sounds reasonable to me," he said. "Not just because I am on your side but because there has to be something that someone is using to keep Ida obedient. She was risking at the least a reprimand from her superiors for not disclosing the letter from Louise. And yet, she blustered that she was in charge of the investigation and only she had the whole picture."

"It doesn't make me feel sorry for her," I stressed, "but at least I can grasp the concept of Ida not listening to reason and not accepting anything I present. It would be interesting to know whether the mastermind has used this in the past or whether he was saving up for this particular escapade."

"It sounds almost unbalanced to put his friend in this position, without regard to her welfare and her reputation."

"Please," I retorted "don't pull on my heartstrings. I would feel a heck of a lot sorrier if it weren't affecting me in a dire way."

"Well, at least we have a possible idea of what is motivating Ida to pursue you."

"And..." I said.

"We'll think of something," he said. I believed him.

What is becoming clear to me now is the presence of tightly woven web, first in the entry in the auction and then in the murder of D.L. And whoever is behind all this, he (or she) is keeping all parties nicely in place, circling in his galaxy. Except for me. I am the loose cannon. And every time I make a move, he is forced to respond to thwart it. Things have been not working very well for him at the moment. I expect that he might have to step up the action. The wheels are falling off. What was he going to do to me next?

# CHAPTER 24: The Planner Goes Mental.

As I approached my apartment front door the following night, I stopped short, shocked to see the lock had been jimmied and the door trashed. I walked into complete havoc.

My living room and kitchen were in mayhem. I felt like someone had slugged me in the stomach. This was a personal attack, meant to intimidate. My computer had been stolen. Drawers were rummaged, the contents thrown on the floor. Some of the furniture was trashed: the sofa and a chair had been cut through the upholstery to the frame. Lamps were smashed into pictures on the wall. Dishes were broken. The vandals had stopped up the kitchen drain and turned on the faucets. Water was running throughout the apartment. Glass was strewn everywhere. The Cuisinart had been smashed into the kitchen floor: several clay tiles were broken. Food was thrown out of the refrigerator and freezer onto the floor. Flour was sprayed on countertops and on the floors in the kitchen and into the hall. It had mixed with the running water into liquid paste. My clothes were out of the closets tossed onto the floor and were soggy from the water. My bathroom was full of empty shampoo bottles and broken cosmetic jars. The tub was overflowing onto the floor.

There was a message on the phone from the janitor of the building complaining that water was dripping into the apartment below. I shut off the water and called Dave. The janitor could wait.

"Heads up. I had vandals. They did a number. The only thing I can see that was stolen is my computer."

"I thought you put in an alarm and everything was nailed down."

"Well, yeah. I thought so, too."

"What about the portable hard drive back-up that we discussed? Did they take that?"

I got off the phone and tiptoed through the debris to the hall closet. I started ferreting through the mess. My coats were on the floor, contents from the shelves opened on top of them. I had hidden the hard drive in my yoga bag. The bag was thrown on the floor, but the zipper was stuck and the drive was wrapped in a towel on the bottom.

I called Dave back. "Ha! They did not take it."

"Good for you," Dave said.

"But I don't like that someone now has access to my finances," I said. "Please tell me what I should do and say to the police. How much do I tell them?"

"Why don't I come over? When I get there, we'll call the police. I'll leave right now. Don't touch anything in the meantime."

Jean's ploy had worked. This, I decided, was revenge for blocking the plan, just another ploy to keep me from continuing my investigation. But my enemy was wrong about my staying power. I could outlast him and would not be intimated. I would hire a cleaner and buy new stuff. What was interesting to me was...this act seemed out of character. It must be draining psychologically to keep juggling the people in this scenario. It only worked as long as each person in the game reacted as planned. But I wasn't doing what he expected, which was to follow the legal course of being the accused. This violent vandalism, even if by his minions, showed that he was desperate and becoming undone.

Dave arrived a few minutes later and looked around. He had a "I told you so" look in his eyes. He said nothing.

"Well, at least I wasn't here when they came in. I think that it was just meant to intimidate me."

"This time," he said. "What happened to the alarm?"

"I don't keep it on during the day because I'm not here. I just worried about me being alone at night. That's when I use it."

"An alarm is no good if you don't use it all the time. Let's call the police." I dialed 911 and recounted my discovery of the break-in and vandalism. The dispatcher said someone would be on the way. A half hour later, two uniforms showed up at the door. Dave gave a wave of greeting. Handshakes all around. The three of them seemed happy to see each other.

Dave took over, explaining just enough to protect me from any questioning on suspects I thought might be responsible. He went with the officers on their investigation while I trailed behind, only answering questions directed at me. They said what I already knew. It was a break-in to vandalize the apartment.

I wasn't required to tell them that the computer had no data on it that could be the vandals' focus. My enemy would be disappointed. Luckily, the computer where I stored all information for my investigation was in my office. It was now locked away in my office credenza. Sorry, bud, whoever you are. I need to find Jimmi or Lana to figure out who this devil is.

Once the police left, Dave told me to call someone to fix the door right away. He gave me a name, told me to mention him. I asked if he knew any-one who could clean vandals' damage. He did, gave me another name and told me to mention him. I called the locksmith, mentioned Dave's name and asked whether he could come over and do it now. He said he could and would be there in an hour. Dave left. I called the cleaner, left a voicemail message. I described the vandalism, mentioned Dave's name and asked for a meeting the next morning before work.

While I waited for the locksmith, I took pictures of the damage for the insurance company. The claim was going to be another painful experience. But my lock fixer arrived on time and replaced the bolt and the lock. He said that he would come back and clean up the door the next day. It pays to have a former cop as a consultant.

After he left, I called Cam and told him about the break-in. He asked whether I had a place to stay that night. I was too surprised to answer for a minute. "No, no place to stay."

"Well, come over here. What are friends for?"

Stunned, I gathered up a few belongings, alarmed and locked the door and went to Cam's place. It looked neglected and disorganized. But it was a place to stay. As I walked in, Cam looked over his shoulder at his living room and said, "I've been traveling a lot." Well, at least it sounded like he wasn't staying at someone else's place.

"Just thanks for giving me a place to land. It's so devastating to see what one person would do to another person."

"Well, you're interrupting someone's plan and they don't like it. Come and sit down. You want a glass of wine?"

"Wow. Wine! That a great idea! Thank you so much."

"Did you have anything to eat?"

"No. That was another thing I didn't think of."

"Leftover Thai carry-out?"

"Yes!"

Soon, we were sitting at his kitchen counter eating warmed up Thai and drinking cold white wine.

"This is so nice," I said. "It's like being rescued from an accident and realizing that you hadn't only come through unscathed but given a reward for surviving it."

I talked about the mess at my house and who could be responsible. I didn't know who was capable of the things that were happening but I suspected I'd know when we found Stanley. We talked about Cam's travels and his work. We didn't talk about our relationship or his relationship. I got a call from the house cleaner and we set up an appointment for the next morning. I was to meet him at my apartment before I headed for work.

All of a sudden, it was ten o'clock. We cleaned up the dishes, like old times. He said that the bed was made up in his spare room, that he had an early morning meeting and if he left before I got up, it had been good to see me and have dinner with me. I thanked him profusely. He hugged me and kissed me on the cheek. "Everything is going to be okay," he said. I was over the moon.

When I got up the next morning, Cam was gone. He'd left a note on the kitchen counter that told me there was coffee made and he wished me good luck. Why had I thrown this man away? Then, I thought that we both had. I wondered if he had any regrets.

I met with the cleaner an hour later at my place. It turned out that the service was owned by Dave's work buddy. The cleaner took a look around, scowled at the damage and quoted a price. It was very reasonable.

"It's amazing what some people will do," he said, shaking his head.

"Well, at least it was the house, not me," I said.

"Set your alarm. And be careful from now on."

He was confident that his crew could have the place organized and cleaned by the end of the day. He would be looking for valuables in the trash. I left it all in his hands, except to say, "Leave the cosmetics containers, so I know what to reorder." On the half-full side, I had the opportunity to reorganize the place now.

It wasn't long after I arrived in my office that I got the first phone call. Someone had probably started a rumor about my break-in. The call was from Adam. I saw his number and let it roll over into voicemail. I didn't want to answer his questions and have them relayed back to my tormentor. I'm sure he would be delighted to hear that I'd been brought to my knees and that I was upset. But I wasn't on my knees. And I didn't want to let on that the vandalism of my house and stealing of my personal property bothered me.

The second call was from Jean. I saw her number and was in a dilemma.

Was she still my friend or did she already know about the break-in and report back to the "group." After all, Adam could have gotten my nemesis to call off Ida, if Jean would switch sides. I sighed. I just had to trust someone. I picked up the phone. She was in a great mood.

"I just wanted to tell you that I put a check in the mail to you this morning. Dick moved the money back into our joint account."

"Progress!" I exclaimed.

"Yeah. We agreed to go to counseling and have our first session today. He seems really interested in making it work. I am, too."

"I'm delighted! He was dumb but he seems repentant."

"He is. He didn't think that I'd tell him to leave."

"And he probably didn't believe he'd get caught. Living in D.C. and listening to the news, this town is full of men who think they're too smart to get caught."

"Yeah. At least, he didn't expose himself on the internet." We both sighed. "Yah, there's that," I said.

"One thing I would like to know, Jean, and I will be discrete here for several reasons—one being, my phone might be, ah, compromised."

"Uh huh," she said. That's my Jean. She is so intuitive that when we set up the date to meet for a drink, she probably already knew that.

"When you had the conversation with our friend, did you detect anything unusual?"

"Yes," she said. "He mentioned mania."

"Do you have any idea who that is?"

"No, and I don't think that Adam knows, either."

"Well, if he doesn't know, how are we going to get Ida to stop her attack?"

"I have a feeling that it's already gone to the proper source."

I knew that, and my apartment is evidence.

"But that means Adam is part of the conspiracy, doesn't it?"

"Not sure that he does know everything."

"Why is that? It can't just be because he loves to gossip."

"Yes. I can see that." She paused. "Anything new with you?"

She was being evasive with me, which led me to worry about her allegiances. I again wondered if someone had turned her.

"Not much," I said, changing the subject. "I stayed at Cam's last night."

"Well! When did that happen?"

"It's a long story."

If anyone was listening out there, I wanted to report some good news to them.

We signed off. Now, it was time to follow up with Dave on Jean's news. I reported the fixed door and the cleaning service and thanked him for his help. Then I mentioned in cryptic terms, my house of cards theory to him. He listened, without comment.

To my surprise, no one appeared to know or at least care about the break-in. It wasn't reported in the paper and I didn't get any calls. So much for my paranoia, or was it my antagonist's paranoia? Perhaps Adam's call wasn't about the break-in, but I wasn't taking any chances. It was now full steam ahead to try to get Stanley. It was bloody time to get this thing done and find out who the perpetrator was before anything worse happened.

I left the office to get some coffee from the kitchen, when I returned there was a second message from Adam. He sounded agitated.

"Leyla, please give me a call. I have some information that might inter-est you."

I returned the call. Adam picked up the phone.

"Hi, this is Leyla, Adam, I got your call. What's up?"

"Well, I wanted to let you know that the gossip from Leon is that Ida has been taken off the investigation."

I was stunned. "What! Why?" I croaked.

"Her superior felt the heat from the Hill on why the letter about the custodian at the Administration had not been given to the Administration immediately. The Commissioners all were ticked off. She was told yester-day that she was off the investigation. They gave it to Evan Randle. She was put on leave, with pay, pending an investigation of her behavior. No one thinks that she will be fired. We think that her superiors will let it simmer and then find that there were no indiscretions on Ida's part."

I signed off quickly and called Gail. She was in court and would return my call.

When I finally talked with Gail later in the afternoon, I relayed the news about Ida. I was expecting some sort of surprise, but she was fairly low key.

"So...I guess you don't think that this will change their approach?"

Gail was non-committal. Maybe she was remembering our discussion about the suspected bug on my line. Good point.

"It's too soon to tell," she said.

"So, we should proceed as we've been going. Is that right?"

"That's all we can do," she said. "We have no other options."

I got off the phone, deflated. I truly thought that she would think that this would change the focus of the inquiry. She was right about it being too soon to tell, but absolutely wrong that there were no other options.

Jesse was out for the day, so I went to his office and called Dave for a follow-up. I told him that I was using another phone and the only item on the agenda was what to do now that Ida had been removed. Dave got Len on the line.

I began, "It was tough to behave normally with Adam. I wanted to jump up and down at first. But Gail seems to think that nothing really has changed. Evan Randle didn't seem very involved in the case. He was a suit but had nothing to add. Correct me if I am wrong, but why should we wait until we find out which way the FBI is going?"

Dave played the devil's advocate, "Well, with Ida gone, maybe no one will have any sway with Randle. Then, the focus could be off of you."

"Hmmmm. Maybe I need to know more about Randle."

"Maybe," Len said. "But assuming Randle does get a handle on the case, how do you think the investigation will proceed?"

"It will be long and I'll continue to be dragged along as I have been to this point." I hesitated. "I think that I might have made my decision. It doesn't matter who's in charge of it, I want out. I don't want to be jerked around anymore. Let's go and do it now."

"That's my..." Dave paused "...client!"

We stuck with the plan, and he didn't call me a girl. So tonight, at Dave's office, we would discuss the specifics.

# CHAPTER 25: Where is Stanley?

A lot of people seemed to be interested in Ms. Stanley: the Administration; the FBI; three undercover police; Dave; Len; Me; Louise; Keith; and I'm sure, my phantom antagonist. Meanwhile, Stanley was slithering around somewhere, trying to avoid all of us.

Dave, Len and I got together at Dave's office at 5:30 that night. The guys had formulated a plan. We talked briefly about the break-in, and I repeated my feeling, confirmed by Jean, that the perpetrator could be losing control of his scheme. I didn't think that I knew the kind of person or lawyer who would unleash destruction like that vandalism. Someone was losing it.

"What about D.L.'s murder?" Len asked. "That wasn't a peaceful act."

"But," I responded, "It was cold and calculated. It was like a lawyer figuring out a solution to a problem: what do we do when someone goes off plan? Do we need that person or is she expendable? When the applications are granted, she'll become expendable and she'll have to be eliminated because she'll cause nothing but trouble. She'd proven that over and over.

"So, the thinking would be...if we hire a killer who can also place a bug in Sam Watson's office to monitor any discussion about her or with her at the Administration, and then we remove it at the same time of the murder, we get rid of the other problem." I gave my two guys a determined look. "But what was done to my apartment was an act of someone really infuriated at my interference with his plan. It wasn't rational. It was a tantrum. True, it was meant to intimidate but that had already been tried several times with friend Ida and the institution she stood for. It hadn't worked with me. Frustrating for our perp. When my friend Jean told me about her demand that Adam tell the pipeline that Ida must lay off about the loan or else, Jean said that he sounded frantic. Maybe it's because Adam is beginning to realize the big picture and he's worried about repercussions. This is no longer just gossip with his group but a wacky plan that has gone awry. His manic friend no longer controls the many parts of his scheme."

Len and Dave listened but their focus was on their plan. They told me that the undercover guys had located a contact for Stanley. They were trying to set up a meeting with her near Hanover Place. The contact was told that it had to do with a personal matter.

"But wait," I said. "How are you making the connection between me and Stanley? Who gives her my information?"

"There's a rumor they put on the street that there is still money to be made from the Administration job, in case Stanley had forgotten. And it's repeating the FBI's insinuation that you were involved. Our guess is that she hasn't forgotten your name: it's sort of an IOU, but for obvious reasons, she put off the collection. Don't forget that Dave got shot working for you. People know. Anyway, our guys heard about it and, for a cut, they will make the introduction. The street says it's $25,000.00."

"Is that good or bad for that kind of job?" I asked. "She had to take a risk to remove the bug."

"Well, she was a custodian and she could get into the office at odd hours. She could take her time and she would bag the prize," Len said.

I shuddered, reconsidering my resolve to end this myself. "Why don't we just tell the FBI where she is once we set up a meeting and let them take her? Then we would be viewed as the good soldiers plus it would be simpler and none of us would get hurt."

"Because we want you totally out of this mess. You said that yourself!" Dave said firmly. "We don't want you to have any taint or any innuendos from her. We want to get everything out there on wire, so that there are no loose ends to drag you back in. You need to be out. Then, we will have done our job."

"I agree with that. I don't want any more trips to the FBI for chats with agents. So, who is going to be involved, Dave? Will it be Len, you and the two undercover guys?"

"No," he said. "We decided that we will need three undercover guys." He paused. "And you will also be involved."

"Oh, my God, how?" I started to fidget in my chair. I stood up and walked to the window. It was a different world out there. People were walking around, people who weren't afraid about being chased by the FBI and/or, in the near future, chased by a thug or possibly by a crazed villain.

"Now I really don't want anyone else involved with this," I said.

"I agree and that's fine, said Dave. "We talked the plan over. But you need to be the trap."

That did not feel at all good to me. In fact, that sounded really dangerous. "You mean, the bait? For whom and how?" I gulped.

"Stanley. We tell her that you want to know more about the note at the murder. You had heard from the FBI that it had something to do with you and you would like her to give you a call to talk about it."

"I don't get that. Why do I care?"

"We are guessing there was going to be a bonus for her."

"Sorry, I still don't get it. Everyone knows that hired killers get paid up front, at least the guys in the movies do."

"Maybe whoever hired her thought she deserved a bonus. There is the planting and retrieval of the remote device. That might have been the reason for payment. D.L. might not have known she had already been paid to kill her, so she might have been involved somehow and offering payment—although, from what I know of D.L., she would not have paid Stanley. D.L. just wanted the evidence back. The meeting at the Administration might already have been arranged before Louise talked to Stanley. Or maybe Louise too had a part in this plan."

"Louise? She's terrified of Stanley. At least that's what she says. Anyway, how do you have any idea of what address is on the note and what was going to happen at that address? All we know is what the FBI told me, which may not exactly be true, that my DNA was on the note—not my fingerprints but my DNA."

"Call it intuition."

"Dave, if you hadn't recovered so quickly, I'd call it delirium."

"Yes, but we need to know about that note. What's on it and why was it so important that your DNA be put on it? Look, trust me. You now know from Louise that D.L. Phillips was involved in a plot that ended with her own demise. According to Louise, she arranged something and she had that note with her. My guess is that she tried to give it to Stanley. She really wanted to recover the device from the Administration office now that her auction applications were granted without any investigation about her or her company or any discussion about whether there were any undisclosed parties. We don't even know who had the device planted. Stanley can tell us. You told me that the Administration did not trust D.L. or her transactions and she knew that there could be trouble. Someone wanted to know about it if an inquiry happened, but it didn't. So, in order to get the device back undetected, someone on the inside needed to get it before it was discovered and an investigation began. Someone set her up with Stanley to retrieve it and give her the note. Who knows why D.L. wanted the bug or, for that matter, the reason for her meeting with Sam Watson. So, Stanley retrieved the device and D.L., known to Stanley only as a redheaded 'contact,' not by name, gave her the note, telling her that she would get paid when she went to that address. But Stanley had already gotten paid to kill her, so why bother with the note? Stanley left the note there, as she was told to do—which would incriminate you. Now, Stanley might have decided that she really did want that bonus for all her trouble."

"Not half bad," I said. "So what am I supposed to do? I go from one version of sitting duck to another, but this one could save me if it doesn't kill me?"

"You just have to sit in your office." Dave said.

"Good and I will get my blood splattered on the walls so that my partners will have to redecorate before re-use. Speaking of which, what should I tell my partners about Ms. Stanley visiting me? As it is, I have to give a weekly status report to them, now I will have to tell them that a thug—probably a murderer—is visiting me during office hours." I had visions of my fairly straight partners—even those people who dressed informally in defiance of the standards—double taking over this Stanley person asking for me at the front desk. And Cecily the receptionist, asking her politely whether she would prefer coffee or water? Uh uh. That scenario wouldn't work at all.

"Ms. Stanley won't be visiting you in your office. She'll be calling you at the office. She'll ask to meet you at another location."

"And will I go?"

"No, we will."

I exhale. "I can do that, I think."

"You'll meet everyone at a different location. We don't want to be surprised by any of Stanley's friends, lovers or creditors."

"Everyone, meaning Ms. Stanley and your folks?"

"Yes."

I sigh. "Where will everyone be?"

"Two visible. Three invisibles. All wearing wires. You will be, too."

"Wow, you guys really do bear grudges." And we all laughed. The Feds are not going to like this. At all. Dave would call me when things were set in place.

I went back to my office and wrote up a memo to Eliot, the firm ethics counsel, advising him that the lead FBI agent had been taken off the case with hypothesis that this dismissal may have due to the agent withholding a witness's letter from the investigation which stated that an Administration staff member may have been somehow involved in the murder. I copied the memo to the firm's managing director and emailed it to the home office.

At 7:30, I packed up and went home to view the damage. The cleaners had been there and had left. Cam had called in the afternoon and asked whether he could drop by to view the place. He brought a bottle of wine as a sympathy gift.

We walked around the rooms. There was a lot for me to do, but the floors and the walls were clean. Drawers were back in the cabinets, bedside tables and desk, but the contents were not in any particular order. The broken glass was gone and so was the broken Cuisinart. All the food had been tossed and the flour and water mess had been mopped. The kitchen floor shone. This guy was good! But then he was used to this kind of stuff, which sometimes involved a body or two.

There were five plastic bags near the door. Everything that had been mashed and trashed was in the bags. A separate bag with questionable throwaways was there for my review. He had taken pictures of my cosmetic jars instead of leaving them out. I had an opportunity to make sure nothing was in there that I wanted before I tossed it. My dried clothes were piled neatly on the bed, waiting for my decisions on washing or cleaning. Smashed pictures and lamps that might be salvageable lined the walls, but at least the place was semi-organized.

Otherwise, things did not go very well. When I told Cam about "the plan." He became livid and accused Len and Dave of putting me in danger.

"But I kind of agree with them." I protested. "I know it means taking a risk, but I just want out of this horrible chapter of my life, which keeps going on and on. These guys know what they are doing because they have done it before."

"Well, what about you? You have not done it before."

"I am relying on professionals." I said, praying that I have put my trust in the right people.

"Do you know how many friends Len and Dave are bringing?"

"Dave tells me two undercover visibles, the guys that Stanley would recognize from the street, and three invisibles which includes Len and Dave," I said.

But Cam kept up his questions. "Do you know if Dave is even healed enough to participate in this disaster waiting to happen? What if Stanley happens to see Dave and recognizes him as the guy who was asking about her before? Is this really smart to put yourself on the line with other people who have had police training and know how to fire a gun, for God's sake? The last I knew, you had never handled a gun, yet they are taking you down into Northeast, probably to some abandoned warehouse and setting you up. You need to talk to Dave now." Cam was behaving like a boyfriend now, and I didn't know whether I liked it or not.

"Look, Cam," I said. "I appreciate your concern. We are friends and I know that friends take care of each other. But they're the guys who have arranged this plan, based on their past experiences, and they are able to carry it out."

Cam insisted that I call Dave; we reached Dave on his cell phone. Cam repeated everything that he had said to me, only more forcefully.

I don't know what Dave thought about this guy on the phone acting as if he belonged in my life. But Dave sounded calm, "Look, there will be five of us there; Leyla won't be with us when we meet Stanley at her designated location. The two undercovers, the visibles, will explain that Leyla wants to be cautious. Leyla will be where we take Stanley once we have her. We will meet Leyla at a less isolated, friendlier location. We will take care of Leyla."

Cam was a little less snarky now. "Why does Leyla have to be there at all?"

"She is going to get Stanley to tell us who hired her and then pay her. Stanley loves money; she loves her power; and she likes to show-off. Odds are she'll want to brag about herself to Leyla, a respected lawyer, and the two men."

Hmmm. I hadn't thought of myself as a respected lawyer for a while now. I felt more like a machine these days, trying to slog through this legal morass that had encompassed my life forever, or so it seemed.

"That's what I'm afraid of," snarled Cam. "It sounds like, Stanley will be free to go and spend the money once she tells Leyla who hired her! What kind of plan is that? How did street guys even get information on Stanley and her involvement with the RFA murder and the note and Leyla? There are a lot of holes in this story."

Dave was still calm, "Everybody knows everything on the street. That's where I heard that Leyla was the suspect. And then there is Stanley dressing up like a janitor for six weeks and working like a straight person for the federal government, leaving for work at 7:30 and getting home at 5:30? Anyone who knows her would know there was something happening there. Then, Stanley shows up with cash to flash and people really start talking.

Our guys hear about it. Stanley knows two of us from the street. They are undercover but she doesn't know that. Stanley also knows about Leyla from the note that she more than likely read. And she knows that the FBI is interested in Leyla."

"I don't like it, I just don't trust any of this," said Cam.

"That's because you live a conventional life. The street isn't like that. It's full of people hustling for a way to make money and maybe not even legally. These people live by their wits. Maybe they even risk their lives, but it's pretty much the only game in that part of town."

Cam was cynical, "So, Stanley will come with you because she wants the money. Is she stupid? I wouldn't if it were me."

"Of course, you wouldn't. But people on the make would. She knows two of the guys and they have always looked and acted like druggies. She would probably think that she could get whatever money they bargained for back from drugs they buy."

"Anyway," I said finally from the background, "all of this discussion relates to me, right? The question is whether I take my chances on the alleged good graces of the FBI, a judge and/or a jury or whether I at least try to find out how and why this whole set-up happened. Call me a risk-taker, but I would rather rely on cops who are my friends and are avenging damage to a fellow, than be a "solved" case by unfriendlies after I lose my job and my money."

"Hopefully, I won't have to go to identify you," Cam grumbled. "Thanks for your confidence." I scowled at him.

We said goodbye to Dave.

"But listen, Cam," I said. "I heard one good thing today. Ida Cramer was removed from the investigation."

Not even that news put Cam in a good humor. He was sulking, like in the bad old days. We said goodbye to each other and he left, with no mention of whether we would ever see each other again.

# CHAPTER 26: No Rest for the Weary.

My phone rang. It was my mother. She asked what time she'd see me at her house tomorrow. OMG, I forgot. We'd decided on this weekend to try and approach April's late father's partner to find out what happened that last night between April and her father. How could I forget so soon? I had no choice but to go. I'd spent the years since her death with guilty thoughts flitting through my head. The chance to finally know was two-edged, though: what if we find that the evidence showed that she had ended her own life? That would confirm my worst thoughts.

We planned to go to the restaurant and see whether we could approach him with our delicate inquiry. We knew that Mr. Sanders made a death bed statement. The question was whether the partner would divulge it to April's best friend. To be honest, my mother is much better than I am with getting information from people. I can do the upfront lawyer thing, but this conversation required a real skill that only my mother with her search-ing eyes and mild manner could bring off.

I needed to go despite wanting to reorganize my house immediately. Having to come home to a disheveled house made me feel unhinged. I'm a lot of things around the house, but I am neat. Things need to be in their place for me to be at ease, and seeing my paintings propped up against the wall with damaged frames was sending me into a fit. But then, in the past, I didn't like the mess that Cam made at times, either. All in all, I would rather have that mess.

I called Dave again and told him that I was leaving town for the week-end, starting tomorrow late afternoon. If there were any updates I wanted to know, but I wouldn't be physically in D.C. this weekend.

I puttered around, packing a bag for the weekend and organizing one drawer in the kitchen. I had to admit the house cleaner knew his business. The insides of the drawers were spotless. Most of the kitchen tools were organized in a reasonable way. I did not have to move much.

I had stopped at the store on the way home and bought some basic stuff since my visitor had destroyed most of my food supplies. I had thought I would ask Cam to stay for dinner. Another plan gone awry. I threw together a salad and some salmon, finishing my dinner with fruit. It was 10:00 PM. I needed to go to bed.

There was a sharp knock on my door. I approached it slowly and looked out the peephole. No one was there. I didn't know what to do, except to call Dave.

The call went straight to voicemail.

"Someone knocked on my door. When I looked out the peephole, I didn't see anyone. What should I do?" I was not going out there until I heard from Dave.

I started to get ready for bed. Dave called me a half hour later.

"I'm in the neighborhood," he said. "I'll be around in ten minutes." What a jewel he'd turned out to be! Either I was his only client or he really was into my case. I was grateful for whatever it was.

There was a knock on the door in a few minutes and I heard Dave call, "Leyla, it's Dave."

I went to the door and looked out the peephole. There, in fact, was Dave.

I opened the door to find him with a small envelope in his hand. "This was left at your door," he said, handing it to me.

I took it. There was no writing on the outside. I opened the envelope and took out a note card. It read: "Next time, it will be worse. Promise." I handed it to Dave.

"Well, I think it's good we're closing in on Jimmi. I can't go through much more of this."

"Look," Dave said. "I'll sleep on your sofa tonight. You're getting out of town this weekend, and one of us will stay in the apartment while you're away. We need to wrap this up soon."

I gave him the alarm information; a comforter and pillow; and offered him food and something to drink. He'd just eaten and didn't want anything to drink. So I handed him the TV remote and apologized for calling it a night. I stopped to make coffee ready for the morning and set the door alarm.

I put in my ear plugs so I wouldn't hear the TV from the living room.

I fell into a deep sleep, realizing how safe I felt with a person in the next room, who was there to protect me. At 2:00 AM, I heard shouting and pulled out the ear plugs.

Dave was yelling, "Get down on the floor, Leyla."

I rolled out of bed and onto the floor. Dave burst through the door. He was putting away his gun when he came into my room.

"Someone was on your balcony," he said. The balcony ran the length of the living room and my bedroom.

"What happened?" I asked, shaking.

"I was trying to sleep. Through the curtains, I saw someone climb over the balcony railing and move outside the sliding door. I had my gun out, slid off the couch, stood off to the side of the door. Whoever was there must have seen me and the gun. He jumped off the balcony."

"It's three stories up!" I said.

Dave cautiously opened the door. He looked over the balcony rail. "There's a figure on the ground. Getting up now, but slow. Looks like bush broke his fall."

I looked over his shoulder and could see someone limping away. I disarmed the alarm. Dave ran out and down the stairs. The elevator was going to be too slow. I saw Dave coming around the side of the building, but by then the figure had disappeared. Dave looked as if he was checking the ground where the person had landed. He gingerly picked up a knife with a tissue, then ran in the direction that the figure was headed. I lost sight of him as he went around a corner. Five minutes later, he was back at the door.

"I lost him. He must have had a car. There was no sign of him on the street."

"Wow. I'm glad you were here." I let out a deep sigh.

"Me, too. I'm also glad you're leaving town. Get some sleep, if you can."

But I was too wide awake now. I walked to the refrigerator and took out the bottle of wine Cam had brought. I opened it and poured a half of a juice glass. "They tell you not to do this, but I can't think of anything else to calm me down. By the way, do we need to call the police?"

Dave opted out of the wine, told me he'd call the officers who came after the break-in, and wished me goodnight.

I went to bed and sipped the wine. I picked up my Kindle and, somehow, managed to fall asleep with the thing still on my lap.

My alarm went off at 6:00 AM and I got up, dressed in my running clothes, disarming the door on my way out. Dave was asleep on the couch. The city was just waking up, traffic beginning to move. I ran to a nearby park and down the path, thinking about the close call last night. Several runners were around me as we ran down a hill along a stream. The traffic was hushed by the trees and it was just getting bright when I reached my 15-minute turnaround point. I ran back, coming in the door with the newspaper as Dave was folding up the blanket. He had turned on the coffee and already had poured two cups. They were on the kitchen counter. I walked toward the coffee and smiled at him.

"Thank you so much, Dave. This is above and beyond, and I am so grateful to you. I just want to tell you that I slept well for the first time in ages, knowing you were here. Thank you! You probably saved my life."

"Well, things have heated up. You're right: someone out there is losing it. I always thought Jimmi would lead us to the mastermind and when it was quiet on that front, I didn't worry. Now, I think that the plan is not proceeding as someone anticipated, and maybe we need to refocus on the people in Ida's group to avoid more violence."

"No, I think that we are on the right track, Dave. We just need to be patient; this has to be over soon. I'll be gone until Sunday. We can put our plan into effect as soon as possible. I'm ready to play my part. Do you think that your guys can locate Jimmi and set something up with her by then?"

"We'll try over the weekend. By the time you get home, we should have some idea of when and where we'll go into action."

"Great. Call me if you need me over the weekend. And if I can ask a big favor, can someone stay with me on Sunday and Monday?" At this point, I didn't care what it cost to protect me: it was worth it.

"We'll get someone."

"Thank you!"

Dave hung around my place until I was ready to leave for work. I gave him cereal, fruit and my newspaper to pass the time. At 8:00, I was ready to leave for the office with my weekend bag packed. We alarmed the door when we left.

I dropped him off at his apartment. "Give me a call after you talk with your guys," I said. Then I headed to my office. What surprises would meet me today? I could only guess.

By the time I got to my office, I had received an email from the managing partner, in response to my email of the previous night. He "invited" me to the firm's board meeting, via teleconference, to give everyone an update. The meeting was going to be held Tuesday at noon. He did not mention Jesse, who was not cc'd on the email. I didn't know what to think of that.

I went down the hall and looked in Jesse's office. He was on the phone and motioned me in. "Yes, she just came in my office. I'll put her on the speaker."

I sat down. "Hi, Leyla." It was Ray. Who called whom? I wondered. "Jesse and I were just talking about your case. He called to tell me that the FBI investigator had been taken off the case. I told him that you had sent an email last night." Question answered. I was ticked.

"Yes, I sent it only to you and Eliot, as you requested that I do. And I just got your email about the Board Meeting." I could tell from his face that Jesse had not received that email, but he recovered quickly. I had no idea why the firm had begun to leave Jesse out of the loop, after strenuously advising us to work together.

"I haven't opened my email this morning, Ray, I assume that I should be attending the meeting with Leyla."

"I don't think that's really necessary, Jesse, if you have other matters to attend to."

"I'll see what my schedule is and let you know," Jesse said.

"Okay. I think that we can discuss the FBI situation more thoroughly on Tuesday, Leyla. I guess that's all we have to discuss right now."

"We'll talk on Tuesday, then. Thanks, Ray." I said, glaring at Jesse. He hung up.

"May I ask why you called him, again?" I said.

"I just wanted Ray to be involved. He wants that."

"These events are happening to me," I said, emphatically. "I should be telling him what is happening to me and I did, last night!"

"Well, the whole process is affecting our practice."

"How is it affecting our practice? I am billing the same amount of hours, or more. We are still getting paid by our clients. I don't understand."

"Our peers are talking about us."

"And how is that hurting us?"

"It's our reputation."

"Again, I am asking you, if we are billing the same hours and we are getting paid and our clients are happy and referring others to us, how is this affecting our practice."

Jesse avoided looking at me. "I just don't like it."

"Well, I don't like it either. It's worse for me than it is for you, and I'm continuing to practice law. I don't like you going behind my back and calling the managing partner, as if I am a naughty little girl. It's degrading. It is also misogynistic, and you need to stop, Jesse. I'll continue to share everything with you, if you promise you won't discuss my life with the firm without telling me."

"I don't like it, Leyla," he mumbled, shifting piles of paper on his desk.

"Me either. But for the time being, we will have to live with it."

Luckily, the rest of the day passed quickly. Just business, reviewing a settlement agreement and writing a response to the Administration request for additional information on another transaction. This was easy stuff, compared with matching wits with Ida.

I had a phone call arranged with my West Coast client who had been recently freed from D.L.'s harassment. I detected a more relaxed attitude by him, although he had always taken each blow in stride. I did not tell him what a rat's nest I was in. Someday, when it was over, I would tell him.

For a change, things went without a hitch and I was in my car and on the road headed to the beach at 4:30. With a little luck, I would be at my mother's house at 7:30. My phone rang. I had forwarded my office number to my cellphone. It was Adam. I let it roll over to voicemail. Great, I thought. That's all I need.

During the interminable ride out New York Avenue, stopping at every red light, I could finally see that Adam had left a voicemail. At the last major intersection before I hit the highway, I listened to his voicemail. "Hey Leyla, it's Adam. I just heard about the break-in at your house. Do you have any idea who did it? It just seems odd. Give me a call. Thanks."

Hmm. It had taken a while for him to get the information. His observation that it seemed odd seemed odd to me. Why would Adam think so? I didn't have any idea, but I needed time to think about it before I called him and the whole network, including Annie Sims and Leon Gallagher, heard about. I turned on the radio, switching from my usual news station to my music stations. I needed just to clear my head. But the task ahead was formidable. Did I really want to know whether April allowed herself to die?

Once out on Route 50, headed to Annapolis, the traffic was fairly light for rush hour in the Nation's Capital. But of course, this wasn't the middle of the beach season. These were just the poor daily commuters who had to sit in traffic, Monday through Friday. My phone rang again. I saw that it was my mother's number and I put it on speaker.

"Hello, darling," my mother said. "Drew ran into Gray at woodworking class and mentioned you to him. Drew told him that you were a friend of April's and that you were coming to town this weekend. Gray was reluctant but Drew got him to agree to at least chat with us at the restaurant tonight."

"I guess that's good," I said. "I hate to put him in a bad spot and I'm really anxious about it but if there is a chance to figure out what happened to her after all these years, it's worth it. I'd thought that I'd never know."

"Yes, when you talked about her the last time you were here, I realized that we hadn't mentioned her for years. It seemed that after her funeral, you barely talked about her again."

I sighed. "I thought about her a lot. I guess I felt guilt that I couldn't prevent her death."

"You couldn't do anything," my mother said. If she only knew what I feared. If that fear were true, then I could indeed have done something, and I didn't. Living with that fear came to the forefront now.

"I'm figuring that I'll be at your house about 7:15," I said. "It was easier getting out of town than I'd planned."

"Good. We'll go to the restaurant right after you get here. Have a safe trip."

"Bye, Mom," I said.

A wave of dread came over me. What would we find out? What had gone on between April and Mr. Sanders on her last day of life? I felt like I was back in that fateful date again, that raw day that I had tried to keep tamped down for years.

Familiar scenery passed: the Severn River; the Chesapeake Bay Bridge that so many people are afraid to drive over. It never bothered me, but I have two friends who couldn't do it. For one thing it is long and the other thing is that it is high. The trick is not to think about it. Just drive. I passed into the Delmarva and through the little towns that never seem to change. Friday night and the one hot spot in each little town was jammed for early dinner.

I turned into my favorite route though horse country in Maryland, off the main roads into the green rural countryside, big puffy clouds in the blue sky. If I hadn't been so cranked, I'd have succumbed to the peacefulness.

What had the fight been about, and why had Mr. Sanders cried when he talked about it? Why was this his last thought? I couldn't imagine. Both of them were upset. It would be terrible to die like that and yet apparently both had. April had been my only friend who had died in her teens. It's a big deal. I switched to news and heard the same thing I'd heard yesterday, last week and last month. Wow. I'm getting cynical. Time to chill. I'll do that, I promised myself, as soon as the D.L. nightmare is over. I'll take a vacation! But maybe it will be a really long vacation after the Board Meeting on Tuesday. I switched back to music.

Slowly I was moving toward my home town. I merged until Route 1 and settled into the Friday early evening traffic. The trees were more colorful than the last time I'd been here. The sun was just sinking and the sky was glorious. Clouds in front of me were golden, reflecting the sunset behind me. At least I could still enjoy nature.

# CHAPTER 27: More Drama.

7:15 almost on the nose, I pulled into my mother's driveway. She came to the door as I got out and grabbed my bag from the backseat.

"Hi, Mom," I said, putting on my happy face.

She looked at me. "Have you lost weight? Are you feeling alright?"

I couldn't fool my mother, but I could tell her that it was hard work that was making me tired.

"It's the end of the work week, Mom," I said, kissing her on the cheek. "You girls work too hard!"

"I'll relax this weekend, after we talk with Gray." I promised.

"Yes. Sukoshi wine?"

"Whew, yes, a little, please."

She poured a third of a glass, and I headed to my room to get ready.

My room was the same, only cleaner than when I lived here. It had a new coat of paint that I had picked out when my mother repainted the house. A year after my father died, she gave herself a project to renew the look of the house. Everything had been on hold when my father became ill. When she started the project, I was relieved. It had taken a while, but my mother became herself again.

I came back downstairs a little refreshed.

"So, what's our game plan?" I said, knowing my mother would have one. I almost wished I could tell her about D.L. because she might have a game plan for that, too. But it was too much to lay on her.

"Well, I will introduce you to him and tell him that you and April were best friends. Then, you'll say that you are sorry to hear that Mr. Sanders died. That you always wanted to talk to him about April, but it was too raw for both of you, so you never did."

"Yes, and then what."

"We will wait for him to say something. And then maybe I can say something like I heard that Lou had mentioned April before he died."

"Better you than me!" I said.

"We will see what happens."

"Hmm. There is a lot of room for mischief there."

"Yes. But he already knows that you were close friends and that you'd wanted to talk with Lou about April."

"Whew. Well, let's get this show on the road."

Since my car was last one in, I drove to the restaurant. We walked in and were greeted by the young lady at the door. She took us to a table by the fire and left two menus and a wine list. I looked at the list and saw my favorite white wine.

The waiter came to our table. We ordered the wine and listened to the specials. We looked around for Gray. He was nowhere in sight. Stood up? Well, at least we'd have a good dinner.

Shortly after we had gotten our wine and given our orders, Gray came to our table. He was a handsome man and had a very kind manner. We shook hands and my mother asked him to sit down. She said, "We're so sorry about Lou's passing. Leyla and April were best friends and sometimes I thought that Leyla lived at the Sanders house."

"April and I knew each other since pre-school," I added.

"So sad," Gray said.

"Traumatic!" I said. He nodded sympathetically.

"Yes," my mother said. "After her funeral, Leyla rarely talked about her again."

Tears came to my eyes and I blinked. This was not acting, this was real. "I always wanted to talk with Mr. Sanders, but I never had the nerve. Then, I finished high school and went to college. I never saw him again." My voice trailed off.

"He mentioned you once or twice," Gray said. "Your name was in the paper when you graduated from college and then when you graduated from law school. He always acted like he wanted to talk about what April would have done: what college she would have chosen, what job she would have gone after. He never did, though. He didn't mention her very often. He might have been too upset, I guess."

"Like me," I sighed.

A woman came up to the table. She spoke quickly to Gray. "Sorry to interrupt but we need your help in the kitchen."

Gray got up and apologized to us. Then he hurried away.

"What a letdown," I whispered.

My mother, usually the picture of patience, made an exasperated face. "We were so close."

Our orders came and we ate them in silence. Gray did not appear again. There must have been a really big problem in the kitchen, or maybe he just did not want to talk to us about April. We paid our checks and left. I was distressed. I had taken myself to a level of grief that I hadn't felt in years and for nothing. I couldn't blame Gray: my feelings were really not his problem. It was just bad timing. Maybe I would never know what happened that night.

I headed to bed, dreaming of April who appeared in the background of a gathering of high school friends. I tried to push through the crowd, but couldn't get to her. And then I woke up. It was 2:00 AM, my "favorite" wakeup time. If I lay there for a while, I would go through the rolodex of worries, so I got up and took an over-the-counter sleep aid and turned on my Kindle. Henry XII was still having problems with pretenders and paying massive amounts to spies and foreign rulers to protect his throne. Better to think about Henry's problems than about Leyla's. The next thing I knew, it was 7AM and I heard my mother down in the kitchen. I put myself together and joined her.

"Good Morning, dear," she said. "I'm glad you weren't wandering around the house last night! Did you have a good sleep?"

"Yep," I said. "What's on your agenda today?"

"Well, I am going to the shop today because Melissa is off this weekend. Her cousin is getting married. Why don't you come down at one, and we'll go to lunch. It isn't a busy weekend so I can take an hour or so off and not lose many sales." She laughed.

"Your people are so faithful, they'll just wait for you." I smiled. "OK, I'm going to run after breakfast and just chill. I need it." Boy, did I need it.

It was fall, no doubt. The wind was always there and constantly shifting. I felt the chill as I came around the corner on a side street and hit the boardwalk. My mother was right about the crowds this weekend: the next big weekend event was Halloween which brought out a throng, dressed to the teeth like Dracula or little Bo Beep. That no longer thrilled me or at least it didn't thrill me now. I had too many other "thrilling" things going on.

My phone rang. I stopped and put my foot on a bench, stretching my leg while I answered Dave's call. "What's up?"

"The guys got the word out to Jimmi's dude."

"And?"

"She'll be in town next week."

"Did they talk about the cash?"

"Yeah. That's the only way to get at her."

"OK. I've got a big meeting on Tuesday noon. After that, I guess I'll get ready for the plan."

"Fine. No one has been around your apartment, by the way. We've been there since you left."

"Sorry that I didn't leave much food. I had a visitor who used it all."

"You had a message on your machine."

"Anyone I know?"

"No, just a long pause, breathing and a hang-up. The call identification was an unknown number. Probably a solicitor."

"Solicitors don't breathe into the phone."

"Yeah. I know. One of us will be there when you come home tomorrow afternoon."

"You are awesome, Dave."

We hung up and I started running, thinking about the phantom caller. I ran the length of the boardwalk and then along the Ocean road, a couple of blocks through a high-end village and back up to town.

I stopped at my mother's shop. She was having a sale and several women were browsing through racks. My mother was in the back of the store helping one of my friend's mother.

"Hi, Mrs. Lewis, how are you these days?" I asked. I was aware that she had gone through a bout of radiation last summer, but she looked healthier now.

"I'm fine now, Leyla. I just wish my hair were a little bit longer."

"You look great! How is Janet?"

"Still living in Wilmington. She has two boys now. And they keep her busy."

"Is she still doctoring these days?"

"Yes, she still works in the emergency room at duPont Hospital. I don't think that she will ever give it up. She loves it. How is everything with you, Leyla?"

If she only knew the half of it.

"I'm good. Still working long hours but, like Janet, I love what I am doing."

Until I get booted out for being on the FBI's most-wanted list on

Tuesday.

"Well, I'm proud of you girls. Back when you all were running around in a herd, I would never have guessed that everyone would settle down into a comfortable life."

"Yes. I guess we have our parents to thank."

"For some of it," my mother said. "The rest was up to you." Yep, the rest will be up to me.

"Well, I just thought I would stop by on my way back home. I'll take a shower and meet you at Fish."

"OK, dear. By the way, Gray called. He said he didn't have your number so he called me. He was sorry that he left us so abruptly last night. He said he could stop by the house before he goes to work at four this afternoon. I told him that you would like to talk with him. So, you need to back home by 3."

I eyed my mother and she raised her eyebrows. I was not sure what that meant. I would find out more at lunch, I assumed. I was apprehensive.

Mrs. Lewis was looking at herself in the mirror. She was thinner than she had been, but the dress my mother chose for her flattered her olive coloring. My mother held up a jacket that would complement both her and the dress. "That dress looks great, Mrs. Lewis! It was wonderful to see you. Say hi to Janet for me. We will have to have a reunion again soon."

"Good seeing you, Leyla. I'm glad you're happy."

Well, not quite happy. Things could be better, but I was working on that.

The house was quiet when I came in. I missed my father. He was always puttering around, either in the yard or somewhere in the house playing Mr. Fixit. He was pretty good at it and my mother relied on him a lot. Then she relied on Cam for a while. It all made me sad.

But I went up to my room and it was beautiful. The bathroom had fluffy towels and wonderful soaps. It felt like a B and B. I just needed to learn to enjoy the simple things and not worry about events coming up: Gray's visit; going home to danger; the firm's board meeting where everyone will be looking at me while I try to explain my precarious situation. Not to mention, the meeting with Stanley.

The shower was lovely and soon I was at the restaurant waiting for my mother. She had been waylaid by a customer. I sat in a booth and watched the door. It was fairly quiet in the restaurant and I didn't see any familiar faces. My mother would, I knew.

I looked at the menu and then at my phone. Cam had texted me, asking how things were going. I guessed that he was over his snit.

I called him. "I'm fine. I'm at my Mom's to try to find out about April. Also, a note was left at my apartment door telling me that things will get worse. They did, but Dave was there. I'll tell you about it later. Dave is looking after my place this weekend. I think the thing is going down next week. And I have a command performance on the FBI investigation with the firm's Board next Tuesday noon. So, nothing is really new at all. What's happening with you?"

"I wanted to let you know that I'm going to Spain tomorrow for a few days."

"Business or pleasure?"

"Are you kidding? Business, with the Secretary."

"That should be interesting."

'Hectic."

"Well, try to have a little fun."

"No fun in this life right now."

I didn't know how to respond. I hoped that he was trying to tell me something. I hoped his squeeze was no longer around. It was too much to hope for, in my sorry state of affairs.

"I know the feeling."

"Well, take care. I'll be thinking about you."

"Hopefully, it will soon be resolved."

"That's why I touched base. I was thinking about you. Good luck. I hope it goes well."

"That's two of us."

"We'll talk soon."

# CHAPTER 28: The Truth at Last.

"Hi, dear." My mother slid into the seat across from me. "Fitting a dress took longer than I had thought. She couldn't make up her mind about the length."

"That's OK. I was talking to Cam."

My mother's eyes lit up. "How is that lovely man?"

"He's good. We reconnected and he helped me with a work project. He is on his way out of town and just touched base."

"Anything exciting happening?"

"I'm not sure. We are both a little reluctant."

Actually, he is reluctant, but I am not going into any disturbing details with my mother.

"So, Gray called you? What do you think he has in mind? I'm a little nervous. I'm afraid of what he will say and afraid that I might fall apart."

"But you could get an idea of what really happened, after all these years."

"What if I find out that I could have done something and I missed an opportunity to help her?"

"You can't control the world, dear. You didn't create the situation."

"But I could have made it a little better for her, maybe."

"Gray is a nice man. Drew and he have become good friends. He will be gentle. To me, it sounds as if he wants to help you because it was clear from our conversation last night that April and you were such good friends and he loved her dad."

"We'll see."

I got home a little bit before three and was preparing some appetizers for cocktails with mother's boyfriend Drew. Something else!

Gray knocked on the door and I let him in.

"Thank you so much for this," I said. "I know that I am asking a lot of you to relive a sad event."

"Lou was so guilt ridden. I think he wished he could have done better with her accepting us."

"I know this sounds lame compared to a father's grief and guilt, but I felt the same. I felt that I should have been able to help her as a friend and I felt hopelessly inadequate when she died. To be honest, I always feared that she had done it herself."

"Oh my God, no, Leyla! Don't even think that. She never would have committed suicide. Lou and I were assured by the State Police that from the angle the car skidded and the direction it was travelling, she was trying to control it. She didn't aim the car at the tree. It's just that the slippery road at the bend was too difficult for her to maneuver. The accident wasn't Lou's fault or your fault. Lou just felt that he should have handled her distress better. Our situation was unusual at that time, and she was having a hard time understanding it. Lou didn't help her. That was his angst. We upset her and may have contributed to her distraction in the dangerous conditions. That's what Lou regretted. He only mentioned it rarely, but I could tell it ate at him."

I felt an immense burden lift. A burden I had carried for 18 years. It wasn't my fault. I could have done nothing to prevent that accident.

"But why didn't the State Police explain that to the reporter who covered her death? The way the story read, there were mysterious circumstances leaving open the possibility that she might have driven toward that tree intentionally!"

"Yes, we thought it was poorly written, too. But I want to reassure you that April's death was accidental. There was no mistake about that. Lou's concern was only due to his fear we'd distressed her enough to make her inattentive. He never even thought she had committed suicide."

It was with great relief that we finished our conversation. Gray headed off to work. I went up to my room and cried all the tears for my long lost friend April that I had held back for so long. I could at last grieve without the guilt.

The door opened downstairs, and Mother called up to me. "How did everything go with Gray?"

I went downstairs, with my makeup washed off from my tears and my eyes red. She gasped. "Was it that bad?"

"No. It's just that I've carried the guilt around for so many years. My emotions were all stopped up. When he told me that the police said April was trying to keep control of the car when it slid at the bend in the road,

I felt that huge burden of guilt lift. It was always there in the back of my mind and I didn't realize how much space it took in my head. Until Gray told me the truth."

"You never told us how much her death affected you. After her funeral, you hardly ever mentioned her."

"But it was there, Mom, hidden all the time."

"I'm glad that you're at peace about it, now." She hugged me tight, and I sobbed some more.

"But I'll always be sad."

"Of course," my mother agreed.

Then she looked at her watch. "Drew will be here in a half-hour and I need to freshen myself."

"I made the appetizers," I said. "After I redo my face, I'll come down and set them out."

Drew was right on time and rang the bell. My mother came down the stairs and held open the door. He hugged her. I was standing in the hall. He smiled at me

"Leyla, this is Drew," my mother said.

"Hi, Drew." I shook his hand.

"I'm happy to meet one of your daughters, Lillian." He turned back to me. "The three of you seem so busy, I feel honored to finally get to see one of you." He had a relaxed, outgoing manner. And he was an attractive man, greying around the temples. He was slim and taller than my mother by a couple of inches. They looked good standing next to each other. I didn't know how I felt about that.

It turned out that we had more to talk about than I imagined. Over wine and appetizers, I asked him about his career. He had been chief executive of a publishing company specializing in legal books. I recognized the company from my law school days and my legal career. He had become part owner of the company over the years and had retired from his position three years ago.

He remained on the board and still had his half interest in the company. We talked about the publishing business and how it had changed over the years. He asked me about my work. I summed it up quickly and was happy to hear from my mother that we were running late for dinner. I didn't want to be reminded right now about my job.

I liked my mother's friend. He seemed a good companion to her and shared her interest in golf and tennis. From what I gathered, they were somewhat evenly matched in both sports. I saw one or two familiar faces in the restaurant. A couple that I had gone to college with was sitting at the bar, waiting for a table as I walked by. I stopped and chatted with them briefly, they had not changed a lot. They were firmly settled in the community: he worked for his father's real estate business and she taught English in high school. They had two preteen children. Hard to believe.

The dinner went well. I enjoyed Drew's company. He had two daughters about my older and younger sisters' ages. They lived in New Jersey, where Drew had lived and worked before relocating. We chatted about their lives and where they attended school. My mother had met the younger daughter and was enthusiastic about her and her family. I wondered whether my mother was ever dismayed about the single status of me and my sister Suzanne.

Before I knew it, the weekend was coming to an end and I was packing my car to head back to whatever was awaiting. For better or worse, my tribulation would be coming to a close soon, I hoped, if I survived it.

On the way home, I called Dave for the latest. He said that he would be at my place when I got home. Check. There had been no more disturbing calls. Check. Things were quiet in my neighborhood and it did not appear that anyone was lurking around my house. Check. We hung up.

The Sunday afternoon traffic crawled past Annapolis into the Beltway and then D.C. Some activity was going on, but I hadn't paid much attention. I was busy with my thoughts of the week ahead and the board meeting. I would like to know the agenda. Maybe I'd ask one of my Texas partners on the board.

At last, I was turning into the garage. I noticed someone standing outside my building looking in my direction. I called Dave.

"I am in the garage. I hope that I don't sound paranoid but there is someone out front who was looking toward the garage when I drove in. Is that a friend or foe?"

"I don't know," he said. "I'm in your place and now I am looking down at the front door. I don't see anyone there."

"OK, I'm coming up on the elevator."

I put my bag and a care package from my mother in the elevator and went up to my floor. There was no sign of anyone in the hall on my floor. I went to my door and unlocked it. Dave was in the living room.

"I guess this place must seem like home to you now," I said. "It's been quiet all weekend."

'Let's hope it stays that way."

"I doubt it," Dave said. "We need to finalize the plan for Tuesday night."

"Tuesday? So soon?" I felt clammy.

"Yes, my guys set it up with Jimmi. Tuesday night is when she is available."

"Well, at least, my Board meeting will be over by then."

"We need you really focused."

"Well, tell me what I need to do." I sighed.

Dave got Len on the phone and they detailed the script for Tuesday night. At last I was going meet Jimmi Stanley. The strange part was, I was somewhat intrigued. It would be fascinating to meet this person who had played such a large part in my life the last six months. Life was presenting me with answers to questions that I thought might never be resolved.

Dave had drawn a diagram of where I was to be standing and where Jimmi was going to be. The street guys were the only other people in the warehouse where we would meet. They would be the deal makers only. They were not to reveal themselves as my protectors. Dave and Len would be outside with another former D.C. officer.

It looked good on paper, but I had to be assured that the plan was fool-proof. Unfortunately, they could not provide that for me.

"Just make sure that she doesn't have a weapon, that's all I ask."

"We'll see what we can do. Maybe the street guys can see to that."

"I mean, really. I need to know that she is not going to hurt me. I just want a simple exchange of money. What happens after we leave the warehouse is up to you guys. My job is to be there, give her the money and leave. And I want to be safe then."

The more we discussed, the more I feared that Cam was right. This scheme was not well enough thought out. There were too many loose ends.

But they had given their word that they would take care of me. And they had so far. So, I just had to trust them, with my life.

We finished the call. Dave had some take-out food, funnily enough, from the Thai place that Cam loved. We ate in silence and I cleaned up. I thanked him again for everything. For staying with me and protecting me in these last few days. We were both tired. I headed to my room to unpack and get ready for a new very eventful week. My fate at the firm and in this interminable case would be resolved for better or for worse. Not a guarantee for a good night's sleep.

Monday morning came too fast for me. I had been briefed for the Tuesday night meeting but at a loss for how to prepare for the firm's Board meeting.

# CHAPTER 29: Where the Rubber Meets the Road.

When I arrived at my office in the morning, I waited until 9:30 Central time to call one of my partner friends in Texas. Steve had been on the board for several years and was plugged into the thinking of the executive committee. We had worked on two transactions together involving energy companies and their internal communications licenses. We had a good working relationship and, when I went out for the annual meeting, we had a friendly conversation at the opening cocktail party. I felt as if I could ask him directly what the meeting was going to involve. From there, I'd at least know the agenda and could fashion my defense, if necessary.

I called Steve, and his voicemail told me that he was out of the office. I decided to be straight forward and left a message.

"Hi, Steve. I got an email on Friday morning, asking me to attend the Board Meeting by video conference on Tuesday. I don't have an agenda of the meeting and I wondered if you knew what the parameters of the discussion will be. I did talk with Ray on Friday about the FBI agent being changed in the investigation in the Radio Frequency Administration murder, but nothing other than that. Is this just a catch-up on what is happening on the case or should I be prepared for something else? I would appreciate any light that you could shed. Thank you and hope to talk to you soon."

Well, I didn't know where Steve was, in a meeting, out of the country, on vacation or trying to avoid me. I would wait until noon their time and call another partner, one of the two women on the Board.

In the meantime, there was a conference call on the resolution of a

four-year-old proceeding between my client, another licensee and D.L.
On the conference call, two attorneys represented the licensees and an
Administration staffer. No one represented D.L. The issue was who that
was going to be. We discussed the arbitration proceeding in New York that
had involved D.L. and her partner who had sued her in a New York court.
The proceeding was referred by the Judge to arbitration. We discussed that
D.L.'s representative, presumably her estate rep, would be brought in as a
substitute for D.L.; whether he was capable of wrestling with telecommunications issues or whether D.L. would need to be represented by another
attorney; and what procedure would be involved. It was decided after a
half-hour conversation that the staffer would call the representative and
attempt to resolve the impasse. I decided that I would research the issue in
the afternoon. My client was eager to wrap up all the proceedings involving D.L. But that wouldn't be as easy as it sounded.

It was now noon central time. I called Lauren to try to get some information on the Board Meeting Agenda. "Hi, Leyla. How are things in
D.C.?"

"Same old thing, Lauren. This town is full of former high school class
presidents and they can't get over it. Type As everywhere."

"That is certainly different from out here."

"Yes, I know. That is why I am happy to be part of the firm."

"What's on your mind?" She asked.

"Well, I got an invitation from Ray to attend the Board meeting tomorrow, and I was wondering what the agenda was going to be on my item. I'd
really like to be prepared."

Lauren paused and she turned cautious. "Well, I haven't been in on
everything. I know they want the latest on the proceeding and your view
of how long you think you will be part of it." I noticed she didn't say, a
suspect, but it was clear the firm wanted to know how long the professional
liability insurance company would be monitoring of my case and worrying
about image damage.

"Well, there is a more likely suspect now and the FBI is looking for her."

"Her. Another her?"

"Yeah, this case has an all-female cast." Neither of us laughed. "So,
have there been any opinions on what the Board might do?"

Lauren hesitated again. "Some partners are concerned about how long
this is going to go on and whether this will affect the firm in any bigger PR
way. Then, of course there is the money that is being spent."

"So, the options are?"

"Well, luckily for you, the money is still coming in from your clients. If that weren't the case, you might have been laid off or terminated a while ago. But let me say, you do have some defenders. Ray has been good and is keeping the faith about you. It's the guys in Houston who are getting restless about expenses, and the long timers fear that the firm name might be damaged."

"So, what you're saying is: my presentation had better be optimistic."

"Realistic, though. And an optimistic timeframe, if possible."

Lauren did not know that tomorrow night was my target for extracting myself from this mess and I was not about to disclose any of that to the firm. It was clear from Ray's directive earlier that I should not practice self-help. That subject would not be part of my spiel.

"I'll let you go, Lauren. You've been a big help. I appreciate your being honest with me. Ray was sounding as if it weren't a big deal, but it seems as if the natives are restless."

"You could say that," Lauren said. "Just be positive. I wish you luck. I know this whole thing can't be easy for you."

"Words fail."

"Yes, I know. I'll see you tomorrow."

After I hung up, I sketched out my defense: there was a more likely suspect, as a matter of fact, a female drug lord, posing as a custodian at the Administration who arrived right before the murder and left her job shortly after; an FBI agent had ignored a piece of evidence disclosing information about this custodian; the public revelation of the piece of evidence to the Administration and the Congress; the subsequent removal of that agent from the investigation; the disappearance of the person who provided the evidence on the custodian and who had previously met with Administration officials verifying it; and the pressure from Congress and the Administration on the FBI investigation to resolve the matter expeditiously. After I reviewed this, I felt a little better about my appearance before the Board. I would polish this throughout the day.

I began my research on the representation in the D.L. proceeding issue. I wondered whether Delilah Lydia Phillips had made a will and how that might affect the proceedings. Of course, I couldn't go over to her office and pillage her files or contact Louise, who might know, but I could inquire into it.

I began by looking through my contacts for D.L.'s phone numbers. I came up with three phone numbers. The first one I dialed was a this-number-is-no-longer-in-service message. The second number rang and rang and then a this-mailbox-is-full message. The third call was on an answering machine which said, "This is the office of D.L. Phillips, please leave your message after the beep." I left a message stating my name, my firm and mentioning the proceeding I wished to discuss. I stated that there had been a conference call about the matter with the Administration this morning and I had some questions that arose about it. I asked that someone return my call. I continued researching the issue of who could legitimately take the place of D.L.

I got an answer of sorts shortly. Richard Waters, D.L.'s Executor, called me an hour later and informed me that under her will, Waters would stand in the place of D.L. I asked whether he had filed an involuntary transfer of control at the Administration. He wavered and then said, "We haven't gotten around to the filings at the Administration."

I said, "It should have been filed within 30 days after her death, but I think that if you filed and asked for a waiver, the staff wouldn't have a problem with it. Are you going to use a telecom lawyer to represent D.L.'s interests?"

Again, he wavered, "No. We haven't gotten around to that either. It has been difficult getting D.L.'s papers organized."

I could imagine that, judging from her filings at the Administration. "I guess Louise Richards is no longer around?"

He said that he had let her go. Of course, I knew that but I just wanted to get a confirmation from him and try to detect his attitude toward Louise. I couldn't tell. He wasn't exactly disdainful. He'd simply stated a fact. I suppose it should have been obvious: D.L. didn't need office help anymore.

"Is D.L.'s office still open?"

"No, we just moved her papers to our office and have someone here trying to organize them."

"Well, as I mentioned in the message, we had a telephone conference with the Administration staff this morning about resolving the proceeding related to the New York licenses of my client; another licensee; and D.L. We need to involve a representative for D.L. The Administrative staff was going to discuss this matter with you."

"According to D.L.'s will, I am standing in her place."

"Then there are really two issues here: no one at the Administration knew about the will because there was no transfer filing; and there is the issue of D.L.'s partner in the company that has a part interest in the New York license. They are in arbitration."

"I have to talk to the Administration staff and get this matter under control," Waters said abruptly. "I'm not going to let anyone interfere with D.L.'s plan. We will talk later." He hung up.

Okay. That was not good. In fact, it was like Frankenstein rising. Although I had my fears, I thought that things would be easier and less contentious without D.L. around. But this conversation set me straight. I called the Administration staffer and left a message to expect a call from a perturbed gentleman named Richard Waters, who was D.L.'s Executor. I tried to explain my discussion with Waters as that I had a client in multiple litigations and wanted to know who would represent D.L. I didn't want the staffer to think that I was barging in. But I guess I was: I didn't know how long it would take the staffer to call Waters. Meanwhile, my client was interested in resolving the New York matter.

This development was not something we had anticipated. It also was probably going to result in litigation at the Administration between the Executor and D.L.'s partner. I dialed the client's familiar number and left a message. Surprise. We were not out of the woods on this by a long shot. Then I called the other licensee's attorney.

"Not good news. D.L.'s Executor, who hasn't filed an involuntary transfer of control for D.L. at the Administration, is now going to exert his control over our proceeding. From what I experienced a few minutes ago, he is a guy who could be as cranky as D.L. was. Let the fun begin."

The rest of my afternoon was taken up with this setback. After a flurry of conversations, I packed up at 6:30 and was about to leave for the day. Jesse stopped by and said that he would attend the video conference tomorrow.

Oh, great. I stayed and honed my notes for my presentation. It looked good on paper, but we would see.

When I got home, there was Dave, bless his heart.

"Thanks, Dave. Only one more night of babysitting. You know how much I appreciate it."

"I do know. Glad to do it. But now we need to talk some more about tomorrow night."

"Well, I thought that I would wear jeans and a turtleneck with a puffer jacket and sneakers."

Dave laughed, "Your attire is the least of our worries."

"It distracts me from thinking about possible death at the hands of a drug lord."

"You are not going to die."

"But you told me that the street guys wouldn't protect me if she goes ballistic."

"We will hear it and intervene."

"What if you can't?"

"Let's start at the beginning. Recite."

"I wait in my office for Stanley's phone call to my burner."

"Yes. And I will be in your office at 7PM. We will wait for Stanley's call to tell you where and when to meet her."

"Check."

"I will call the street guys and the other invisibles."

"That would be Len and your fellow traveler."

"Yes."

"You will wait with me until the street guys and Stanley arrive at the alternative location."

"That's where I have the problem. What if she doesn't want to go with you to a location not of her choice?"

"There is the money."

"I suppose."

"I will have dropped you off a block away around the corner to the alternative location."

"And you have researched this location and I won't be seen getting out of your car and you won't be seen at all."

He looked at me with a well-duh expression.

"OK. I get it. The three of them will already be inside."

"So, I come in. I schmooze with her, asking for information on the kingpin of the kill D.L. plan in exchange for the money. Is that right?"

"Yes."

"So that's another question that I have: what if she won't tell me? Then, I will be out the cash without a lead."

"Do you think we are going to let her get away?"

"Well, that could happen."

"Maybe. But we don't think so. We will have already separated her from any of her friends who might have followed her."

"Another maybe."

"Remember that there are three of us listening to what is happening."

"What if she has some sort of location device."

"Perhaps, but we still are out there listening."

"OK. She tells me, maybe. I give her the money. She leaves with the street guys?"

"Yes. Then, the three of us get her."

"And I do what again?"

"You stay back."

"If she will let me."

"She goes with us. You then go to the car and drive away."

"End of story. What do I do for an encore?"

"Go home and wait to hear."

"Great. End of movie."

"It'll be fine."

"Sure. But first, I need to get through the Board Meeting at noon. I'll give you my presentation."

I looked through my laptop and gave him a preview of what I was going to say. He listened nodding.

"All good points. Hopefully, the partners will have a little more patience after you tell them that the spotlight is off you."

"You'd think, but what I perceive is they just want it to be done. Me, cleared, the firm untouched and the case, history."

"Would they settle for you solving the murder?"

"The last time that was discussed, I was told to leave it to my attorney to extract me. They didn't like the idea of me solving anything, except how to bill my requisite hours per week, month, year. They definitely did not want me sleuthing."

"Blame that on me."

"For sure. I will bring you in with me to 'splain it to them."

"It's a deal."

"OK. I guess that I better get myself together for tomorrow. I'll try not to roam around the house tonight, wringing my hands."

"Everything will be fine."

"Sure. Goodnight."

My sleep was spotty, nothing new. Henry XII was still having trouble.

# CHAPTER 30: What a Day This Will Be!

I was distracted in the morning. I filled a backpack with jeans, sneakers and other necessities for the night's adventure. Then I took a shower and got ready for work, just like any normal business day, except I put on my best suit with a silk blouse and scarf picked out by my mother. It actually looked good and Dave gave his approval.

My day was hardly normal, but I had two conference calls and comments in a proceeding to complete and file for a client in Denver. I needed to have the document drafted and emailed to her by the time she came into the office. We would collaborate on any changes she felt necessary before I filed it late in the afternoon. This was something to keep me occupied and distracted until the Board Meeting at 1:00 PM Eastern. Jesse stopped in and we exchanged greetings. He asked if I was prepared for the meeting and I said yes and that the recent events seemed positive. He shrugged and said, "I hope so."

I finished the client comments and sent them out before 11:00 AM, 9:00 AM mountain time. My client and I had a bit of back and forth about strategy and edits. I produced a final draft and gave the document to my assistant to finalize for filing.

A little before 1:00 PM, Jesse and I were sitting in the conference room with the video screen on. A partner or two walked by and peered in. I waved and mouthed, "Command Performance." The screen came up at 1:00 PM, and we all exchanged greetings. Seated at the table were 11 out of the 15 members. I assumed that the remaining members were in Houston, which I could not see on screen.

Ray opened the meeting and told the Board, "As we discussed last week, we wanted Leyla to bring us up to date on the status of the FBI

investigation into the murder of a woman at the Federal Radio Administration. Leyla has been questioned on a couple of occasions by the FBI and
the investigation seems to be moving along. Leyla, would you tell us where
the investigation is at this point."

"Thanks, Ray. First, the most important news is that there now seems
to be a more likely suspect of interest. She is an alleged member of an
organized drug/crime gang, the Warriors, who operates in D.C. and Baltimore. This woman was employed as a custodian at the Administration
about a month before the murder and she left that job a few weeks after
the murder. This was not known until recently because the FBI agent in
charge of the proceeding set aside a piece of evidence, a letter that was sent
to her by a woman who was secretary to D.L. Phillips, the murder victim.
The letter disclosed information about this custodian and her involvement.
The writer of the letter publicly released it, after hearing nothing from
the FBI, to the Commissioners and the General Counsel of the Administration and the members of Congress who are on the Administration's
oversight committees. Following that disclosure and the blowback from
the Administration and Congress, the FBI removed that agent from the
investigation. In her defense, the FBI agent claimed that she had gotten a
great deal of information on the murder by crackpots, and she viewed this
letter in that category. During that time, the witness who wrote the letter
disappeared. She had recently met with Administration officials verifying
the information in the letter. She had also told individuals that the alleged
suspect called her; tried to enter her boyfriend's apartment; and showed up
at her daughter's school. Finally, I am of the opinion that the matter will
be resolved soon because of the intense pressure on the FBI from Congress
and the Administration. This murder at a federal facility, coupled with the
bungling at the FBI, is a black mark on both agencies, and the matter needs
to be resolved quickly.

"Where is this suspect now?" Ray asked.

"She is on the run, from what I hear," I said. "Apparently, the FBI is
trying to find her and she has eluded them so far."

One of the firm's jesters muttered, "Your FBI in action."

I stopped and waited for more questions. The Board sat absorbing the
information.

Steve then said, "When do you think you will be released as a witness
in the proceeding."

"My attorney is discussing that with the new Agent in Charge. We
should know more soon." If Gail hadn't discussed it with Evan Randle yet,

I would tell her to, immediately.

"So, basically, you are still a witness?"

"Yes. The agent replacement happened at the end of last week. The government doesn't move as quickly as I—and you all—would like."

Jake, a longtime partner from the beginning of the firm and deeply invested in it, put his hands together in a pyramid in front of him mouth and said, "Leyla, as you know, we have been concerned with the effect of this investigation on the brand of this firm."

"Yes, sir." I said. "I know. I am concerned also. I am proud to be part of the firm and I would not want to harm it in any way."

Jake sat back and said. "You have been a loyal member of the firm and we appreciate your work. We just don't want any of this tainting the firm."

Someone who I could not recognize on the screen said, "A possible approach to avoid any contamination would be to have Leyla take a leave of absence." This was what I feared. A sense of dread came over me, too close to being let go.

"I don't think that measure is necessary because I really do think that this matter is going to be resolved sooner rather than later," I said. Jesse rustled in his seat and started to sit forward as if he was going to say something and I put my hand down firmly on the table as if to warn him not to. I hoped that no one had seen that gesture. Jesse sat back and kept silent.

The unknown voice came again. This time the screen split to show the members in Houston. "But how do you know that, Leyla? How can you protect the firm while still practicing law here?"

"I know that because of all the recent events that I have laid out for you. There is an actual suspect who is far more viable than I am, who was at the Administration and had access to the conference room on the day of the murder. In addition, there is evidence that the FBI agent withheld any reference to that suspect intentionally. The FBI has now turned its focus away from me. I haven't had contact with them in ten days."

"But who is to say that you are off the list?" asked Eliot, the firm's ethics guru.

Before I could answer, one of the Houston contingent spoke up again, "They could keep you—and us—dangling for months while they prepare the case against the woman who seems to have disappeared. In the meantime, the press may get ahold of it. We need to cut our losses here. We cannot continue to be part of this spectacle." This meeting was turning into a kangaroo court.

Jake spoke again. "Gentlemen. There has been not a whisper of scandal at all from Leyla's involvement in this investigation. She has been cooperating with the FBI. There has been no reporting on her appearances in any media. We only know about it because Leyla has kept us up to date."

"I agree." Ray said. "Leyla knows that we are concerned. We've told her from the beginning where we stood, and she has followed our guidelines."

I went stiff because later, like tonight, events would show that I didn't strictly follow their guidelines. Except, I rationalized, I did follow their demand to leave the investigation to my investigator. I had done that as best I could. Participating in tonight's operation was at the direction of my investigator. This would be my argument, after the fact. Hopefully, the result would outweigh that insubstantial excuse.

Meanwhile, Jake appeared to be taking on the role of my advocate! He is the leader that the senior partners always followed. I couldn't help thinking that Ray might have helped make this happen. Ray knew that a group of younger partners wanted me and my problem to disappear. I barely knew that group, and that has been a problem in the past. I'm in Washington, they are in Texas.

Without waiting for further discussion, Ray began to wrap up the meeting. "Okay, Leyla, we will talk it through as a group and make a decision, but for the moment, just keep on doing what you're doing and let us know when anything significant comes up." Significant! I let out a sigh and then began mentally gearing up for the night's events.

"Thank you, everyone. I will keep you informed," I said. The video went black.

I turned to Jesse. "I think that I got a reprieve, for a while."

"Those guys in Houston were after you," he said. Obviously.

"I know. For the time being, I think the gentlemen from Dallas have kept them in line. We'll see what happens next."

Jesse and I got up and went back to our offices.

The day continued without leaving me time to panic. My filing was due, and I was putting the last touches on the final version when Cam called.

"How did the Board Meeting go?" He asked.

"Thank you for remembering and calling me from Spain! It was interesting: turned out that it was the Dallas old guards that defeated the Houston upstarts: an All-Texas Play-off. Now, for the next stress point of the day. The meeting with Stanley is set for tonight."

"It sounds like you are having a hell of a day. By the way, I'm back in town. The meeting ended yesterday evening. Good luck tonight. I'll be thinking about you," he said, gently.

"Thanks. Nothing bad will happen. After tonight, I'll be done with all this stress about Stanley. Whether the FBI will call me in again or not, and even though I dread it, I'm looking forward to getting this behind me."

"Don't say it like that. It sounds like a gospel singer: 'Soon, I'll be done with the troubles of the world'."

"Mahalia Jackson. I never pegged you as superstitious. You are too smart for that."

"Anyway, I'll be thinking about you. Take care."

At four, there was a group conference call on the joint frequency transfer project we had been working on for three months. The call was full of lawyers one-upping each other. I gave up playing the "who is the smartest guy on the call" about ten years ago. It's a waste.

Then, it was six o'clock. My filing at last had been made, and I was off the conference call. I began to prepare for the night. I closed my office door and changed into jeans, turtleneck and sneakers. Apprehension set in.

I sat in my office and waited for a call on my throw-away phone, unable to muster interest in any of the work on my desk. An hour went by. I was fully frightened, anxious, uneasy and all the other emotions I had felt during these past months of torture. I now, however, also feared for my life. I sat at my desk, feeling helpless.

At seven, Dave came to my office. He gave me the marked money. I put it in my backpack. Then, he wired me. I looked in the mirror: he did a good job, nothing showed. He sat across from me, but that was small comfort. The burner phone rang. I set the phone so Dave could hear it, too. When I answered it, a surprisingly genteel voice said, "You wanted to talk with me?"

I looked at Dave and raised my eyebrows. "Yes, I want to talk to you about the note that was left at the Federal Radio Administration on March 28."

"I don't know anything about that." She either was a good actress, or we had gotten the wrong person.

"OK. But I thought that you were supposed to get paid for an assignment you did for D.L. Phillips."

There was a pause. "D.L. Phillips?"

"Yes, the woman who was killed. It was in the news in March."

There was another longer pause. "I was out of town during that time and didn't hear the news," she said dismissively.

"Did you know D.L. Phillips?"

"I knew her name. She was a, a friend of a friend of mine." She sounded unsettled now. "I never met her before."

"Well, I was told by a contact that you are owed money for something you did for her."

There was a pause. I waited for her to think this through. I looked at Dave. He nodded and smiled a little, as if he approved of how things were going.

"Oh, that money," she said. "You have it?"

"Yes. I guess with her death, you somehow didn't get paid. I want to get it to you. But I need an answer to one question, first."

"A question?"

"Who arranged it," I asked.

"Who arranged what?"

"You know what I mean," I said, giving Dave a perplexed look. "I want to know if your contact is the same as my contact, or if one of us is being set up. I'm sure you don't want any surprises, any more than I do."

Silence.

Had I said something to make her suspicious? I took a deep breath. "Listen," I said when a minute had passed without her saying anything, "I don't care whether you get paid or not. But I'm not walking into a set up to hand money over to a stranger."

Dave was nodding his head, as if pleased that I had my act together.

Suddenly, her tone shifted and she was all business. "You don't need to worry about anything. When we meet, I'll tell you whatever you want to know. And I'll make sure neither of us are being set up. Meet me at the Way Out Inn on North Cap between N and O at nine o'clock."

"Fine. The Way Out Inn on North Cap." Dave grimaced. It wasn't your best D.C. address. It was also likely that Stanley would be bringing friends from the hood.

"That's the neighborhood I was visiting when I got shot," Dave said after I hung up the phone.

"Something's wrong here," I said. "She was flustered, I mean, really flustered when she heard that the person who was killed was Phillips. She sounded almost afraid when she said that she was a 'friend' of her buddy. Could it be that D.L. had been more like a "girlfriend" of her friend? If my intuition about that is right, the friend is a member of the Warriors who is not going to be happy with Stanley when he finds out who really killed his girlfriend. I can't figure out how she didn't know this already. It must have been all over the street, no matter where she was."

"Maybe not," Dave said. "Remember she said she was away. Maybe she meant away, away. Like in hiding. The FBI gave her a reprieve for a while."

"Another thing, she said that she knew D.L.'s name but didn't know what she looked like. It is just odd; she sounded so off. It's almost as if she had had other indirect dealings with her but still had not associated the name and the face. There really are a lot of missing pieces here. I'm confused. Why didn't she know the name of her victim? Why didn't her friend, D.L.'s friend or someone tell her about D.L.? Why did she not know who she had killed until we just talked on the phone?"

Dave shrugged and looked at his watch. It was 7:30 now. Dave called his team. The plan was for them to meet at 8:30 somewhere near the Way Out Inn to scope it out. I was staying in my office. Dave who was going to be one of the "invisible" guys who would drive me close to the location where the team would take Stanley.

I was shaking and sweating. I had to rely on two people I had just recently met and three people I had never seen before to keep me alive. I was on my way to a nightmare. Even when I reminded myself that it was eat or be eaten. That didn't make it better. At all.

The address where we would meet was near a section of NE advertised as being revitalized, NoMa, which had been the site of a spate of killings in the past. Dave would drive me close to a warehouse near Florida Avenue and North Capitol Street.

In a while, Dave left my office and went to his car. When he had pulled up outside, he flicked his lights outside my office window. Some attorneys were still working. There was a big white-collar fraud trial coming up next week. Lights were on in a conference room and several paralegals were handling documents for discovery in another proceeding. As grueling as trials were, I would rather be doing that than what I was about to do.

Deep breath, Leyla. It will all be over in a couple of hours. One way or the other.

# CHAPTER 31: The Gig.

Things had not gone well at the Way Out Inn, where the two team members had met up with Stanley. She was not happy with the change. In fact, she was belligerent. The team guessed that her friends and probably her partner were somewhere in the bar, anticipating that something might go awry and ready to defend her. She obviously wanted the money, but she now would not be surrounded by her friends and would be at another less public location.

She also had somehow assumed that I'd arrive alone. Apparently, she thought that a woman, who is a lawyer, might not guess that she could be walking into a possible trap. It said something about her mindset. She wasn't afraid, so why would I be? Despite her reluctance, the money as well as her acquaintance with the two street guys overcame her irritation at the relocation of her "meeting" with me

At 9:15, Dave dropped me off at a taxi stop, told me where he would be parking and gave me a duplicate car key. I caught a cab to the warehouse, followed by Dave in his car. I arrived at 9:30. The visible guys, Ken and Jim (I doubted these were real names) and Stanley were inside the warehouse. Ken stood near the door and let me in.

Stanley looked like a person I might have seen while commuting on the metro, not a drug lord or gun moll, as I had imagined. She had dark straight hair with bangs and a pouty full mouth. She was about 5'8", had an athletic build and wore a silver Ankh cross necklace and diamond stud earrings. She wore a black sweater and pants and sparkly athletic shoes. Did she look like a hit person? I didn't know. Certainly if she dressed like a custodian, covered her hair and toned down her jewelry, she wouldn't stand out. Her demeanor was mild at the moment, but I couldn't tell what she was capable of. Maybe that made her the perfect person for the job.

She eyed me up and down. Measuring me as an enemy or a competitor? At last, she nodded, as if thinking—this one seems harmless enough. I put down my backpack. I was either going to have to put on an act or run screaming from the warehouse. I took a deep breath.

"I have the money," I said. "But first, I need the name of the person who contacted you for the job; and the address on the note."

She shrugged. "Listen, I don't know anything."

"But you told me we could talk here, now. And you still you came for the money," I said. "Why should I give you the money if you don't know why you are being paid or who your contact was? I could be handing over all this cash to the wrong person."

"OK. Some messenger at the Inn asked me to find someone to help him out."

"Messenger?"

"Like one of those guys riding bikes with packages."

"Who hired him?"

"I didn't ask him."

"Weren't you concerned about some kind of a sting?" I asked.

"No. I knew the guy."

"Do you know who the guy worked for?"

"Could be anyone. He has lots of contacts. He works for a friend of mine."

Ken nodded his head. I wasn't sure why.

"OK, I am confused. If your friend wanted to hire you, why did he send a messenger?"

"He doesn't get his hands dirty."

"So, now we need to talk to the messenger to compare contact names? I'm worried that there too many people involved here and bad things may happen...to both of us. That is why I need the information from you. To protect us."

"The messenger was some guy who used to work at a law firm."

"What was the name of the law firm?"

"I don't know, a law firm downtown."

"Was the law firm Gallagher?"

"Yes, I guess that's it. Gallagher."

"And another thing about the timing of the murder. How did it happen that the victim's meeting was postponed at the Administration?"

"That lawyer Gallagher had a meeting with some staff person before

she met with him. Gallagher arranged a last minute conference call with
the client about something important and so she was waiting. I was supposed to find my target and walk her to the conference room in the North
building to give her the bug. I told her that I did not want to be seen giving
it to her. I never saw her before. I didn't know her or her name. I went by
looks not names. They said red hair."

"Yes, you said that on the phone that D.L. was the girlfriend of your
friend."

"Yeah, Sid, my partner's friend, was her boyfriend and helped her with
her father."

"He worked with her father?"

"In a way, yes."

"I don't understand."

"Sid said that his girlfriend's father ordered her to stop seeing Sid or he
would cut her off, so his car developed a problem and crashed. After the
crash, Sid fixed the problem." She smiled, showing perfect teeth. She was
beginning to scare me. Her companions remained passive with no reaction
from that news.

"That's why the investigation showed that nothing was wrong with the
car."

"Yeah."

"Did D.L. know?"

"Maybe she did."

"Beforehand?"

"She might have."

"My God. Are you saying that D.L. helped kill her father?"

"Not exactly."

"But close enough."

"I didn't know who she was. I never saw her before. I was supposed to
get rid of a red-head. I took her to the conference room."

"Didn't she protest?"

"No, she thought it was about the bug. She was supposed to pick it up.
She wanted it and I brought her there to give it to her where no one else
would be around."

"And to kill her?"

She did not deny it, but she said nothing. But she was spilling all the
beans, for some extra cash. Maybe she was also bragging?

"Who hired you to kill her?" She said nothing.

"Was it Leon Gallagher?" She smiled.

"I assume that is a yes." She did not respond.

"OK, when you left, she was dead."

She just could not help herself. Apparently, she wanted to keep talking. This was confusing to me. Once Pandora was out of the box, she needed to tell me how good she was in her business. I remember seeing the Roger Rabbit movie a long time ago. Roger got caught because he couldn't keep his mouth shut. Just like Jimmi here. She needed to talk.

She said, "Yes."

Close enough for wires, I thought.

"OK. So now, what was the address on the note?"

She told me that she had written it down, after she left. It was my address. A double whammy: my DNA and my address. No wonder the FBI was interested. But even an amateur would think that all this was a set-up, wouldn't they?

I paused. "Did D.L. give you the note?"

"Yes. She said that someone at that address would pay me."

"For what?" I said.

"For the bug."

"Gallaher had already paid you for the other thing."

"Yes, he paid. She didn't and I want the rest of it, now."

And before anyone could move, she had pulled a gun on me.

I had thought that Ken and Jim might have checked that part. But then, they were supposed to be playing on her side of the street. I wondered what they thought about Stanley's tell all. I did not look at either of them now. I had been bewildered by the confession, but now I knew her plan. I was expendable. It did not matter what I knew because I was never going to be able to tell anybody. She didn't care what her street buddies here knew. They were never going to tell on her either. She had fooled me.

"I'm taking her backpack and her. You guys get nothing and say nothing. I did the work. My partner is outside because I am wired and he knows I am ready now. So, don't move," Stanley ordered.

The two inside guys looked on passively, while I stood in front of Stanley and her gun. I had no illusions that I would survive this. The other undercover guy and Len and Dave were not showing themselves to Stanley and no one could move without getting me shot. Stanley started backing out of the warehouse, holding me tightly in front of her. She was strong. I was between the two immobile men and Stanley. Cam was right, this plan sucked. I should have listened.

In front of the warehouse door, a car idled. Stanley moved around me, pushing me toward the backseat of the car. A shot came from inside the car and hit Stanley in her chest. She dropped the gun and fell. Stanley looked dead. I tried to run away from the car, away from the driver who was obviously armed.

But before I could get very far, Keith sprang from the backseat and I was grabbed in midflight and was thrown onto the floor of the backseat of the car. I kicked and flailed at him, to no avail. Within seconds he'd tied my wrists and ankles and wrapped a blindfold over my eyes. I felt a blanket thrown over me. Keith must have gotten into the car; I heard a door slam. Then the car was moving

Where were my bodyguards?

"So now you know everything." The voice sounded familiar. "I heard everything she said."

"Leon?"

There was silence.

"Is that you, Leon?" I asked again.

"You are always getting in the way," he whined. "I had to take care of all of it for the client."

"Whoa, Leon," I said. "Is that the disbarred client? He may have spent a lot of money with the firm, but this is murder. You can't do this. It is not worth it. We can say that you rescued me. We can get you out of this somehow. You don't want to do this."

"Yes, I do," he insisted. "I must get rid of the people who are in the way." He sounded a little off. Well, then maybe a lot off, like manic.

As we picked up speed, I could hear traffic. It was quiet in the car for a while, then I felt the car turn onto a ramp. Probably Route 50.

"Well, you got rid of D.L. and Jimmi Stanley, or was she Lana to you?"

"It doesn't matter. She was talking too much. It would have been fine if she had kept his mouth shut. Maybe she was trying to impress you. Stupid girl."

"Yeah, maybe. You do know that everyone in the warehouse was wired, don't you? And she confessed to being at the Administration, taking D.L. to the conference room and admitted that when she left, she was dead."

He said nothing.

"And she told us who hired him."

"It was Keith. I can't be responsible for what a paralegal does. He left the firm."

"Right. All paralegals go out and hire killers to help keep a client at the firm. And he is here with us now."

"That will all be taken care of."

"Yes," said Keith. "Leon said that he will take care of me."

"OK, I'm wondering what that means, exactly."

"Leon will give Louise and me money and we will move away."

"Really, Leon?" I hoped that question would raise fears from Keith.

"I said that I would and I will." Leon said defiantly.

"So now, the list of the dead is D.L. and Stanley, right?"

"Darius Phillips, too."

"Why, Darius?"

"He was getting in the way of the deal."

I had been struggling with the bands around my wrists, but now I froze at the realization of how insane and beyond reason this guy must be.

"Yeah," he said, "the client knew Darius would cause trouble for him with his plan to use D.L. Darius would naturally try to get involved. The client didn't want another hand in the till."

"I thought Darius died because he discovered that D.L. was dating a thug and that D.L. knew that was the plan."

"Yeah. That's what Keith told Sid. It made it easier. A good excuse."

"And how did Stanley know that D.L.'s meeting was delayed?"

"I was in the meeting causing the delay. We brought up an issue of concern to the FCC staff about the auction late in the meeting. I told Sam that my client was standing by to discuss it by phone."

"Convenient."

"The client wanted her dead."

"Why?" I hoped my bodyguards were following us and listening.

"Because D.L. was getting greedy and threatened to expose him."

"But she was in on it, too."

"D.L. said that she would say that the client had threatened to kill her like her father, if she didn't help him. She claimed she had forged papers to prove it. And he thought that she had set up a meeting with the staff that day to tell them."

Leon turned off the highway and soon was bumping along on a rural road. I had no idea of the time or how long I had been in the car. Branches brushed against the car. I was by myself with this guy and his helper who were going to kill me and dump my body in the woods.

"Leon, what happened to you? You were so straight. You came to my office to discuss a client conflict and you acted as if you wanted to follow an ethical plan!"

"Things change."

"But murder?"

"I'm not going to murder you. Someone else is."

"Accessory?"

"No one will know."

"The accessory will."

"We won't tell," Keith quickly volunteered.

"But that's four people, Leon. Their blood will be on your hands."

"Yeah, it's really too bad. Some people are just no good. You all had me fooled."

The car stopped and he and Keith got out. They opened the back door and I felt the cold air. I would be like thousands of people in this world, killed and disposed of in a field or ravine, like trash. Maybe next spring, someone would come along and notice my bones. They grabbed me out of the car. My legs were untied and I was told to walk. I walked.

Keith held me on one side and then there was another person on the other side. I whispered, "I think that you will kill me and then Leon will kill you. He wants no witnesses."

"That's not true!" said a voice. It was Louise.

"Ohhhhh. So, this is where you were hiding," I said. "You were always part of Leon's scheme."

"Not always, but there was money in it, and I needed it," Louise said brusquely. "D.L. stopped paying me after Darius died. Leon recruited me after she started screaming at his client for more money. It was easy. I hated her. Ginny needed the money from her father. D.L. would never let that happen if she were alive. I was glad to be part of it. Leon had me call you to set you up for this. And you took the bait."

"Well, here's hoping that you survive this," I said. "Oh, don't you worry about that," she insisted.

That was the last thing I heard before a gun went off. I dropped to the ground.

Even through the blindfold, I could tell that bright lights had come on.

Nearby, someone yelled, "Drop the gun!"

I lay on the ground, shaking and sobbing. There was more gunfire, it sounded as if it were coming from the car. Was Leon shooting at others? Had he shot himself?

Someone came running to me and dropped down beside me. "It's me, you're safe." Dave's voice. He removed the bands from my arms and mask from my eyes. Len was examining Leon who lay by the car. Apparently, my bodyguards had followed us and picked an opening to rescue me.

Then, everything went even more ballistic.

More lights came on. Maryland State Police cars sped in, sirens blaring. An ambulance arrived and a cop went with the EMTs to take Leon to the hospital. I figured it was too late. Leon had found a way out of this for himself. There would be no one to shield his client Carlton Edwards this time.

Louise and Keith were taken away in a police van. I was taken to the Maryland State Police station with Dave and Len. We had all had been wired: everyone would soon know about everything, except for the identity of the silent invisible helpers. Now I knew why Ken and Jim had not spoken. They just disappeared into the night, without a sound on the wire. I have no idea what the protocol was on that. I didn't ask. The police would sort that out, I was sure. Or not.

I had to tell my whole, long side of the story that night, not to the FBI this time but to the Maryland police. They gave me coffee and water and treated me kindly. I was not a suspect now, just a traumatized witness. There would be problems down the line, I was sure. The first one would be jurisdiction. The activity took place in Maryland, but former D.C. police had been involved and, of course, the FBI was conducting the murder investigation. Not my problem. I would talk to whoever was not trying to frame me for a murder. But then, D.L.'s murder had been solved. A wave of relief rolled over me. I was exhausted.

Finally, at 1:00 AM, I crawled into Dave's car and we drove back into the District. We did not talk at all on the ride. Dave dropped me off at my house and I hugged him. "Thanks, Dave. Let's talk tomorrow." He had retrieved my backpack, and I carried it into my apartment house.

As I started to put the key in the lock, Cam surprised me by opening the door. He held out his arms. He had come back from Spain and into my life. The sight of him smiling and my gratitude for just being alive would get me through the next few days and the endless meetings with police, my lawyer, the FBI and my partners. Maybe not in that order. But I was free! That was something to celebrate. Cam opened a bottle of champagne and we toasted our future.

# Don't miss out!

Visit the website below and you can sign up to receive emails whenever A. Eveline publishes a new book. There's no charge and no obligation.

https://books2read.com/r/B-A-GPXL-LGOIB

Connecting independent readers to independent writers.

# About the Author

A. Eveline is a mystery writer who loves to spend time by the ocean and think of ways in which people can be murdered.